Praise for

The Alehouse Murders

"I loved *The Alehouse Murders*. Combining marvelous period detail with characters whose emotions and personalities would ring true in any era, Maureen Ash has launched a terrific new historical mystery series. I'll be standing in line for the next Templar Knight Mystery."

—Jayne Ann Krentz, *New York Times* bestselling author

"A delightful addition to the medieval mystery list. It is well researched and, even better, well written, with distinct, interesting characters and plot twists that I didn't expect . . . I look forward to more books in the series."

—Sharan Newman, author of *The Outcast Dove*

"Fans of quality historical mysteries will be delighted with this debut . . . The first in what will hopefully be a long-running series of Templar Knights whodunits . . . Ash's period detail and plotting are first-rate, superior to many other representatives of the rarefied subgenre."   —*Publishers Weekly*

"Maureen Ash masterfully creates a medieval world full of rich historic detail and peopled with fascinating characters. Her complex hero, Sir Bascot de Marins, immediately engages the reader as he tracks a ruthless killer in a mystery that will keep the reader guessing until the very end."

—Victoria Thompson, national bestselling author

"A perplexing mystery with its flawed but sympathetic hero . . . An enjoyable read."   —*Gumshoe Review*

"Good, old-fashioned mystery. I look forward to more."

—*Meritorious Mysteries*

"Maureen Ash's series will be very popular if the future novels are the quality of *The Alehouse Murders*."

—*Midwest Book Review*

"Interesting reading."   —*San Jose Mercury News*

Berkley Prime Crime titles by Maureen Ash

THE ALEHOUSE MURDERS
DEATH OF A SQUIRE
A PLAGUE OF POISON
MURDER FOR CHRIST'S MASS
SHROUD OF DISHONOUR

Shroud
of
Dishonour

A Templar Knight Mystery

MAUREEN ASH

BERKLEY PRIME CRIME, NEW YORK

THE BERKLEY PUBLISHING GROUP
Published by the Penguin Group
Penguin Group (USA) Inc.
375 Hudson Street, New York, New York 10014, USA
Penguin Group (Canada), 90 Eglinton Avenue East, Suite 700, Toronto, Ontario M4P 2Y3, Canada
(a division of Pearson Penguin Canada Inc.)
Penguin Books Ltd., 80 Strand, London WC2R 0RL, England
Penguin Group Ireland, 25 St. Stephen's Green, Dublin 2, Ireland (a division of Penguin Books Ltd.)
Penguin Group (Australia), 250 Camberwell Road, Camberwell, Victoria 3124, Australia
(a division of Pearson Australia Group Pty. Ltd.)
Penguin Books India Pvt. Ltd., 11 Community Centre, Panchsheel Park, New Delhi—110 017, India
Penguin Group (NZ), 67 Apollo Drive, Rosedale, North Shore 0632, New Zealand
(a division of Pearson New Zealand Ltd.)
Penguin Books (South Africa) (Pty.) Ltd., 24 Sturdee Avenue, Rosebank, Johannesburg 2196,
South Africa

Penguin Books Ltd., Registered Offices: 80 Strand, London WC2R 0RL, England

This book is an original publication of The Berkley Publishing Group.

This is a work of fiction. Names, characters, places, and incidents either are the product of the author's imagination or are used fictitiously, and any resemblance to actual persons, living or dead, business establishments, events, or locales is entirely coincidental. The publisher does not have any control over and does not assume any responsibility for author or third-party websites or their content.

FIRST EDITION: October 2010

Library of Congress Cataloging-in-Publication Data

Ash, Maureen.
    Shroud of dishonour : a Templar Knight mystery / Maureen Ash. — 1st ed.
        p.   cm.
    ISBN 978-0-425-23790-8
    1. Templars—Fiction. 2. Murder—Investigation—Fiction. 3. Middle Ages—Fiction. 4. Lincoln (England)—Fiction. I. Title.
    PR9199.4.A885S57   2010
    813'.6—dc22   2010014030

PRINTED IN THE UNITED STATES OF AMERICA

10   9   8   7   6   5   4   3   2   1

"Courage is rightly esteemed the first of human qualities . . . because it is the quality which guarantees all others."

WINSTON CHURCHILL

List of Characters

PRINCIPAL CHARACTERS
Bascot de Marins—a Templar Knight
Gianni—a mute Italian boy, former servant to Bascot
Nicolaa de la Haye—hereditary castellan of Lincoln castle
Gerard Camville—Nicolaa's husband and sheriff of Lincoln
Roget—captain of Gerard Camville's town guard
Ernulf—serjeant of Lincoln garrison
John Blund—secretary to Nicolaa de la Haye
Lambert—clerical assistant to John Blund

THE TEMPLARS
Everard d'Arderon—preceptor
Emilius—draper
Hamo—serjeant
Alan of Barton—man-at-arms
Thomas of Penhill—man-at-arms

IN LINCOLN TOWN
Elfreda—nicknamed Elfie—prostitute
Adele Delorme—prostitute
Terese—former prostitute

Verlain—stewe-keeper
Constance Turner—perfume maker
Agnes—Constance's maid
Jehan—infirmarian at Priory of All Saints

IN GRIMSBY
Peter Thorson—Grimsby bailiff
Sven Grimson—boat owner
Joan Grimson—Sven's wife
Askil—steersman
Dunny—seaman

IN INGHAM
Gilbert Roulan—lord of Ingham manor
Margaret Roulan—Gilbert's wife
Jacques, Hervé and Julia Roulan—Gilbert's younger brothers and sister
Savaric—bastard son of Gilbert's father

Shroud of Dishonour

Prologue

✦✝✦

Acre, Outremer—Late autumn, 1201

THE TEMPLAR COMMANDERY ON THE SOUTHWEST SIDE OF ACRE lay still and silent under the silver shimmer of a crescent moon. Just before midnight, two figures slipped out of the postern gate and melted into the darkness of the city streets. They were both brothers of the Order and wore black cloaks with hoods over plain dark tunics from which the Templar insignia had been removed. Under their cloaks they were lightly armed, each wearing a dagger at his belt. Their faces were shrouded by the hoods so that only their beards could be seen, one dark in colour, the other tinged with a coppery hue. The dark-bearded man's stride seemed confident as they reached the main street and started down its length, but there was a nervous agitation about his movements that belied his certainty. His confrere regarded him worriedly as he followed in his wake.

It did not take them long to reach the entrance to the souk, a marketplace which, in the daytime, was filled with stalls piled high with bolts of cloth, silver jewellery, shoes, hides and spices. During the hours of daylight, it bustled with activity and sound—the babbling voices of merchants and their customers, the rumbling growl of camels, and the plaintive importuning of beggars—but now, in the darkness of the night, it was quiet and almost deserted. A few mendicants, young children amongst them, slept curled up on the ground here and there, protected from the chill night air by tattered rags swathed haphazardly about their bodies. The sliver of moon cast little light, but both men knew the way to their destination and threaded the labyrinth of mean streets around the perimeter of the souk with ease. The air was redolent with the pungent stench of excrement. Camel and goat droppings slimed the ground underfoot and human dung overflowed the sewage runnel that ran along the edge of the byway. Neither man took any notice of the offensive reek; both had been in Outremer for over a year and had become inured to the intense heat and noxious odours.

The Templar with the dark beard continued to lead the way and did not falter until they approached the entrance of a brothel. As he came to a halt, his companion put a hand on his arm.

"I do not think this venture is wise," he cautioned. "Our absence from the enclave is certain to be noticed before long. There will be a dire punishment awaiting us when we return."

"If you are so fainthearted, go back!" was the angry response. "I did not ask you to accompany me. It was your own choice to do so." His manner softened as he saw the concern in the eyes of his comrade. "Try to understand, I beg of you. You know I have not long to live, that in just a short time, I will be gone from this world. Before I get too weak, this is a task that must be done."

At these words, the other Templar's shoulders slumped in resignation. "So be it, but I refuse to be an accomplice to this act. I will wait outside and keep watch."

With a nod of grateful thanks, his friend pushed aside the leather curtain that screened the door of the bawdy house and went in.

A babble of voices was briefly heard before the curtain swung back into place. Among them, mingled with the native tongue, were accents from many nations. The port of Acre attracted traders from all parts of the world—France, Venice, Portugal and England, as well as travellers from eastern climes. The brother who had remained in the street slipped into the shadows a small distance from the entrance to the brothel. Nearby, a couple of burly Arabs stood, drinking from a goatskin flask. Both had curved daggers swinging from belts wrapped crosswise around their muscular torsos. These were the guards employed by the owner of the brothel. At the first sign of trouble, the whoremaster would bang on a drum and the two men would come running and use their fists and, if necessary, their blades, to restore order.

After a few moments, the waiting man began to relax. There was no sound of disturbance from inside. Perhaps his companion would carry out his mission without his identity being discovered. If so, it might be possible for them to return to the Templar commandery and slip back inside, their absence unnoticed. How he prayed that would be so. As the minutes passed, he began to believe his prayer had been answered.

Suddenly, the sound of voices raised in argument came from inside the brothel. It was followed seconds later by the crash of furniture being upended and the frantic beating of the whoremaster's drum. The two guards dashed towards the entrance, pulling their curved swords loose as they ran. Just before they reached the doorway, a figure came hurtling out. It was the dark-bearded Templar.

"Quick!" he said. "We must get away from here."

The pair ran back along the perimeter of the souk and melted into the darkness of the winding side streets. Not until they could be certain they were not being followed did they halt to catch their breath.

"What happened?" asked the Templar who had waited outside the brothel. "Did you find the girl?"

"Yes. But that is not why the alarm was raised." The response was made in a tremulous voice and streams of perspiration ran down the ailing Templar's face and trickled into his beard. The night's exertions had taken a toll on his weakened body. With a shaky hand, he held the dagger up to the dim light of the moon. On the triangular blade, blood glistened darkly. "I think I may have killed someone," he said. "An Englishman. If he is not dead, then he is sorely wounded. I cannot stay in Acre. I must get away from here as quickly as possible."

One

Lincoln—May, 1202

JUST OUTSIDE POTTERGATE IN THE CITY OF LINCOLN A PROS-
titute stood. Her slim frame shivered slightly in the pre-
dawn chill. She was a comely girl, not as pretty as some of
the other whores in the stewe where she worked, but attractive all the same. She had pale blond hair, an impudent
manner and a mischievous smile. Now her expression was
touched with a hint of anxiety.

She looked up the track that led alongside the city walls
but could see no more than a few feet in the inky darkness.
Daybreak would not lighten the sky for two hours yet, but
this was the time she had been told to arrive and she was
certain she was not late. Impatiently, she waited for the man
she was to meet and, when a figure at last materialised from
the gloom, breathed a sigh of relief. She had been promised
ten whole shillings for her help in winning a wager that had
been made, and she needed the money desperately. It would
take only a couple of hours of her time, she had been told,
and she could do it after she finished work for the night. At
first, when she heard what was expected of her, she had been
frightened, but the assurance that it was only a jape and she

would not get into trouble had persuaded her to consent. She had to admit, even though the venture was daring, she was experiencing a pleasurable thrill of excitement at the prospect.

A quiet word of greeting came to her as the man approached. "Hello, Elfie. Did you wear the cloak I gave you?"

Elfreda nodded and twisted around so that he could see the hood hanging down her back. Her companion wore a similar garment; both were of brown wool and capaciously made. Hers hung well below the hem of her kirtle, almost sweeping the ground.

"Good," he said approvingly. "Now, pull the hood up over your head. Your hair is far too bright to escape the notice of any who might see us, even though it is so dark."

She did as she was told, pushing her blond hair back and covering it with the cowl.

"You remember what you are to do?" he asked.

"I am to pretend I am a man," she replied dutifully, "so we can get through the gate of the Templar preceptory. Once we are inside, I am to hide in the chapel behind the statue of the Virgin Mary until the monks come in. Then I am to show myself."

The man nodded. They had known each other only a few hours, since he had come to the stewe where she worked last evening. It had been while they were in the cubicle where she entertained her customers that he had proposed the scheme, claiming he wanted to win a wager he had made with a friend. The stake hinged on a challenge that it would be impossible to smuggle a woman into the Templar enclave and he was willing to pay Elfie for her assistance in winning the bet. The convincing argument that it would also be an enjoyable caper to play on the sanctimonious warrior monks had added an extra incentive to accept. His words still echoed in her ears. "They take a vow of chastity and swear to avoid the company of women, but Christ revered the Magdalene, did he not? Why shouldn't a harlot, or any other female, be made welcome in their place of worship?"

The words had been spoken in an educated fashion and the clothes he was wearing were of good quality. Probably the son of one of the rich merchants in the town, she thought, a lazy clodpoll that had nothing better to do than get up to mischief.

"We have to walk along the outside of the city wall until we get to the enclave," he told her. "Once we're at the gate, don't say anything, even if the guard asks you a question. Just nod or shake your head if he speaks to you, lest your voice betray you are a woman. I'll do any talking that needs to be done. Do you understand?"

With a saucy smile that carved two dimples in her cheeks, Elfie gave a solemn nod.

The man chuckled, not loudly, but distinct enough to be heard. "Good. Here is the two shillings I promised to give you before we start; the rest will be yours when we are inside the chapel." He handed Elfie a small leather pouch. She felt inside to make certain it truly contained silver pennies and gauged the weight by hefting it. When she nodded her acceptance, he gave her further instructions.

"Now we have a brisk walk ahead of us. We must be in the preceptory before the Templars go into the chapel for the service at Matins. So step out, my girl, and lengthen your stride. You must walk like a man, not mince your steps like a female."

Motioning for her to go ahead, they walked along the

footpath. It led upwards, for the city of Lincoln was built on the side of a hill. At the top of the knoll were the castle and Minster and, on the eastern shoulder, just before the slope began its descent, was the Templar enclave. It was surrounded by a high stone wall and no one was allowed entry without permission. To their right, at the bottom of the hillside, the distant light of a torch could be seen and, on the soft spring air, came the occasional sleepy whicker of horses.

"Like I told you," her companion breathed in Elfie's ear, "there are so many Templars in the commandery just now they haven't got room in the stables for all the horses, so they've put some of them into a makeshift pen down there."

As Elfie nodded her understanding, additional details were given. "That's why my ruse will work. The commander had to hire some local men to help look after the mounts. I'll tell the guard on the gate we're two of the men that have been taken on and were told to arrive early. He won't suspect a thing."

"Are you sure?" Elfie asked nervously.

The man nodded impatiently. "The monks sleep until it is time for them to attend Matins. And they will be sleeping soundly, for it is only recently that the hour of the service has been put back to comply with the earlier arrival of dawn in the summer. They will not yet be accustomed to waking betimes and will value their rest. The guard won't dare rouse them to check if we are telling the truth."

Elfie shivered. Suddenly her stomach began to quiver with fear. She had seen the Templar knights a couple of times, riding along the streets of Lincoln. They had been wearing chain mail covered by white surcoats with a red cross emblazoned on the chest, their faces sober and forbidding. And they were monks, too, protected by God, religious soldiers who travelled to far off lands to fight against the enemies of Christ. Would she be mocking God by going into their enclave? Would her soul be damned for what she was about to do?

The harlot's step faltered a little as misgiving gripped her.

"Don't worry, Elfie," her companion said, giving her a gentle push in the small of her back. "You will suffer no recriminations. And you do want the rest of the money I promised, don't you?"

Reluctantly the bawd nodded her head and stepped out a little more boldly. The man smiled at her naivety and fingered the leather cord he had wrapped around his wrist, concealed by the sleeve of his tunic. It would make an excellent garrotte. His promise had not been a lie. No one, not even a Templar, could punish a woman who was dead.

Two

***

Two days later, Everard d'Arderon, the preceptor and senior officer in the Lincoln enclave, stood with two other Templar monks watching a troupe of knights and men-at-arms leave for Portsmouth on the southern coast of England. The bright spring sunshine glittered on their polished helms as they rode through the gate, and illuminated the black and white pennant held aloft by the standard bearer. The banner was not in the rigid rectangular shape of the Beauseant that is carried into battle, but was formed of two streamers that fluttered in the breeze, the black representing the sinfulness of the world the monks had left behind and the white the purity of their life in the Order. Once the contingent reached Portsmouth, they would board a galley and sail across the Bay of Biscay to Lisbon in Portugal, and then travel on horseback a little over eighty miles northeast to the Templar castle at Tomar.

"May the hand of God speed their ship," said d'Arderon, a solidly built older knight of over sixty years with a broad weathered face. "Our brothers on the Iberian peninsula are hard pressed by the Moors."

His companions added their prayers to his. Long exposure to the sun while on duty in hot climes had permanently darkened all of their visages. One of them was Emilius, a knight who held the post of draper and was second-in-command to Preceptor d'Arderon. He was a man of middle years, with sandy-coloured beard and hair, the wiry texture of both clipped extremely short. His left arm, irreparably damaged by a sword slash, was strapped to his chest in a sling.

The other monk was a younger knight named Bascot de Marins. Although barely past his mid-thirties, his dark hair and beard were threaded with grey, premature signs of aging resulting from the ordeal of having spent eight long years as a prisoner of the Saracens in the Holy Land. Over the socket of his missing right eye—a legacy of the torture he had been subjected to while in captivity—he wore a black leather patch. He also walked with a slight limp, his ankle having been badly injured during his escape from the infidels. Until recently, he had been in the retinue of the hereditary castellan of Lincoln castle, Nicolaa de la Haye, and had spent two years in her service after his return to England. A crisis of faith had made him reluctant to immediately rejoin the ranks of the Templar Order on his return but, while staying in the castle, he had recovered both his bodily strength and his devotion to Christ. Now he had finally rejoined his Templar brothers and was looking forward to taking up arms in the ongoing battle against the encroachment of the infidel.

"It will be only a few days now, Bascot, before you go on the same journey," Emilius said, sensing his companion's eagerness. "I wish I were going with you."

"And so you would be, Draper, were it not for your arm," Bascot replied. It had been just outside the walls of the Templar fortress at Tomar, during a skirmish with a band of marauding Moors, that Emilius had sustained the wound that had sliced through the muscles of his upper arm and smashed the bone beyond healing, rendering the limb useless. No longer fit for active duty, he had been sent to the Lincoln preceptory to assist d'Arderon in running the enclave. The duties of both men were diverse—along with overseeing the training and outfitting of new initiates, they also bore the responsibility of administering the many properties in the Lincolnshire area that had been donated to the Order. The fees obtained from these lands were used to provide supplies and arms for brothers on active duty in overseas commanderies, as was the revenue obtained from a small trade in commodities imported from Outremer. Although both were aware of the importance of the parts they played in support of their brethren, it did not lessen their longing to wield their swords in protection of Christians too weak to defend themselves.

The three knights turned and walked across the compound towards the refectory. The enclave was modest in size, encircled by a stone wall with buildings lining the inside of the perimeter. On the northern side was a round chapel; next to it a two-storied building with an eating hall on the lower floor and a dormitory above. Adjacent to the chapel, alongside the western gate into the compound, was the armoury, a capacious granary and a storehouse. At the southern end stood the stables and blacksmith's forge and, lining the eastern perimeter, was a gate out onto the hillside, the kitchen, a well and a wooden shed housing the latrine. The open area in the middle of the compound was used as an exercise and training ground.

As the gates swung closed behind the departing troupe, the rest of the men in the commandery resumed their duties. Some of these would join Bascot in the next contingent, scheduled to depart in a few days. Now, under the watchful eye of Hamo, a brown-robed serjeant, a dozen brothers picked up blunted swords and returned to practise in the centre of the compound. The serjeant was a rangy monk with a craggy face and taciturn demeanour. He had been with d'Arderon for many years in the Holy Land, serving the knight as squire. When d'Arderon had been sent back to England in a weakened state from recurring bouts of tertian fever, the serjeant had accompanied him. Hamo's devotion to the Templar Order was absolute, but his allegiance to d'Arderon ran a close second.

As the three knights walked around the edge of the exercise area towards the refectory, the air was filled with the clash of steel and the grunts of the men as they strove to overcome their opponents. Dust swirled, the clang of the blackmith's hammer rang out from the forge and horses whickered in excited anticipation as grooms led them out for exercise on the hillside below the enclave.

Suddenly Hamo yelled at one of the men-at-arms on the practise ground. The soldier was young, a recent initiate into the Order, and although he had proved to have remarkable archery skills, he was having difficulty in gaining proficiency with the short sword he was now attempting to wield.

"Keep your arm up!" Hamo shouted and strode over to the lad. Pulling his own weapon from his belt, the serjeant took the youngster's position opposite his opponent, a seasoned man-at-arms of mature years. With two sharp lunges and a vicious slash, Hamo disarmed the veteran. "That's how it's done," he said to the new recruit. "You won't get a second chance if you're facing a Saracen, for you'll be dead. Make sure your first attack is the enemy's last."

Shamefaced, the young man-at-arms nodded and, with renewed vigour, recommenced his struggle. This time he was more aggressive and Hamo nodded in satisfaction. "Keep at it, lad. By the time you leave, we'll have you more than ready to confront those heathen bastards."

As d'Arderon, Emilius and Bascot approached the dining hall, the preceptor mentioned that more recruits from one of the northern preceptories were expected to arrive within the next two weeks. There had been many men through the commandery since Eastertide. Pope Innocent III had sent out a call for a new Crusade, and it was planned to begin later in the year. The response to the pope's summons had been enthusiastic and, because of it, an influx of suppliants had requested admission into the Order, preferring to take up arms in the ranks of the Templars rather than in a secular capacity. A few were men who had given their pledge of poverty, chastity and obedience for a defined number of years—two, five or sometimes ten—and had made a donation of land or money as proof of their sincerity. Of these, a small number were married and had obtained their wives' consent to join the Order for a limited period. Many of the suppliants were men of knight's rank, but there were also a substantial number of freeborn villeins, often younger sons of a family overburdened with children, but nonetheless genuine in their devotion for all that. The latter would serve as men-at-arms.

The town of Lincoln was centred around Ermine Street and was the main route to the south of England and ports along the coast. Nearly all of the recent arrivals came from northern preceptories, gathering at the Lincoln enclave before setting out on the last leg of their journey to travel to Templar strongholds in various parts of the world. For most of them, their destination would be the Holy Land, but some—like the recently departed contingent—would go to Portugal, others to Spain or Cyprus.

"If more men are expected, I'd better take inventory of our stock of small clothes," Emilius said in response to d'Arderon's pronouncement, referring to his duty to ensure that all Templar brothers were, as the Rule demanded, correctly attired. "We are running low, and I may need to send to London for more."

D'Arderon nodded and Bascot offered to assist the draper in his chore. Emilius's disabled arm made certain tasks difficult, even though his sound arm was heavily muscled and he was surprisingly agile in using it. But the tedious chore of taking the clothing out, counting the number of garments and replacing them, was more easily done with the use of two arms than one.

At the preceptor's dismissal, the two knights walked towards the chapel. The Order's raiment was stored in coffers in the vestry, along with a small aumbry containing the altar vessels.

As they entered the church, the pleasant aroma of incense met them and they genuflected in front of the altar before going into the vestry, a chamber situated behind a statue of the Virgin Mary. When Emilius opened the door of the room, a faint, and unwholesome, odour overlaid the pervasive smell of incense. Bascot remarked on it to the draper.

"Yes, Brother John mentioned it after he conducted the dawn service this morning. He noticed it when he came in here to fetch the chalice and paten," the draper replied. "It is probably a rat that has worked its way into the rubble infill between the stones of the wall and died. If it doesn't dissipate soon, I will send into town for a rat-catcher and see if his dogs can locate the source."

Three large wooden chests were ranged against one wall of the chamber and a few black flies hovered over one of them, others were crawling on the lid.

Bascot motioned towards the coffer. "I do not think you will need a rat-catcher, Draper. The dead rat must be in, or behind, that chest. The weather has been unseasonably warm of late. Its carcass would begin to smell very quickly."

Emilius had a disciplined nature, a love of order which made him well suited for command and the post of draper. With meticulous care, he checked every article of apparel and equipment on a regular basis to determine if repairs or replacements were required. Leather gambesons, boots, sword belts and wrist guards were also subjected to scrutiny, but these items were kept in the armoury. Another of the draper's duties was the responsibility of ensuring that the hair and beard of each brother was clipped short and neatly trimmed, and tonsures not overgrown. It was important that brothers of all ranks paid obedience to conformity in appearance and dress, for allowing personal taste to take preference increased the danger of being tempted into the sin of pride.

One of the coffers held the white surcoats worn by knights. Next to it was one packed with the brown and black robes of serjeants and men-at-arms—all emblazoned with the blood-red cross pattée of the Order. The third was filled with the lambskin girdles that all Templars wore under their outer clothing as a reminder of their vow of chastity. This chest also contained a selection of hose and undershirts. It was to this last coffer that the flies seemed attracted.

"Shall I pull the chest away from the wall?" Bascot asked.

"Let me check the contents first," Emilius said. "I do not believe the smell can be coming from inside; the covers are made to fit tightly to prevent the invasion of insects or rodents. But, even so, it might be that one got in while I left the lid open for a short time."

The draper lifted the lid and let it fall back against the wall. As he did so, a nauseating odour arose and both men fell back, placing their hands across their noses. The flies began to swirl in a sudden buzzing frenzy.

"Sweet Jesu, all the raiment will be tainted," Emilius exclaimed.

"The carcass must be underneath the clothing," Bascot replied and, brushing at the flies with one hand, he reached inside the chest with the other, grasping the girdles lying in an untidy bundle on the top.

"I did not leave the garments like that," Emilius exclaimed. "They were all neatly folded the last time I . . ."

His words trailed off as Bascot pulled the heap of woolly circlets clear of the coffer. As he did so, a dead body was revealed, but it was not that of a rat. It was human. Crammed tightly into the chest, the corpse lay in a foetal position on its side, legs folded up tight against the stomach and the arms pushed down into the folds of a pale blue skirt. Bright blond hair spilled over the shoulders and, around the neck was an indentation that cut deeply into the flesh. It was the type of mark left by a strangling cord.

"God have mercy," Emilius breathed. "It is a woman. And she has been murdered."

Three

✦

Just over an hour later, Gerard Camville, sheriff of Lincoln, rode into the preceptory. With him was Roget, the former mercenary who was captain of Camville's town guard. The two men dismounted and walked towards Bascot, who was waiting for them at the entrance to the chapel.

Camville was a man of bull-like proportions and irascible temperament. Now his broad features, usually fixed into a scowl, were solemn with disquietude. Beside him, Roget, a fearsome looking man with the scar of an old sword slash bisecting the flesh on one side of his face, had a similar expression. As they paced across the enclave, the Templar knights and men-at-arms of the commandery stood in small silent groups around the perimeter of the central training ground, watching with apprehensive eyes.

Bascot nodded to both men when they reached the chapel. The Templar knight, from his time in the temporary service of Camville's wife, Nicolaa de la Haye, knew the sheriff well. The same was true of Roget. During his stay in Lincoln castle, Bascot had assisted the castellan in seeking out the perpetrator of four previous cases of secret murder and the captain had been involved in most of the investigations. They had formed a liking for each other and become fast friends.

"The preceptor is waiting for you inside the chapel, lord," Bascot said to Camville. "The body of the murdered girl is in there."

The sheriff grunted a response. "D'Arderon's message said the victim's identity was unknown," Camville said as they went into the small church. "I have had no report of a missing female within the town, so have brought Roget along to see if he recognises her."

As captain of the sheriff's guard, Roget was familiar with most of the town's inhabitants. If the dead girl was from Lincoln, it was likely he would know her identity.

Bascot led the two men into the vestry. Additional incense had been set burning and it had, in part, masked the rank smell of death. D'Arderon and Emilius were both inside the chamber, kneeling alongside the preceptory's priest, Brother John, as he intoned Prayers for the Dead. Camville, Roget and Bascot knelt beside them until the priest was finished and Brother John's gloved hands, kept continually covered so they were pristine for the celebration of Mass, moved in the sign of a cross over the body.

"I have done what I can for the soul of this unfortunate woman," the priest said as he and the others rose to their feet. Brother John was an elderly man, fussy and precise, and his face was drawn downward in lines of sadness. "As soon as she can be moved, her body can be taken to the nunnery in the Priory of All Saints. There her earthly remains can be properly cared for by those of her own gender."

The priest moved towards the vestry door. "Please inform me when that has been done, Preceptor," he said to d'Arderon. "The chapel has been defiled by this violence and will need to be reconsecrated before it can be used again. Until then, I will conduct our services outside, under the clean air of God's heaven."

"Thank you for coming so quickly, Gerard," d'Arderon said to the sheriff as Brother John departed, well aware that in most cases of a reported crime, Camville would send Roget or one of his household knights to take down the details. The import of this crime, however, was serious enough to bring the sheriff in person. Not only had murder been done, it had been committed in a house of God, a heinous act compounded by blasphemy.

Camville and Roget moved to the open coffer. The girl still lay as though in foetal sleep; only the angry purple circle around her neck marked the violence that had been done to her. Her blue kirtle was of cheap material, and the skirts were gathered above her ankles, exposing small feet encased in shabby boots. Her hands were almost hidden from sight in the folds of her gown, but two slim fingers protruded, the nails ragged and bitten to the quick.

Roget reached in and gently brushed the bright hair back from her face, so that her features could be seen more clearly. The flesh had a waxy appearance from the effect of encroaching decomposition, and her once pretty hazel eyes were bulging and bloodshot. From between her lips, the tip of her tongue protruded. The death rictus had come and gone.

"*Le pauvre petite*," Roget said as he crossed himself. "She is known to me, lord," he said to Camville. "She is one of the prostitutes from a stewe in Butwerk. I do not recall her name, but the stewe-holder will know it."

The sheriff nodded and looked at d'Arderon. "She's been

dead for a couple of days at least. Do you have any idea how she, or her body, could have got into the preceptory?"

D'Arderon shook his head. The preceptor's face was ashen. "None at all," he said. "There have been many brothers through the commandery in the last few weeks, but for one of them to smuggle in a woman . . . and then murder her. . . . It is too incredible to contemplate."

"She must have been placed in the coffer during the last two days, lord," Bascot said. "Brother Emilius received a supply of new girdles from London three days ago and added them to the few that were left. Her body has been put in here since then."

Emilius nodded and pointed to the two chests containing surcoats, the lids of which were open to reveal the garments inside, all neatly folded. "I also received a few new surcoats, not many, and I added those to the inventory as well. As you can see, the other chests have not been disturbed."

"After the preceptor sent his message to you," Bascot said to the sheriff, "I spoke to the guards who have been on the gate for the last two days. The only way a female could have been brought in here is if she was disguised as a man. All of them are certain that no one of suspicious appearance has been admitted, except for one. He is one of the younger men-at-arms and told me that two men hired from the local populace to help the preceptory's grooms were admitted an hour before Matins two nights ago. Both of them wore cloaks and hoods which shielded their faces, but one of them was small and slight; the guard assumed he was a young lad. It was his companion who requested entrance, saying they had been ordered by Serjeant Hamo to report early for instructions about their duties. The guard knew that Hamo had hired extra men because, with so many brothers passing through on their way to enclaves overseas, there are too many horses for the preceptory's grooms to care for. He admitted them without question."

Bascot paused. "I then spoke to Hamo. He hired only three local men; and none of them were told to report early."

"So that is how the girl got into the enclave," Camville said. "Even though it would seem she came willingly, it was probably her companion who murdered her."

"It would appear so, lord," Bascot replied.

"But why?" d'Arderon demanded angrily. "This is more than simple murder, much as that evil act is to be decried. To kill anyone, man or woman, in the precincts of a church is an abomination. Surely no Christian would damn his soul in such a terrible manner."

His words chilled them all. The preceptor was right, only an infidel would have such blatant disregard for a house of the Christian God.

"But if that was the intent, why choose our chapel?" Bascot said musingly. "It would have been much easier to commit this sacrilege in any of the churches in town, or even the cathedral. Their doors are open to all at any hour of the day or night. Why was the girl brought here, where access can only be gained through a gate protected by an armed guard? It would seem the murderer's intent was not only to defile a chapel, but that it must be a Templar one."

The others reflected on Bascot's comment as Emilius went outside and called to one of the men-at-arms to take a message to the prior of All Saints and ask his permission for the corpse to be taken to the death chamber in the nunnery. Two other soldiers were sent for a makeshift bier on which to place the body.

"Perhaps knowledge of the girl's identity will make the matter clearer," Camville said. He spoke to Roget. "Go to the stewe where she worked and find out her name and anything else that is known about her, especially if she has any connection with the Templar Order, such as a family member that belongs to it. Ask also about her customers. It may be one of them that used her as a tool for his own vengeful purposes."

While he was speaking the stretcher arrived and the preceptor gave a terse order for the soldiers to lift the woman's body out of the coffer and place it on the litter. With grim faces, they did as they were bid, taking care to be gentle. As the harlot was lifted up, a sound coincided with the movement, a dull thud that startled both of the men-at-arms.

Motioning for the men to move aside, Camville strode to the chest and looked in. "Were any monies kept in this chest?" he asked as he reached in and drew forth a leather pouch that chinked with a metallic clatter as he picked it up.

Emilius, to whom the sheriff had directed the question, gazed at the pouch, his expression astonished. "No," he assured Camville. "Only clothing."

The sheriff hefted the purse and then opened it, spilling half of the contents into the palm of his hand. "There is a goodly quantity of money here. At a guess, I would say there are thirty pence."

Silence reigned as the men took in the implication of the number of coins. It was the amount of silver pieces that Judas had been paid to betray Jesus.

Camville was the first to speak, looking at Bascot as he did so. "Your question is answered, de Marins. It seems the murderer used a Templar chapel because he is accusing someone in your enclave of forswearing their vow of chastity, mayhap with this particular harlot."

Four

"Is this villain's allegation a true one, Everard?" Camville demanded of the preceptor. "Have any of the men under your command been consorting with prostitutes?"

D'Arderon's heavy jaw tightened. "If any had, you are well aware that I could not disclose it to you, Gerard," he answered stiffly. "All that passes within our brotherhood is private and not to be revealed to those outside the Order."

If discovered, punishment for any Templar found to have had congress with a harlot was severe. At the very least, he would be whipped, but the chastisement was more likely to be confinement in manacles for a specified period. But any disciplinary measures that were meted out, as with all other affairs concerning the brotherhood, were kept strictly to the knowledge of those within the Order. To reveal these matters to an outsider was considered a grave infraction of the Templar Rule and could result in expulsion.

Camville's eyes narrowed in suppressed anger at d'Arderon's refusal to answer. The two men had a great deal of respect for each other and the confrontation between them was not an easy one. "Damn it, man," Camville spat out, struggling to keep his choleric temper under control. "A harlot has been murdered in your church. If I am to discover the identity of the miscreant who is responsible, I must have your cooperation. At least tell me if the accusation is warranted."

D'Arderon relented a little, although his reply was constrained. "That much I can divulge. I have no reason to believe that the behaviour of any of the men who regularly serve in the Lincoln enclave, including the lay brothers, is the cause of such enmity."

Camville nodded brusquely. "What about the Templars who are just come to Lincoln? Can you give me your assurance about them as well?"

The preceptor shook his head. "No, I cannot. Do not go too far, Gerard," he warned. "I have told you all I can."

Despite d'Arderon's warning, the sheriff pressed for more information. "Your lay servants are not included in your dictate, since they are not members of the Order. Have any of the men who are employed here, in the preceptory, or on properties held by the Order, been lately dismissed for lascivious behaviour?"

"Only one," the preceptor replied, "but that was almost a year ago. And you already know of the incident, Gerard. The man was Ivor Sievertsson, the one who was hated by the poisoner that killed so many people in the town. But, after I dismissed him from his post, I believe Sievertsson returned to his family home in Norway."

"He did," Camville replied, "and has not returned."

"There have been no others," d'Arderon assured him.

"Then we must assume that either one of your brethren is keeping his sin well hidden or that the maggot eating into this murderer's brain has been falsely spawned," the sheriff said resignedly. "I shall send Roget to the stewe where the harlot worked and see if he can discover any information that may help. Apart from that, there is not much else that can be done."

As Camville turned to leave, the preceptor called him back and asked him to wait for a moment. As the sheriff and Roget paused in the doorway, d'Arderon turned to Bascot.

"The person who murdered this poor girl is attempting to destroy the honour of our Order, de Marins. Since you have some experience in tracking down murderers it might be helpful if, with the sheriff's consent, you assisted him in his investigation. It is not a duty that a member of our Order would normally perform, so I will not command you, but instead would ask if you are willing to do so."

Bascot did not hesitate in giving his assent. He knew that his experience with previous investigations into secret murder was not the only reason d'Arderon was asking for his help. It was in the preceptor's mind, as it was in all of those standing there, that Camville's hands were tied in his enquiry by the fact that the Templar Order stood outside his jurisdiction. The brothers were answerable only to the pope in Rome for their actions; not even a king could command the Order's compliance in any matter. If the implied sin proved true and one of the men in the enclave had visited a prostitute, only his Templar brothers could be made privy to his transgression. As a member of the Order, Bascot might therefore learn some detail that would reveal the identity of the murderer. Although the Rule forbade him to disclose the name of the offending brother to anyone not in the Templar ranks, in the few days that were left before he was due to leave for Portugal, such knowledge, if carefully given, might guide the sheriff in the direction his investigation should take. It could prove to be a delicate task and Bascot appreciated d'Arderon's tact in asking, instead of commanding, that he undertake it.

Camville readily agreed to d'Arderon's suggestion. The tension was eased between the two men as the sheriff recognised the preceptor's willingness, within the confines of the Templar Rule, to collaborate in the enquiry. He was also aware, more than most, of Bascot's ability to seek out men with evil lurking in their hearts, for it had been on Camville or his wife's behalf that the Templar had carried out his previous enquiries. The sheriff would have welcomed Bascot's assistance for that proficiency alone.

Bascot and Roget accompanied the sheriff back through the preceptory gate and left him as he rode off back in the direction of the castle. Most of Lincoln's brothels were situated in Butwerk and, as they guided their horses down the track along the outside of the city wall that led to the suburb, Roget told the Templar that the stewe to which they were going was run by a man named Verlain.

"I have been in that brothel before," Bascot said. "Ernulf took me there when we were looking for the person responsible for the murder of four people found dead in an alehouse. I do not remember seeing the dead girl amongst the harlots we spoke to, but I remember the stewe-keeper. An unsavoury individual, with a face closely resembling a ferret's. Ernulf did not seem to have a high opinion of him."

Roget laughed. Ernulf was the serjeant in command of the castle garrison, a grizzled old veteran that was a friend of them both. "He is right. Verlain is a parsimonious bastard, and keeps his girls on short money if he can," Roget replied. "But he is no worse than most and probably better than some. At least he does not physically abuse his bawds; not that I have heard, anyway."

Entering Butwerk through Claxledgate, they rode past the evil-smelling ditch called Werkdyke and into a street named Whore's Alley. The buildings here were dilapidated and of cheap construction, leaning towards each other as though in danger of imminent collapse. The shutters of every one were closed; it was too early yet for the bawds to be at work. A couple of mangy dogs scoured for scraps and a few crows were pecking at remnants of garbage in the refuse channel that ran down the middle of the street. The birds watched the two men with inquisitive black eyes.

Pulling their horses to a halt outside the first of the houses on the lane, they dismounted and Roget banged on the door of the stewe. It was some moments before the door was finally pulled ajar and the close-set eyes of the brothel keeper peeped through. Alarm spread over his face when he saw Roget and, when he noticed Bascot beside him, his features fell even further.

"Open up, Verlain," Roget commanded. "I have some questions to ask you."

Reluctantly the door was pulled open to its full extent and the visitors allowed entry. With an unctuous smile that revealed teeth black with rot, the stewe-keeper showed the two men across a shallow entryway and into a room where the harlots were paraded for inspection by prospective customers. A number of stools stood along the perimeter of the chamber and in one corner a table was laid with a flagon and wooden cups.

"Can I offer you both a cup of ale?" Verlain asked obsequiously. "It is not of the best brew, but palatable. . . ."

Again Roget cut him short. "You have a girl who works here, hair as blond as a Saxon. What is her name?"

The question took the stewe-keeper by surprise. "I have two or three who are fair, Captain. There is Rosinda and Jolette. . . ."

"Not fair, Verlain," Roget said brusquely, "I said blond, the colour of a wheat sheaf."

The stewe-keeper nodded. "You mean Elfreda, Elfie we call her." He shook his head, running his hands nervously up and down the front of the greasy jerkin he wore. "She is not here at present, Captain, but perhaps one of the other girls would suit your purpose. They are all lovely maids. . . ."

"I have not come to sample your wares, keeper," Roget said roughly. "Elfreda—when did you last see her?"

"Not for the last three nights," Verlain admitted. "She has probably gone to visit her daughter; she sometimes does that, although she usually tells me when she is going and this time she did not. If she has done something wrong, Captain, it is nothing to do with me. I keep a clean house, and obey all the town ordinances. My girls are inspected regularly by the bailiff and there are none with pox, of that I can assure you. . . ."

Roget did not let him finish. "Elfreda is dead, Verlain. Murdered." The stewe-keeper's jaw dropped. "I want to know the names of all her customers," Roget went on. "And to speak to the rest of your harlots; see if they can tell me anything about her movements on the night she was killed."

Verlain almost fell over himself complying with Roget's order. He quickly reeled off the names of a few men who had been Elfreda's regular patrons although, he added, there were some whose identities he did not know, customers who came only infrequently.

Roget glanced at Bascot as the stewe-keeper came to a halt. One more question about Elfreda's customers needed to be asked, but the captain was reluctant to do it. The Templar gave him a nod and spoke to Verlain directly.

"Among those customers you did not know, did any of them seem likely to be a Templar brother or one of the laymen from the Lincoln preceptory?"

His question took Verlain aback, and he stuttered to find the words to reply. "I am not sure. . . . I do not know. . . ."

"The truth, Verlain," Roget interjected, the scar of the old sword slash that ran down the side of his face whitening as he gritted his teeth in impatience. "If you lie, I will tear your panderer's heart out and feed it to the dogs in the street."

Verlain's furred tongue flicked out and worked nervously over his lips as he viewed the angry visage of the former mercenary glaring down at him. "I am not familiar with the faces of the men who live in the enclave, Captain, and so cannot swear to the truth of my answer, but as God is my witness, I do not believe so."

Roget nodded, satisfied that the stewe-holder was, out of fear, telling the truth. Relieved that no violence to his person was forthcoming, Verlain scurried away to rouse the harlots who were, at this early hour, taking a hard-earned rest in the tiny cubicles on the floor above.

There were eight bawds altogether, most of them past the bloom of youth, but one or two still had a freshness in their complexion, even if their eyes had already acquired the hardness common to those who plied their trade. Most wore only a flimsy wrapper to conceal their nakedness, but a couple had cheap cloaks thrown over their shoulders. When told of Elfreda's death, the younger ones began to weep, but the older bawds responded only by a tightening of their lips and one of them muttered a foul expletive beneath her breath.

All of them readily answered the questions the captain put to them. None had been aware that Elfie had not been in her bed on the night of her absence, or of any reason she may have left the stewe, except for one, an older prostitute named Sarah.

"She snuck out of the house a couple of days ago," the bawd said. "It was early in the morning, just after my last customer—a greedy bastard who made sure he got his money's worth—had gone. I heard her and asked where she was going. . . ."

"Why did you not tell me?" Verlain interrupted. "You know I have been asking if anyone has seen her."

The bawd looked at him with distaste. "Why should I? All you're interested in is the money you're losing by her not being here, not if anything untoward has happened to her."

Roget quelled any further protest Verlain might have made with a glance and asked the bawd where Elfreda said she was bound.

"She wouldn't tell me," Sarah said. "Just said she was going to earn a plentiful measure of silver to put by for her little daughter. I thought mebbe she'd hooked herself a rich customer, one who'd pay good money for a session away from this place." The bawd's shoulders drooped in a disconsolate fashion. "I wished her well. If I'd guessed for one minute she was goin' to her death I would have stopped her."

Roget asked to see the belongings that Elfreda had kept in the stewe. At a nod from Verlain, one of the bawds went upstairs to the cubicle the dead girl had used and returned a few moments later with a bag made of rough, cheap, material. The contents were pitifully few—a change of kirtle and a worn pair of hose, a comb of bone with a few teeth missing, a much-knotted length of bright yellow ribbon faded by time and two wedge-shaped fourthings of silver, penny coins that had been broken in half and then broken again. At the bottom was one of the dyed horsehair wigs the women wore when they were abroad in the town. The only thing of value was the fourthings which were, no doubt, tips from satisfied customers.

The paucity of the dead bawd's material wealth brought tears to the eyes of all the prostitutes. Roget carefully replaced the possessions back inside the tawdry bag and told the stewe-keeper he would see that they were kept for Elfreda's daughter, and then asked Verlain where the child could be found.

"There's an old woman who lives nearby that takes care of prostitutes' children for a few pennies a week," Verlain said. "Her name is Terese and she lives here in Butwerk, two streets over from the Werkdyke."

As the captain and the Templar left the brothel to go and speak to the childminder, Bascot said to Roget, "It would appear it was the enticement of money that persuaded the harlot to accompany her murderer to the preceptory. Do you know any of the customers Verlain mentioned?"

"All of them," Roget replied. "But none seem likely to have had a part in this devil's scheme. They're all citizens of the town—a couple of older men with wives past their prime and the others regular tradesmen who visit a stewe when they have an itch in their loins. It might have been one of the others Verlain mentioned, the customers whose names he did not know."

"And it may just as easily have been someone she knew, or met, outside the brothel," Bascot opined.

The captain nodded glumly. "Perhaps this woman, Terese, will know his name."

Five

✠

When Gerard Camville returned to Lincoln castle, he went to the chamber where his wife, Nicolaa, attended to the many details involved in managing the vast demesne she had inherited from her father. Although nominal lord over her estates, Gerard was a restless man, his temperament more suited to the excitement of the hunt than the mundane administration of the fief, and he left all such matters in her hands. Nicolaa had also inherited the constableship of the castle and, while the country was at peace, supervised the fortress's household. It was she, rather than her husband, who was referred to as the castellan by the local populace. Only in matters concerning the shrievalty did Camville take an interest. It was a lucrative post, and he guarded his rights jealously.

When Gerard entered her chamber, Nicolaa was engaged in a scrutiny of the fees collected from one of the Haye estates with her *secretarius*, John Blund. The castellan was a short, slightly plump woman of mature years, her figure encased in a serviceable dark blue kirtle and white coif. She looked up in surprise when her husband entered the room. It was rare for him to interrupt her when she was at work and she felt a brief frisson of alarm.

"I have just come from the Templar preceptory, Wife," Camville said brusquely. "There has been murder done in their chapel; the victim was a harlot from one of the stewes in town."

Both Nicolaa and Blund, an elderly clerk who had served his mistress for many years, listened in horrified silence as Gerard related the circumstances of the murder. When he had finished, Nicolaa rose and poured her husband a cup of wine from a jug sitting on a small table.

"This is a serious business, Gerard," she said to her husband, "and a crime that will be difficult to solve." She waited until he had taken a good mouthful of his wine, contemplating what she had been told. Then she said, "Have you considered that someone in the preceptory may be responsible?"

The sheriff shook his head. "Why would I? This is an attack on the honour of the enclave. It does not make sense that someone belonging to the Order would commit the crime."

Nicolaa sat back down and paused before she continued, judging her next words with care, not wishing to set her impatient husband chasing after a false quarry. "As we have sorry cause to know, Gerard, it is often those that seem to be friends who are the enemy."

For a moment Camville glared at his wife, and then he nodded, recognising the truth of her words. It had not been so long ago that a member of their household had been guilty of secret murder and had, for a long time, screened his evil nature behind a mask of genial bonhomie. The lives of both Nicolaa and their son, Richard, had been placed in jeopardy before Bascot de Marins had finally tracked down the culprit.

Seeing her husband's agreement, Nicolaa leaned back in her chair and extrapolated on the thought that had come to her. "A life of chastity is not easy for some men, even though they have given their sacred word to be continent. Supposing, as you suspect, one of the Templar brothers is guilty of consorting with prostitutes, and while his transgression is not known to the preceptor, there is one other in the preceptory that is aware of it. Would not most men find it difficult to battle with their own sexual frustration while watching another break his vow with impunity?"

"The solution would be to report the erring brother to d'Arderon or Draper Emilius."

"But what if it is one of the lay brothers, or a lay servant?" Nicolaa persisted. "The former have sworn, as do lay brothers in other monastic institutions, to devote their life to Christ, but they are not fully fledged monks of the Templar brotherhood. They give the gift of their labour so that the Templar brothers can devote their energies to the ongoing battle against Christ's enemies. To witness the transgression of a monk betraying his vow of chastity would not be easy to swallow and yet, because of their lower station, any protest they made might be disregarded; and if there was no proof of the charge, might even earn punishment for the sin of bearing false witness."

She paused for a moment, and then continued, "And if one of the lay servants is privy to such a secret and could not corroborate his claim, he would have even more to lose, for his livelihood would be at risk. Even though the lay servants have not taken a vow of chastity, they are expected to comport themselves with circumspection, and so must eschew the pleasure of a woman's company. The knowledge that one of the brothers was enjoying what was denied to them could easily cause a rancorous burn in the gut."

Camville took a few moments to carefully consider his wife's words and found they had merit. John Blund, the secretary, had kept silent during the exchange, but it was obvious from the look on his face and the slight nodding of his head while Nicolaa had been speaking that he found her premise worthy of consideration.

"I hope you are wrong," Camville finally said. "My writ has no authority over any member of the clergy and even less within the Templar Order."

His statement brought to their minds the struggle that the late King Henry II had waged with Thomas à Beckett, when the king and the archbishop had come into violent disagreement over the church's autonomy in matters relating to crimes committed by those in clerical orders. Even though Beckett was now dead, murdered by a few of Henry's loyal, but rash, knights, the issue had not been resolved. Gerard faced a similar problem to the one that had plagued the late king; if the murderer belonged to the Templar Order, he could not lay a charge against the killer. Only the pope, or a Master Templar, could take action against the guilty party.

"I think d'Arderon will cooperate to the fullest extent he is allowed," Gerard said slowly. "But if the murderer is a man under his command, he has no choice but to obey the dictates of the Order."

"Then we must hope that my postulation is an erroneous one," Nicolaa said.

"Just so, Wife," Camville replied with a concerned look on his face.

* * *

THE DWELLING WHERE TERESE, THE OLDER WOMAN WHO LOOKED
after the children of prostitutes, lived was in a row of houses
even more shabby that the ones in Whore's Alley. The stench
from the Werkdyke was almost overpowering; the ditch
contained all of the refuse collected from the streets of the
town and, in the increasing heat brought by the spring sunshine, had begun to renew decomposition. The house they
were seeking had only two floors, but the doorsill had been
swept and the iron knocker rubbed free of rust. Terese had
once been a prostitute herself, Verlain told them, and now
that she was too old to entice customers to her bed, earned
the few pennies she needed to live by caring for children that
younger and more attractive harlots had the misfortune to
accidentally produce.

When Roget knocked on the door of the hovel, the former bawd opened the door. She was not the old crone that
both men had expected. About fifty years of age, she was
extremely thin, but upright in her bearing and even though
her face was marked with old scars of some disease, probably
the pox, a trace of lingering beauty could be seen in her dark
eyes and high cheekbones. Her clothing was shabby, but
clean, and the coif she wore over her greying hair was whiter
than some of those worn by affluent goodwives in the town.

When Roget told her of Elfreda's death, tears sprung into
her eyes, but she kept her composure and asked them to
come in.

Her dwelling place was comprised of only one room
on the lower floor of the tumbledown house with a small
scullery at the back. The sounds of tapping could be heard
coming from above and Terese explained that the noise was
being made by a tinker who lived upstairs. "His work con-

sists mainly of repairing household vessels from goodwives in the town," she said. "Thankfully, he does not labour at night."

In the chamber were half a dozen children, all female, and ranging in age from about a year old to a child of around nine. Terese pointed to one of the smaller ones, a little girl just past the toddling stage, and told them she was Elfie's daughter, and was called Ducette. The child was a pretty little thing, her hair startlingly blond, and there were two large dimples in her cheeks.

"She looks just like her mother," Terese said with a catch in her voice. "I don't know what will happen to the child now that Elfie is dead. As far as I know, Elfie had no family, not hereabouts, anyway. I can keep Ducette for a little while, but I am not a rich woman, as you can see."

She gestured around the room, which was sparsely furnished with a pile of skimpy straw pallets and a few wooden bowls and spoons lying on the surface of a rickety table.

"Did Elfie ever mention to you that she knew one of the men from the Templar enclave, mistress?" Bascot asked. "Or that she had any intention of going there?"

Terese shook her head. "I cannot recall her ever speaking about your Order, Sir Bascot, even in passing. But if it was a recent notion, she would not have done so, for I have not seen Elfie since a week past, when she came to pay me the four pennies I charge each mother for the children's keep. She said nothing to me then that was out of the usual. She played with Ducette for a while and gave her a kiss before she left."

"One of the women who worked with Elfreda told us that she was expecting to earn a substantial sum of money for her services on the night she left," Bascot said. "And a well-filled purse was found alongside her body, so we believe it was the promise of monetary reward that lured her to her death."

"I am sure that is so," Terese agreed. "The mothers of every one of these children are desperate for money. Harlots do not willingly have babies. It only happens when the medicants we use to prevent such an occurrence fail. We know the fate that awaits our offspring—especially the girls. Most of them will end up in the same trade as their dams. I do my best to keep the little ones clean and fed, and teach them what manners I can, but their destiny, unless there is enough money to save them, is to be harlots. There are a few foundling homes available for such children, but not nearly enough."

She looked towards the little girls. The eldest was keeping a couple of the younger ones amused by throwing a small coloured ball back and forth, another was drawing in the hard-packed dirt of the floor with a stick while the other two—aged about three or four—were clapping their hands as they repeated a nonsense rhyme in a singsong fashion.

"I do not tend any male children here. All these little ones will have more than enough congress with men once they are past childhood," Terese said with a catch in her voice. "For a short time, I save them from that fate."

One of the younger children began to cry and Terese picked her up and soothed her. Her world-weary eyes looked straight into Bascot's blue one as she held the child against her withered breast. "I am sorry I do not have any knowledge that will help you, lord, but there is only one thing I can tell you for certain, and that is Elfreda would not have been tempted to go into the preceptory for love of a man."

* * *

Bᴀsᴄᴏᴛ ᴀɴᴅ Rᴏɢᴇᴛ ᴘᴀʀᴛᴇᴅ ᴏᴜᴛsɪᴅᴇ ᴛʜᴇ ꜰᴏʀᴍᴇʀ ᴘʀᴏsᴛɪ-tute's house, the captain to go to the castle and give his report to the sheriff, and the Templar to return to the preceptory. As Bascot rode up the track outside the city walls, he pondered on the motivation for the murder. On the surface, it appeared that it was an attack on the Templar Order, and intended to expose hidden vices. But his thoughts, although he was not aware of it, soon began to echo those of Nicolaa de la Haye. Reluctant as he was to consider it, he came to the realisation that it could have been someone in the Templar enclave who had murdered the harlot, and also desecrated the chapel, in retaliation for what he saw as an unacceptable sin on the part of one of his brethren.

Viewing the situation dispassionately, he had to admit that there were some in the Order that found the strict dictates of the Rule difficult to obey. Brothers inclined to garrulousness found keeping the Grand Silence during meals irksome; others thought the stricture against hunting a deprivation almost beyond bearing, while some of the knights complained of the forbiddance of adding ornate bridles or reins to the accoutrements of their destriers.

But most of these were viewed as minor inconveniences; it was the need to be chaste, in accordance with the vow they had taken, that a few of the lustier men found extremely difficult to cope with. For that reason, the punishment for this particular transgression was harsh and every care was taken that none of the brothers, denied access to female flesh, lapsed into the sin of sodomy. Every Templar, of whatever rank, was forbidden to disrobe completely, even when he lay down for his night's rest. Lights were kept burning all night in dormitories, and the lambskin girdle of chastity, which was donned at the time of initiation, must not be removed.

From d'Arderon's assurance to the sheriff, it was apparent that none of the brothers under the preceptor's regular command had been punished for such a transgression, but that did not mean that the sin had not been committed and kept hidden, at least from the preceptor.

He considered the characters of the men who lived in the enclave on a regular basis, not even pausing to include d'Arderon, Hamo, Emilius or the priest, Brother John, in his reflections. The preceptor was a man of strict honour and the serjeant the same. Both would rather sacrifice their lives than betray the brotherhood. As for Draper Emilius, even though Bascot felt his probity, too, was beyond question, his withered arm precluded him from suspicion. It would have taken two strong hands to overcome and strangle the young prostitute, a physical ability that Emilius did not have. And it was most unlikely that Brother John, a devout and elderly priest, had gone publicly into town to lure a harlot to her death.

Apart from these brothers, there were seven men-at-arms who, during the last few years, had been posted more or less permanently in Lincoln. All were veterans who had served in the Holy Land and sent to the Lincoln enclave to man the garrison and help train newly initiated brothers. Bascot knew them all well and found it hard to believe any of them had broken their vow to remain chaste.

The same could be said of the lay brothers and servants in the enclave. The lay brothers were few in number, comprised of the blacksmith, the elderly cook who prepared the meals they ate, and a widower with carpentry skills that had joined the enclave a few years before, shortly after his wife died. All of them had been in the Lincoln commandery for some time. It seemed improbable that, after so many years of faithful service, one of them would have erred.

As for the lay servants, menials hired to attend to some of the more tedious tasks in the enclave, again, it was doubtful that any of them could be responsible for the outrage. There were a few grooms who mucked out the stables, a spotty-faced lad who assisted the cook and ran errands, and a young man who had suffered the misfortune of being born with a twisted spine but who, despite his disability, swept out the bail, dusted sleeping pallets with crushed pennyroyal to deter fleas and cleaned out the midden. All of them were biddable and seemed content with their lot. None had ever, to Bascot's knowledge, given cause to be suspected of lasciviousness.

If his judgements of all those within the Lincoln enclave were correct and, as d'Arderon believed, none guilty of forbidden congress with women, then it followed that it could not have been one of them that had inspired the deep outrage that had prompted this terrible crime.

That left only the men who had passed through the enclave in the weeks since Eastertide to be considered. Nearly all of them, both those still in the commandery and the men forming the contingent that had recently left, were from commanderies far to the north of Lincoln, from York and another preceptory at Penhill, high in the Yorkshire Moors. Only a couple of the men that were still in the Lincoln commandery were from a closer enclave, the one located at Temple Hirst, a few miles to the northwest in South Yorkshire. But was it reasonable to consider any of these men, all of whom had been in Lincoln for only a short period, and would not be familiar with the location of the numerous brothels in the town?

Bascot was about to dismiss all of the transient brothers as likely suspects when the thought struck him that one of

them could have witnessed lewd behaviour in the commandery he had just left. If so, was it possible he had contained his
rage at the immorality until he was on a journey that would
take him out of the country, and so free him from discovery,
before seeking a way to relieve the poisonous envy that was
festering in his soul?

The Templar shook his head to clear it. These speculations were wild and fanciful. He must look for solid facts
before forming any hypothesis about the murderer's motivation. He had yet to speak to the three young men Hamo had
hired to help with caring for the horses in the preceptory.
They had reported for their duties at Prime on the morning
that Elfreda and her companion had been admitted to the
preceptory. That was not long after the time she must have
been killed. It may be that one of them had seen someone
leaving the enclave and could identify him.

His musings had taken him almost to the gates of the
commandery and he gave the gateward a salute as he approached the entrance. Before he went any further with
the investigation, he needed to make a report to Preceptor d'Arderon about what he and Roget had learned at the
brothel. It would make disappointing news.

Six

✦━┼━✦

THE NEXT DAY, AS NEWS OF THE MURDER SPREAD THROUGHOUT the town, the reaction was mainly one of shock, but there were a few who, envious of the wealth that had been donated to the Order, voiced the opinion that the prostitute's death was certain to be connected to a Templar brother's licentious behaviour. During the daily services in the numerous churches throughout Lincoln, priests sent up a plea for heavenly aid in catching the murderer, and one or two of the more sanctimonious prelates begged God not to take vengeance on the town for the desecration of a chapel that was not attended by any of its citizens.

Bascot and Roget went into Lincoln, intending to speak to the three young lads Hamo had hired to assist the enclave's grooms and then question the men Verlain had said were regular customers of Elfreda. None of the former had turned up for work that morning, probably because the boys, or their parents, were fearful of them returning to a place where a murder, with its terrible overtones of sacrilege, had taken place. It had been through the agency of the town bailiff, Henry Stoyle, that Hamo had hired the lads, and so they would need to go to the guildhall, where the bailiff spent most of his working day, and ask him where the boys could be found.

Both Bascot and the captain doubted whether any of the three lads had been involved in the murder, because the man-at-arms on the gate at the time Elfreda and her companion had been admitted to the enclave had been adamant that no one else had either entered, or left, the preceptory before the young townsmen turned up for work over an hour later. Since the other gate into the commandery, the one out onto the hillside, had been locked and barred, it would have been impossible for any of the three to have gained early access to the commandery, killed Elfreda, and then reappeared outside the walls at the hour they had been told to report for duty. But Bascot was hoping that when the youngsters had been on their way to the enclave they might have seen the person responsible for the crime. Unless it was a Templar brother who had committed the murder, whoever had carried out the deed must have hidden somewhere in the preceptory until the inmates were astir, and then slipped out through the hillside gate when the horses were led out for exercise. There was a slim chance that one, or all, of the boys had seen him on the streets as he made his way back to town.

As the pair walked down Mikelgate, the Templar badge on the shoulder of Bascot's tunic caused passersby to turn their heads and stare pointedly in his direction. The expression on most of the faces seemed merely speculative, but there were some that were openly hostile and the Templar realised, for the first time, how quickly the opprobrium caused by Elfreda's murder had spread. As he and Roget approached the intersection of Mikelgate and Brancegate, Bascot was beginning to feel stirrings of anger within his breast for the unfairness of their judgement. Even if it had been a Templar who was responsible for Elfreda's death, that did not mean that all of the brothers should be stained with one man's guilt. He quickly cautioned himself not to give way to resentment. Fear, especially of heavenly wrath, often prompted the need for a scapegoat.

Suddenly, the emergence of a small procession from a narrow turning near St. Cuthbert's church drew the attention of everyone on the street away from Bascot. At the head of a forlorn little group was a priest carrying a crucifix attached to the top of a pole. As he paced slowly forward, he intoned the words of one of the seven penitential psalms recited at funerals. Behind him were two more clerics, one on either side of a young man clad in a rough knee-length garment of cheap wool and holding a clapper in his hand. The youngster was crying copiously, twirling the clapper as he walked. The two pieces of wood crashed together with a loud cracking sound. As the procession moved out farther into the main street, it could be seen that the young man's cheeks were covered with a bright red rash, as was the back of the hand that held the clapper. Following a few steps behind him were two women, one old and the other young, both sobbing loudly.

People drew back in alarm as they realised what they were witnessing. The young man must have recently been diagnosed as carrying the contagion of leprosy, and the procession was the commencement of a funeral rite for his diseased body. Henceforth, the leper would be considered dead, forbidden to have any contact with healthy people, including his family. Lepers were not allowed to enter a church, attend a fair or marketplace or wash their hands or any of their clothing in a stream or fountain. They were also denied the liberty of going abroad among the populace and, if necessity declared they must travel, warning of their approach must be given by means of the clapper or the ringing of a small bell. From this day on, the afflicted youngster would spend the rest of his life in a lazar house just outside the city walls. The Templar's heart filled with compassion for the leper's sad fate and, glancing at Roget, saw that the captain felt the same.

As the procession began to wind its way down Mikelgate towards the gate that led outside the city walls, Bascot noticed Roget, who was standing on the Templar's sighted side, suddenly focus his attention on a knot of people standing a little way along the street. Then, with a bellow of rage, the captain darted towards the group, yelling imprecations at a slightly built man attired in shabby clothes. The fellow's head came up and, seeing Roget running towards him, took to his heels, slipping frantically through the crowd that had paused to watch the leper's passage. People drew back in alarm as the captain shoved his way through them to chase the man, who was doing his best to circumvent a corpulent merchant that had, at the captain's shout of alarm, placed himself stolidly in the fugitive's way. It was only moments before Roget had grabbed ahold of his quarry, seizing him by the long straggly hair that lay lankly on his shoulders and then grasping him firmly by the arm.

"You miserable little worm," Roget growled at his captive. "Give me what you have just stolen or I'll lop your thieving fingers off."

With shaking hands, the captive reached inside his tunic and handed a leather scrip to Roget. At the same moment, a tradesman who was standing near to Bascot let out a yell of alarm. "My purse is gone," he cried, holding up two pieces of leather thong that had once held his scrip in place on his belt but had been cleanly sliced in two.

Roget shook the thief violently and there was a clatter as a small curved knife fell from the man's clothing. The captain scooped it up just as one of the town guards came running from where he had been standing on the other side of the street.

"Take him to the gaol to await trial," Roget ordered, handing the cutpurse into the custody of his subordinate, along with the knife. "He'll not find it so easy to steal after he's had a couple of fingers sliced from his hand."

As the thief was led away and Roget took the scrip back to the townsman from whom it had been stolen, a burst of applause rang out along with cries of "Well done, Captain" from the watching bystanders. When Roget rejoined Bascot, he had a wide grin on his face and, as they resumed their journey to the guildhall, said to the Templar, "Perhaps, *mon ami*, this is a harbinger of the day's good fortune. A thief has been caught, maybe we will also catch a murderer."

THEY FOUND STOYLE, A QUIET CONSCIENTIOUS MAN, AT WORK in a little chamber at the back of the large building that was used by those responsible for the administration of Lincoln's civil regulations as well as a meeting place for the guild masters in the town. When Hamo had needed extra help in the commandery, he had asked the bailiff to recommend three industrious young men of good character. Stoyle had subsequently sent the youngsters—one approaching his seventeenth year and the other two a couple of years younger— to the enclave and, after a brief interview, Hamo had hired them. After Bascot and Roget explained to Stoyle their need to question the boys and why, he told them to go to the flesh market on Spring Hill. The father of two of the lads had a stall there, he said, and would most likely know the whereabouts of his sons, and possibly the third boy.

After walking back up Mikelgate to Spring Hill, enquiries among the stallholders led them to a squat man with burly forearms who was hard at work chopping up half of a pig with a large cleaver. The huge apron that the fleshmonger wore was splattered with gore, as were his hands and face. The stall he owned was a large one, with chunks of beef, lamb and skinned carcasses of rabbit set out on display. The air was heavy with the metallic tang of blood. Hordes of flies circled around and crawled over the raw flesh, while stray cats and dogs lapped at the blood that lay in pools on the ground. Around the fleshmonger were other stalls carrying similar wares, but in smaller quantities. Goodwives from the town were inspecting the various cuts of meat on offer, many of them haggling over the price before making a selection and then wrapping their purchases in old cloths brought for the purpose and placing them in the wicker baskets they carried on their arms.

When Bascot and Roget approached the fleshmonger, he paused in his work to listen to the captain's request to speak to his sons and, after wiping the sweat from his brow with one of his blood-stained hands, answered Roget gruffly, waving his cleaver in the direction of a neighbouring stall where three youngsters were setting out trays of offal.

"My lads and the other boy are over there," he said and then, with a defiant glare at Bascot, added, "Meself and their mate's father didn't want 'em goin' back to the preceptory in case that murderer is still hangin' about, so I put 'em all to work here."

The three youngsters had watched Roget and Bascot's exchange with the fleshmonger and there was excitement on their faces as the Templar and captain walked over to them. When asked what their movements had been on the morning of the prostitute's death, they responded eagerly, deriving a grisly satisfaction from their peripheral involvement in the murder. The fleshmonger's family and that of the third boy lived close together, the eldest one said, and so he and his brother had gone to their friend's house just after Matins, and they had walked to the enclave in each other's company. Their journey had taken them up through Bailgate into the upper portion of the town where the castle and Minster were located, then through the grounds of the Minster and out of the gate in the eastern wall to the path that led to the preceptory. When asked if they had seen anyone during that time, the answer had been disappointing. There had not been many people on the streets that early in the morning, they were told, and only one of the guards under Roget's command making his regular patrol and a few attendees at early morning Mass, all goodwives with young children, had been seen. Apart from those few, there had been no one else about.

Disappointed, Bascot thanked the youngsters and gave them leave to return to their chore of filling the offal trays. Then he and Roget left the flesh market, and walked back down Mikelgate to commence the tedious task of finding, and questioning, each of the men that the stewe-keeper, Verlain, had said visited Elfreda on a regular basis.

In the preceptory, the atmosphere was subdued. Even though the chapel had been reconsecrated, at every service the eyes of the men strayed towards the vestry, unable to rid themselves of the thought that for two whole days, while they had been engaged in worship and prayer, a woman's body had lain secretly decomposing in the chamber. The prostitute's murder had cast a blight over them all.

In the hope that strenuous exercise would restore the men's spirits, d'Arderon decided to hold a series of mock skirmishes on the hillside below the preceptory, using the rolling slope of the hill to simulate the arid terrain in the hot climes of Outremer and the Iberian Peninsula. Directing all eighteen men of the contingent to don full armour, he told them to assemble outside the gate onto the hill. He also ordered them to clad their horses in the protection that was worn while on a march into enemy territory or in battle— lengths of chain mail draped over the animals' withers and back to shield the chests and legs of the mounts, padded covers on rumps, and fitted head-guards of either leather or mail. He then told Hamo to equip each of the men-at-arms regularly based in the enclave with one of the speedy, light-weight horses usually used by the Order's messengers and also with bows, blunted arrows and lances. They were then to be dispersed among the hillocks of grass on the rolling slope below the enclave.

"We are going to simulate the method of attack most favoured by the Saracens when they encounter a troupe of Christian soldiers," he informed the men of the contingent when they were all assembled. "The heathen will do their utmost to entice you into breaking out of formation. Sara-cen horses are smaller than ours and therefore fleeter of foot, and they will dart in, feint an attack, and then retreat, at-tempting to lure you into chasing them. If you are foolhardy enough to fall into that trap, you will find a dozen infidels hidden behind the next sand dune. One or two Christian soldiers, no matter how well armed, are no match for such a large number. You will be captured or killed. It is essential you obey your commander and do not engage the enemy until you are given the order to do so. This is a lesson you must learn for, if you do not, you will pay for your ignorance with your life."

Leading them down onto the grassland until they were about a mile and a half distant from the preceptory, he gathered the men of the contingent into a troupe behind him, knights and squires in the van, men-at-arms behind, and led them in repeated charges up the hillside towards the enclave. In seeming cooperation with the preceptor's intention, the sun shone down with a brilliance unusual for this time of year, and more in keeping with the later months of summer. Although the temperature was not nearly as high as it would be in the Holy Land, it was warm enough that perspiration soon began to trickle beneath chain mail shirts and helms, and the dust thrown up by the horses' hooves stung the men's eyes and clogged their nostrils. As d'Arderon led each charge up the grade of the hill, the brothers from the enclave staged the rapid assaults the preceptor had spoken of, riding just close enough to be out of reach of the swords carried by the men in the troupe and then firing an arrow or throwing a lance before darting back to a safer distance. Although the missiles were blunted, if one managed to find its way past the kite-shaped shields, the impact struck sharply against protective mail shirts and leggings, delivering painful bruises. And there was always the chance of serious injury if one should happen to land on the exposed portion of a face only partially protected by the nasal bar on helms. It was a gruelling drill, but d'Arderon hoped it would distract the men from contemplation of the circumstances surrounding the harlot's death. Again and again, the preceptor led them through the exercise, admonishing the men who followed to keep close together and not allow the encircling men-at-arms to tempt them into retaliation unless he gave the command to do so. It was the strength of the Templar forces that obedience to their leader was absolute. A moment of impatience in a lonely stretch of desert could cost a man his life.

Emilius took up a position at the rear of the band. Despite the physical disadvantage of his crippled arm, years of battle experience made him an implacable deterrent to any who strayed from the tightly packed formation ahead of him. Wrapping the reins of his horse around the pommel of his saddle, in his strong right arm he carried a mace from which the flanges had been removed. To any who seemed about to swerve out of line, he kicked his mount forward and, guiding the animal with his knees, swung the mace onto the offending Templar's shield. The hefty blow resulted in a bone-shaking jar that was sufficient to remind any negligent brother of the need to keep within the tightly packed formation.

The preceptor kept the men at the exercise for most of the morning. As the hour of noon approached, he separated the knights and squires from the rest and, taking them down to the flatland at the bottom of the hill, drilled them in repetitions of wheeling their horses en masse to face different directions, always keeping together in a solid bloc. When under attack, the ability to turn and present a united front to the enemy was of prime importance. Since men-at-arms often fought as infantry, Hamo took over their training, marching them forward and back in a solid rank and, at his command, pivoting shoulder to shoulder with shields enarmed. By early afternoon their passage had scarred the side of the hill with a wide swathe of churned up earth. The only breaks permitted were to rest the horses, or exchange tiring mounts for fresh ones. None were allowed to take a midday meal and thirst was quenched by a few meagre swallows of ale from a keg placed at the top of the hillside. At the hours of divine office, a short respite was allowed while the required number of paternosters for each service was repeated, just as if the men were on active duty and unable to attend services in their chapel.

At two hours past midday, the preceptor gave the little band a brief rest after which, he said, the knights would engage in combat with lances. The men-at-arms were to set up butts and improve their archery skills.

There were four brothers of knight's rank in the contingent and these, with their squires, took up places on a level stretch of ground. D'Arderon and Emilius rode down to watch the contest, leaving Hamo in charge of the men-at-arms. The preceptor and draper watched the knights' manoeuvres with interest, weighing up the expertise of each. Two of the knights were young men who had only recently received the buffet of knighthood and had little battle experience. The other two were older, both men who were approaching their fortieth year. One of these had told Emilius he had once served with King Richard's forces in Normandy in the years before the monarch's death, and had fought alongside William Marshall, a famed paladin despite his advancing age, in the attack on the French castle at Milli, near Beauvais, in '97. Having returned to England shortly after that encounter, the knight's reflexes had slowed somewhat during the intervening years of peaceful inactivity, but the training he had undergone since joining the Templars had encouraged their sharpness to return. After only one pass, he and the other older knight, a crusader who had followed King Richard to the Holy Land in 1192, had unhorsed both of the younger knights and prepared to pit their skills against each other. Twice the pair ran a course across the hillocky grassland, the twelve foot lances crashing onto each other's shields, but with both managing to deflect the blow and maintain their seats. As they drew apart and wheeled their destriers for the third time, the knight who had fought with William Marshall tried a different tactic. Instead of aiming the blunted twelve-foot shaft at the shield of his opponent, he held it low, as though he was tiring and could not couch the lance firmly under his arm. The former crusader was quick to take advantage of this seeming weakness and spurred his horse forward, his lance levelled for a clear hit on the shield of his adversary. At the last moment, his opponent raised his lance and, with a swift movement, knocked the other shaft aside and then, with the full weight of his body, thrust himself sideways and drove his shield into that of the former crusader, toppling him from the saddle. Shouts of admiration burst forth from the watching men and a groan of despair from the fallen knight's squire.

"That man will be a valuable addition to the commandery in Portugal," d'Arderon said to Emilius.

"And I thank God for him," the draper replied with enthusiasm. "They have great need for men of experience."

As it was now approaching Vespers, d'Arderon called a halt to the training and ordered the men to return to the enclave, hoping the day's demanding activity had put new heart into all. For a short time, as they lined up to ride through the gate into the preceptory, there was a brief burst of exhilaration as tactics and weapons were discussed, but it was short-lived. Once inside the commandery, an unnatural silence fell, and it was not broken as the Templars stabled their horses and then crossed the compound to attend the early evening service in the chapel. Despite d'Arderon's efforts, a pall of despondency still engulfed them all.

IT WAS LATE IN THE EVENING BY THE TIME BASCOT RETURNED to the commandery. He and Roget had spoken to all of the men Verlain had named and every one had witnesses to their presence on the morning in question. In the case of three of them, it was the customer's wives who provided their spouses' alibis—with angry glances at their husbands as they did so—and for the rest of them, who were all unmarried or widowed—it was a member of the household in which they lived who confirmed their whereabouts at the pertinent time. Before they parted, Bascot and Roget agreed that, on the morrow, the captain would visit all of the houses in Butwerk, especially those close to the stewe where Elfreda had worked, and ask if any of the inhabitants had seen the prostitute after she left the bawdy house. In the meantime, Bascot would speak to the men in the preceptory, asking each one if they were certain they had not noticed anything untoward during the time Elfreda and her companion had been admitted to the enclave. Preceptor d'Arderon had already made this same enquiry, but it had been at a general assembly of the men after Elfreda's body had been removed, and the response had been negative. Perhaps by Bascot speaking to each brother individually, as well as to the grooms that slept out on the hillside where the surplus horses were penned, he might find some small trace of the prostitute's presence and a description of the man who had accompanied her.

That night, Bascot's sleep was restless. As the rest of the men in the dormitory snored on their pallets, the Templar gave more consideration to the notion that one of the men in the enclave was guilty of the crime. In the small radiance cast by the rushlights kept burning all night long in the sleeping place, Bascot stared into the wooden rafters above him with his one good eye and pondered if the idea was feasible. In order to have gained Elfreda's company, it would have been necessary for the man to have left the command-ery the evening before, and to have done so unnoticed. If he had been able to accomplish that, he could have regained admittance in the guise of one of the lads Hamo had hired as extra help, killed Elfreda and secreted her body in the chest, then returned to his pallet. Apart from the danger of his earlier absence being noticed, the task would have been much easier for an inmate of the preceptory to commit than an outsider. He would be familiar with the daily routine, cognizant of the layout of the chapel and other buildings and, since he was expected to be present in the enclave, had no need to be concerned about a surreptitious exit.

If his suspicion had merit, it was possible that the guilty person's absence had not been noticed. Sleeping quarters in the dormitory were cramped due to the excessive number of men in the enclave; priority was given to those of knight's rank and their squires, requiring that the overflow take their night's rest wherever they could find enough space to lie down. Some of the men-at-arms had spread their pallets in the stables, others on the floor of the granary or in the con-fines of the storehouse, squeezing in beside the lay brothers and servants who regularly slept in the buildings. And there was always the possibility that the culprit was a brother who had left the preceptory with the recently departed contingent. When those additional men were in the enclave, sleeping quarters had been even more inadequate. It was unlikely one man's absence would have been noticed.

Short of asking every brother to vouch for the presence of his sleeping companions, there was no way in which Bascot could verify that all of the Templars, as well as the lay brothers and servants, had remained within the precincts of the commandery for the entire night. Another concern was that if he asked the question too boldly, it might exacerbate the existing feeling of disquietude; he did not want to plant the suspicion in their minds that a Templar might have carried out the murder. If that happened, morale would fall even lower than it was now. Still, he decided, by taking care to be judicious with his questions, it might just be possible to ascertain the presence of everyone without revealing his purpose. He hoped it would prove a fruitless exercise, but felt it to be a necessary one, if only to eliminate the possibility that, God forfend, a Templar brother was the murderer.

IN THE CASTLE, GERARD CAMVILLE GREW EVEN MORE TESTY than usual as one day passed and another began, and still no trace of Elfreda's killer was found. Finally, Nicolaa suggested that he take a hunting party out into the greenwood and use his pent-up energy in pursuit of an animal quarry instead of a human one, perhaps even stay overnight in his hunting lodge while he did so. She would, she told him, send a message to him at once if any new information was unearthed. When her irascible husband agreed to her suggestion, there was a sigh of relief not only from his wife, but from every member of the castle household.

Seven

✦⊶✦

ᴇARLY THE NEXT MORNING, AFTER PRIME, D'ARDERON HAD
all of the men from the contingent assemble in the centre
of the commandery and declared that, since they were to
leave for Portsmouth in two days' time, they were to spend
the intervening period preparing for the journey. Horses
were to be rested, weapons put in good order, and repairs
made to any tears or snags in clothing. They were also to
ensure that the beards which every brother was constrained
to grow in accordance with the Templar Rule were neatly
trimmed, as well as their hair shorn to an acceptable length.
The next morning, the preceptor said, all of the men-at-
arms in the contingent would present themselves for inspection by Draper Emilius, while the knights would take the
responsibility of ensuring that they and their squires were
ready to embark.

The preceptor's decree made Bascot's task of speaking to
each of the brothers, both those regularly based in the commandery and the ones belonging to the contingent, much
easier. Within the organised muddle of men honing swords,
repairing rips in tunics with needles and lengths of gut, or

sitting patiently while a comrade used a sharp knife to shear off excess growth in hair or beard, he was able to approach small groups of two or three brothers at a time and tell them the preceptor had asked him to confirm, before the contingent left the enclave, that no one had noticed anything suspicious on the night of Elfreda's murder. He also asked each of the men in which part of the enclave they had been sleeping.

All of the men's responses to the first part of his question were, as he had expected, in the negative. None claimed to have heard or seen anything unusual and had, for the most part, taken their night's rest undisturbed. By taking note of those who had slept in the same locations, he was able to crosscheck that their claims were true. The men stationed with the horses in the makeshift pen out on the hillside had also passed a quiet night and had neither seen nor heard anything untoward. Only one of the brothers he questioned, a young man-at-arms from the contingent, had said that he could not be sure, since he had been taken with gripes in his belly for almost all of that night.

"A couple of hours after I lay down on my pallet in the stable, I had to rush to the jakes," he admitted shamefacedly, and guffaws broke out from the men who were with the young soldier when Bascot asked the question. "I was back on my pallet before the bell for Matins sounded," he added, "but if anyone was about in the preceptory, I don't think I would have noticed them, 'cause the pains were really bad."

He was the recent initiate, Bascot recalled, who had received a reprimand from Hamo for not being in command of his short sword on the day Elfie's body had been found. It was more than likely his sour stomach had stemmed from anxiety about his lack of proficiency with the weapon.

The Templar had then questioned each of the men-at-arms regularly based in the enclave as well as the lay brothers and servants. The responses were the same as those from the men of the contingent. He was relieved to find his careful enquiry had been pointless.

At a late hour in the afternoon, Roget came to the commandery to tell Bascot the result of his questioning of the inhabitants of Butwerk. The captain's disappointment was evident in his manner when Bascot came out to the gate to speak to him.

"I have found nothing that can help us find this *chien, mon ami*," Roget said. "No one saw either Elfreda or her killer or heard anything of their passage to the preceptory. It is as though the pair of them were wraiths that moved in the shadows, invisible to all." He looked at the Templar hopefully. "Have you learned anything? Anything you can tell me, that is."

Bascot, in turn, shook his head. "Nothing, either that I am allowed to tell you, or otherwise."

"Then I fear we will never discover who committed this despicable crime," Roget said disconsolately. The captain hawked and spat. "I am off to find a jug of good wine and the company of a complaisant woman," he said. "I hope I will see you once more before you leave but, if I do not, I bid you fare well against the infidel."

As the evening drew to a close, and there remained only one more day before Bascot was due to leave, he found himself with a surprising reluctance to depart. It seemed that God had endowed him with a talent for tracking down the perpetrators of such atrocious crimes but now, when that ability was so desperately needed, it had failed him. Although he had never felt any conceit for his accomplishments—it was

God's gift and not his own skill that was the cause of his success—he wondered if he was now in danger of falling prey to the sin of pride. If it was God's will that the identity of the murderer be revealed, it would be done, whether Bascot was in Lincoln or not. With a prayer beseeching heaven to aid d'Arderon in his dilemma, the Templar ruminated on the other cause of his disinclination to leave.

In the spring of 1199, when he had finally managed to escape the Saracens after his years of incarceration in the Holy Land, he had stopped on the island of Sicily as he made his way back to England. There, begging on a wharf in the port of Palermo, he had noticed a young mute boy who was suffering from malnutrition and looked to be near death. Bascot had been struck with pity for the lad's plight and had persuaded the boy to become his servant. As he had found the youngster on St. John's day, he had given him the name of Gianni, a diminutive of the Italian name of the saint. Together they had travelled back to England and, during the two years Bascot had stayed in Lincoln castle, the lad had served him devotedly. With the passage of time, the Templar had come to regard Gianni with the same affection he would have bestowed on a son of his own loins.

Leaving the boy behind when he rejoined the Order had been difficult, even though the castellan, Nicolaa de la Haye, had promised to personally keep watch over him. Due to the lessons in scribing that Bascot had given Gianni during their stay in the castle—at which the boy had proved both his acumen and diligence—Nicolaa had given Gianni a place in her retinue, working in the scriptorium under the direction of her secretary, John Blund. Bascot had been certain that after he left to rejoin the Order, the boy would thrive and be safe from harm. But now, with a murderer once again loose in the town, Bascot felt uneasy. If Elfreda's killer had been clever enough to gain entry into a stoutly walled compound guarded by armed soldiers, the villain would have little difficulty gaining access to the castle. A murderer had breached the security of the fortress once before and a clerk in the scriptorium—where Gianni now spent his days—had died a horrible death from the effects of a lethal poison.

Bascot castigated himself for his fear but, all the same, could not rid himself of it. In just thirty-six short hours he would leave Lincoln and, with it, Gianni, the lad who had come to hold a special place in his heart. He fervently prayed the evil knave who had murdered Elfreda would make no attempt to breach the castle walls.

IN THE CASTLE SCRIPTORIUM, THE YOUNG BOY WHO WAS THE object of the Templar's concern was also anxious, but not out of fear for his own well-being. A small, slim young boy of about fourteen years of age, with a head of dark curly hair and liquid brown eyes, he was seated at one of the lecterns the clerks used to carry out their tasks, making an archive copy of an accounting sheet from one of the Haye properties. With him were the secretary, John Blund, and an older clerk named Lambert who was Gianni's tutor and also his friend. Lambert had taken the trouble to learn the sign language that the boy and his former master had used to communicate and, just a few months before, had compiled a book of the gestures for the use of a scion of the English nobility who had difficulty speaking because of a cleft lip and divided palate.

Gianni was bent over his task, but his concentration was not wholly on the document in front of him. His leave-taking from his former master had been a few weeks before, at Eastertide, on the fourteenth of April. It had wrenched the boy's heart to watch his master leave to rejoin his Templar brothers, but the boy knew it was right that Sir Bascot do so. While Gianni was fully aware of his former master's heartfelt regard, he was just as cognizant that the Templar's soul belonged to the Order.

At first Gianni had found the new routine unsettling and had missed Bascot's reassuring presence but, as the days went on, Gianni had grown accustomed to his new life. He slept in the barracks with the men-at-arms under the watchful eye of Ernulf, the veteran serjeant of the garrison. Ernulf had a gruff affection for Gianni and the boy knew he need have no fear of harm while the serjeant and the soldiers of the garrison, all of whom treated him with kindness, were nearby. Gianni's days were spent in the scriptorium. Master Blund was also well-disposed towards his new clerk, even though the secretary could be a little stern at times. But his faded blue eyes would light with praise as he monitored Gianni's work and his elderly face crease into a smile of pleasure at each new proof of his young assistant's aptitude for the tasks he was given. All in all, Gianni's future was one he could look forward to with confidence.

It was not his new circumstances that were causing Gianni concern, but the news Master Blund had related about how the murder of a prostitute had taken place in the Templar preceptory. The secretarius had related the conversation he had overheard between Lady Nicolaa and her husband, and that the castellan had suggested it might be one of the Templars in the preceptory who was responsible for killing the bawd. Gianni had no fear of his former master's ability to defend himself in an open confrontation—the boy had seen the muscles that swelled in the Templar's arms when he practised with a sword in the training ground of the castle bail—but if the murderer was one of the brothers in the Lincoln commandery, and Bascot came close to discovering his identity, his former master could be in danger of an attack by stealth. A knife in the back while Bascot took his night's rest on his pallet, or was absorbed in prayers in the chapel—the boy's vivid imagination conjured up a dozen ways that the life of the man he had come to love above all others could be snuffed out with the quickness of dousing a candle flame.

The boy turned away from Master Blund and Lambert's scrutiny and, slipping down from the stool on which he was seated, walked over to a huge cupboard filled with rolls of parchment and scribing implements that stood at the back of the room. Determinedly emptying his mind of his fears, he shut his eyes tightly and, under the guise of sharpening the point of a new quill, sent a silent prayer heavenward, beseeching God to keep the Templar free from harm until he had ridden safely away to Portugal.

ᴇARLIER THAT MORNING, A LINCOLN PROSTITUTE NAMED Adele Delorme was startled out of sleep by a knock at the door. She was not a common harlot like Elfie, forced to earn her living under the protection of a panderer in one of the stewes in the lower part of town, but a woman of great beauty who, by using her physical attributes in a discriminating fashion, owned the house in Danesgate where she entertained a select number of wealthy men.

As Adele rose from her bed on the upper floor to respond to the knocking at her door, she mentally castigated herself for not replacing the maidservant who had left her employ a couple of weeks before. But the position required a girl who was willing to endanger her own reputation by working in the household of a harlot and also had the good sense to keep a still tongue in her head about the men who came to enjoy Adele's favours. Such a discriminating servant was not easy to find and, so far, there had been no suitable candidates.

Hastily throwing a light cloak about her nakedness, the elegant prostitute went downstairs. Her caller stood close to the step, a hooded cloak partially shielding the face. It took Adele a second or two to rub the sleep out of her eyes and recognise her visitor but, when she did, she evinced surprise.

"I had not thought to ever see you again," she said.

"Nor I you," the caller replied. "Will you allow me to come in? I have an urgent matter I must discuss with you."

Reluctantly, Adele nodded. "I suppose I owe you such a favour," she said. "But you will have to wait downstairs while I get dressed."

The visitor followed Adele into a small chamber just off the entryway. The prostitute bid her guest be seated in a comfortable chair and poured a cup of wine, which she set on a table near the chair.

"I will only be a few moments," Adele said and, pushing back the thick locks of auburn hair that had fallen over her shoulders, hastened from the room.

As she made her way up the staircase to the upper floor, she was unaware that her caller had not waited in the chamber as she had bid but had, after a few moments, followed her up the stairs with stealthy steps. Nor, as she donned a kirtle of embroidered sendal, did she hear the door come softly open behind her. The first indication that she was not alone was when a length of strong leather cord encircled her neck and was pulled so tight that it choked off her breath. Her hands scrabbled uselessly at the cord that was strangling her and she tried to scream, but to no avail. Within seconds, she was dead.

Adele's body was not discovered until late in the evening when one of her wealthy patrons, an armourer, called at her dwelling for his regular appointment. Just like Elfreda, Adele had been garrotted, but this time additional injuries had been inflicted on the prostitute's dead body. The armourer, a man of strong physical and mental constitution, nonetheless felt his senses reel when he saw what had been done to her. After ripping the harlot's gown from neck to navel, the point of a sharp knife had been used to carve a symbol on the delicate flesh of Adele's left breast. It was a cross pattée, the emblem of the Templar Order.

Eight

+‡+

THOUGH THE WEATHER OVER THE PRECEDING DAYS HAD BEEN
exceptionally fine, the next morning dawned with a heavily
overcast sky that promised rain. Well before report of the
second prostitute's death reached the preceptory, Bascot went
to ask Preceptor d'Arderon if he would accompany him out
onto the hillside and give his opinion on one of the mounts
that Bascot had chosen to take with him to Portugal. Every
Templar knight was allowed to have three horses; if they
didn't bring the animals with them when they joined, or if
the mounts became incapacitated, they were provided by the
Order. The preceptor had bidden Bascot take his pick from
the steeds in the commandery and now that he had made his
choice, he wanted d'Arderon's approval of the animal that
was to be his destrier. The preceptor was a good judge of
horseflesh and his opinion worth having.

As the men-at-arms began to assemble in the middle of
the commandery for Emilius's inspection, the pair rode out
of the preceptory gate and down onto the grassy slope below,
Bascot paying particular attention to the gait of his mount.
The horse was a sure-footed sorrel stallion. It was smaller in

stature than some of the other destriers in the stable, but it had a solid stance and alert temperament. Bascot was confident it would serve him well in any confrontation with the enemy and it looked to have enough stamina to withstand a long journey. He had chosen another stallion, a mature grey that Hamo had recommended, as an alternate war horse, and a black gelding to use as a packhorse, leaving them both with the blacksmith to have new shoes fitted. As he rode the sorrel up and down the grassy stretch, guiding it into swift turns and abrupt halts, the preceptor sat atop his huge black destrier and watched Bascot put the stallion through the manoeuvres. D'Arderon's wide muscular figure was immobile, but every so often his eyes would stray to dark clouds that were beginning to gather on the southern horizon. Bascot would, afterwards, think of those clouds as a dire omen of events to come.

Bascot felt more than a little concern for the preceptor's state of mind. The death of the harlot and defilement of the chapel had shaken him badly, as did the depressed morale of the men. D'Arderon took his responsibilities with great seriousness. Even though it was impossible for him to have prevented Elfreda's murder from taking place, Bascot knew the preceptor nonetheless felt a share of the responsibility, if only for the fact that it was one of the men under his command—the guard on the gate—that had admitted the bawd and her killer into the enclave. During the time a poisoner had been loose in Lincoln a year before, when one of the bailiffs employed by the Order to supervise a Templar property had been found to be of a loose moral standard, d'Arderon had blamed himself for not having been more scrupulous in checking the man's credentials.

Bascot was certain that, at this moment, as d'Arderon

gazed towards the south coast of England, the preceptor wished to be a part of the contingent due to leave the next day. D'Arderon had been stationed in the Holy Land for many years and, during that time, had pitted his considerable strength and military expertise against the Saracens. It was probable that Emilius felt the same. Although the draper was two decades younger than the preceptor, he had, until his injury deprived him of the use of his arm, spent ten years fighting the Moors in Portugal. Neither man made complaint of their present situation, both content to serve Christ to the best of their abilities in any way they could, but now, contending with the murder of a woman in the preceptory's chapel, and the resultant accusation that a Templar brother might be the cause of her death, both officers must long for the uncomplicated life of active duty.

Roget came riding down the hill just as the two knights were preparing to return to the enclave. The captain's expression was grim and, when he came up to d'Arderon, he saluted the preceptor and told in a blunt fashion the grisly news of Adele Delorme's death.

"Another harlot's been murdered," he said. "In the town. She was found last night, but it looks as though she has been dead for at least twelve hours. The sheriff went to his hunting lodge yesterday and Lady Nicolaa has despatched a servant to inform him of the death. It was she who sent me here."

The former mercenary hesitated for a moment before he continued. "This bawd was also garrotted, Preceptor, but there were other injuries inflicted on this latest victim that Lady Nicolaa thought you should be told of immediately."

D'Arderon's face blanched as Roget related the grisly details of the butchery that had been done to Adele's body.

After a moment of complete silence, the preceptor rammed his spurs into the flanks of his destrier and the startled animal leapt forward. D'Arderon kept the horse at full gallop up the hillside, heading for the enclave. Taken off guard by the suddenness of the preceptor's reaction, it was a few moments before Bascot and Roget followed in his wake.

When d'Arderon reached the preceptory gate, he charged through and came to a sliding halt in the middle of the compound. Dismounting in one fluid motion, he tossed the reins of his horse to a groom, and strode off in the direction of his office.

"Emilius! De Marins! Attend me," he barked, never once turning his head.

The draper, who had just begun his inspection of the men-at-arm's equipment and clothing, looked up in surprise at d'Arderon's abrupt entrance into the commandery, and hastily told the brothers standing in line to await his return before hurrying after the preceptor. When Bascot caught up with him, he told the draper in a few succinct words of the murder of a second harlot and that a Templar cross had been carved on her chest. Emilius's gaze grew cloudy with dismay as he assimilated the blasphemous nature of the wanton cruelty.

When they entered the preceptor's office, d'Arderon was standing by the one small window the room possessed, gazing out of the narrow aperture at the men under his command, now standing in puzzled groups looking towards his office.

The preceptor turned and spoke as Bascot and Emilius entered the room. "This murdering bastard must be caught," he rasped. "Not only has he killed two women, he has placed the Order, and this enclave, under attack."

D'Arderon moved to the desk, the expression on his face rigid with suppressed wrath. "Until I order differently, no one is to leave the commandery without my express permission."

"But, Preceptor," Emilius protested, "the contingent going to Portugal is due to leave tomorrow. . . ."

"Their departure must be delayed," d'Arderon replied abruptly. "Someone in the preceptory is the cause of this devil's hatred. I would stake my life that it is not one of the brothers that are based here in Lincoln, nor any of our lay brothers or servants. The two murders must be connected, so the men of the cohort that just left can be exonerated. Therefore it must be one of the men in the contingent that is still in the enclave. Until I discover which of them has committed the sin that is enraging this madman, they will stay."

Emilius said no more, but his expression mirrored his disappointment of the preceptor's decision. The morale of the men was already low; to be told they would not leave as planned would deflate it further.

"The only information we have on these brothers was contained in the missive sent from London to warn us of their arrival," d'Arderon continued. "It states only their name, rank and length of service." He barked an order at Emilius. "You will write immediately, Draper, to the preceptories from which they came and ask for more information about each man, especially whether any have been subjected to punishment and, if so, the reason for it."

"Many of them have only recently joined the Order,"

Emilius replied repressively. "It is hardly likely they would have transgressed in such a short space of time."

At the implied criticism in the draper's voice, the anger that d'Arderon had been holding in check finally exploded.

"You will follow my orders, Draper, and without question, as you are sworn to do." The preceptor had not raised his voice, but there was no mistaking the depth of his emotion.

Emilius, whose steadfast commitment to his vow of obedience had wavered for a moment, flinched at the reprimand and nodded his acceptance of the rebuke.

D'Arderon walked over towards the window and stood looking out the grilled opening for a few long moments in silence before turning once again towards the two knights. When he spoke, his words were milder in tone. "If this devil's objective is to cause dissension among us, we must take care that he does not succeed. There is another reason for my keeping the contingent back, Emilius, and it is that we cannot be certain that the man committing these outrages is not a Templar."

The draper reacted to d'Arderon's words with a shocked countenance and the preceptor looked at Bascot. "My charge comes as no surprise to you, does it, de Marins?"

When Bascot gave a brief nod in response to the question, the draper looked at him in puzzlement. For all his battle experience, Emilius's forthright nature still contained a touch of innocence. His devotion to Christ and the Order had blinded him to the fact that it was not only infidels who were capable of evil acts, and had certainly never led him to envision that the murderer might be a fellow Templar.

"I have considered the whereabouts of all of the men on the night the harlot was smuggled into the chapel," d'Arderon said to the draper. "At that time, the men of both contingents were here. With the press of bodies it would not have been difficult for one of them to steal out before Vespers or Compline and go into the town."

The preceptor began to pace as he went on. "The same is true of this latest murder. Captain Roget said she was killed sometime yesterday morning. There was a lot of movement about the enclave yesterday—the men were preparing themselves for today's inspection, grooms were exercising the horses out on the hillside, and others were helping to unload a supply of grain. It would not have been impossible for a lone man to slip out and go into Lincoln; the track down the hillside gives easy access to a gate into the city. And he need not have been gone long enough to be missed. I do not imagine it would take a great space of time for a man to murder a helpless woman and desecrate her body." These last words were uttered in tones of disgust.

"But surely the man who did this must have local knowledge?" Emilius said. "These men have only been here for a few days—how would they know where to find prostitutes within a town that is strange to them?"

"That is why I want to know more about each one," d'Arderon said. "It is quite possible that one of them has been in Lincoln before, or even lived here. May God prevent my suspicion proving true, but we must be certain."

Dismally, Emilius nodded his reluctant acceptance of his superior's opinion and his disciplined nature reasserted itself. "Do you wish me to also write a letter to Master Berard in London, Preceptor," he asked, "to give warning that the contingent will not leave tomorrow as planned? It will be necessary to inform the captain of the ship on which they are to travel that their arrival will be delayed."

"No, I will do that myself," d'Arderon replied.

The preceptor spoke to Bascot. "My stricture that no one leaves the enclave does not include you, de Marins. I want you to pursue this villain with every capability you possess. If need be, you are excused attendance at any of the daily services."

Bascot nodded his understanding and the three men closed their eyes in prayer, offering up a supplication for heavenly guidance.

Nine

✛

IN THE CASTLE KEEP AS TIME FOR THE MIDDAY MEAL AP-
proached, trestle tables were set up in the hall and laid with
platters of cold meat, bowls of pottage and bread. The sheriff
had not yet returned in response to the messenger Nicolaa
de la Haye had sent to inform him of the second murder
and the castellan sat at the table on the dais alone, barely
touching the food a page placed in front of her. Her slightly
protuberant blue eyes gazed unfocussed over the sea of heads
below. From time to time she took a small sip from her wine
cup.

As the clerks in the scriptorium came down to the hall for
their meal, Gianni glanced quickly around to see who had
entered and then signed to Lambert that he would not take
his accustomed place at their table, but eat in the barracks
instead. The clerk looked surprised, but made no comment.
Grabbing some slices of cold pork and a couple of chunks of
the coarse rye bread meant for those of lower station, Gianni
ran out of the keep, down the steps of the forebuilding and
into the bail. Everyone in the castle knew about the killing
of the second prostitute and that Roget had been sent by

Lady Nicolaa to tell the commander of the preceptory what had happened. Gianni knew that once the captain had done that he would return to the castle and await the sheriff's return. Since Gerard Camville had not yet arrived, and neither Roget nor Ernulf was in the hall, Gianni reckoned they were both in the long low building that housed the garrison. The boy, out of concern for his former master, hoped to learn from Roget more details about the murder that had taken place that morning.

When he ran into the barracks, it was almost empty. Most of the men-at-arms had gone to the hall to eat the midday meal but, aware that Ernulf usually kept a supply of food in the cubicle he used for his private sleeping place, Gianni was sure that was where the serjeant and Roget would be.

He heard a low murmur of conversation as he approached the stout leather curtain that separated the serjeant's compartment from the large open space where the men-at-arms slept and knew his assumption had been correct. Rattling the leather screen to warn of his approach, he slipped inside.

Both men looked up as he came in, but beyond a nod of greeting they paid him no mind. During the two years that the Templar had stayed in Lincoln castle, the boy had often accompanied Bascot while he had shared a pot of ale with Roget and Ernulf and they were accustomed to his silent company.

Moving quietly to the corner and sitting atop his usual perch on a stack of rolled up straw mattresses, Gianni munched quietly on his bread and meat as he listened to Roget tell how Adele Delorme had been killed and of the terrible wound on her chest.

"It was a sight to chill a man's blood," the captain said as he recalled the prostitute's face, her mouth agape and jaw stiffened. "She was a woman of rare beauty. For someone to destroy such loveliness is in itself a sacrilege."

Gianni had seen the woman Roget was speaking of. She had, indeed, been beautiful, with hair the colour of burnished copper and green eyes that were reminiscent of limpid pools in a forest glade. Her figure had been tall and willowy, and the boy had seen men catch their breath at sight of her slim, swanlike neck.

"The *bâtard* must have strangled her first," Roget went on, "because only a little blood had seeped from the wound."

"And you say he carved a Templar cross on her?" Ernulf asked disbelievingly.

Roget nodded. "Aye, he did. A downward slash and a sideways stroke on one breast. He even splayed the ends out like they are on the crosses the brothers wear. He wanted to be sure there was no mistake of his intent."

Shaken by the recollection, Roget took a hefty swallow from the wine cup he held. Ernulf, too, was staggered by the captain's description. His broad callused hands tightened around the cup he was holding, the knuckles turning white. "Hanging is too good for the villain that did this," he growled. "He should be hung, drawn and quartered."

"I think both the sheriff and preceptor are of a like mind," Roget replied. "D'Arderon is furious and Camville will be doubly so when he learns of this second murder. When we discover the identity of this *chien,* he will rue the day his mother bore him."

"What about the man who found her? Are you sure he isn't the guilty one?" Ernulf asked.

Roget shook his head. "I do not think so. He is one of her patrons, a wealthy armourer in the town. He says he found

her when he turned up for his weekly visit and I think he is
telling the truth."

Gianni recalled some gossip about the prostitute that had
circulated among the servants in the castle household some
months before. It was said that, about two years previously,
she had arrived in Lincoln riding a fine palfrey and accompanied by a manservant who left her company just after their
arrival. There had been much speculation about her identity
after she had taken up residence in the house in Danesgate,
since the house, it was said, was owned by a man of high
birth who lived in Newark. The rumour went that he had
married a woman of his own class just after Adele's arrival.
The gossips also said that the harlot had been the noble-
man's leman and the house—a dwelling situated on a street
inhabited by people of moderate means—had been his pay-
ment to her for leaving Newark before he wedded his young
wife. After she had settled in, Adele had patronised shops
in the town and let it be known by her manner and sugges-
tive glances that her charms were for sale, and that the price
of buying them would not be cheap. It had not taken long
before men were knocking at her door, but she turned away
all except for a select few.

"He might be lying," Ernulf said in response to Roget's
opinion that the armourer was not guilty. "Maybe she had
decided she didn't want him to visit her anymore and he was
angry for the dismissal. You are sure it wasn't him?"

Roget shook his head. "She had been dead for at least twelve
hours when he found her last evening and raised the alarm.
This morning, early, I went and questioned his family—
he is a widower but has two sons and a daughter—and his
servants, and they all gave witness that he had been with

them all through the previous night and the morning until he went to the shop where he fashions the armour he sells. One of his apprentices lives in his house and he was with the armourer for the rest of the day. It could not have been him."

"Did the villain leave anything behind in Adele's house that might help you find out who he is?" Ernulf asked.

"Only one thing," Roget said grimly. "Just like was done with Elfreda's body, Adele had a leather pouch full of coins lying close beside her. I counted them. There were thirty silver pennies."

IN THE PRECEPTORY, BASCOT AND EMILIUS REVIEWED THE LIST that had been sent from London with details of the men belonging to the delayed contingent. As d'Arderon had said, the only information it contained was each man's name, rank and length of service. Before the draper sat down to write letters to all the preceptories from which they had come, the pair discussed each one, trying to recall the little that had been said during snatched exchanges of conversation while the newcomers had been in the commandery. It was not much and, except for the two knights that had told of their previous battle experience—the one who had fought with William Marshall on the continent and the former crusader—none had mentioned any personal details, either of their lives before they joined the Order, or in the time since.

Of the eighteen men, apart from Bascot, that had been scheduled to leave for Portsmouth the next day, nine were from Penhill, a preceptory some miles northwest of York. Of these, eight were comprised of the four knights in the contingent, and included the two young men who had recently received their spurs of knighthood, and their squires. Both of the older knights were widowers and had requested admittance to the Order for a period of five years. The ninth man was a man-at-arms, a veteran Templar, who had been reassigned to active duty.

Of the remaining nine men, five were from the preceptory at York. All were of men-at-arms rank and had been stationed in the northern preceptory over the winter months while they waited to be sent overseas. The other four were from Temple Hirst in South Yorkshire. One was a man-at-arms who had proved himself to have an exceptional skill with horses and was to take charge of the contingent's animals and see them safely to their destination. The other three comprised of two men-at-arms who had joined the brotherhood some years before and the last was the recently initiated young lad who had suffered from gripes in his belly on the night Elfreda had been killed.

Taking the Templar seal, an image of two men astride one horse, from the wooden box where it was kept, Emilius then laid out some parchment, an inkpot and quill, and prepared to make a start on the messages. Despite the handicap of performing the task one-handed, he was surprisingly adept at handling the scribing tools. Once the letters were finished, he would roll them up and seal them with some melted wax, and press the seal into the surface. They would then be taken by messengers to their destination. As he picked up the quill to start on the first one, he gave a sigh.

"These are to be sent off directly after I have completed them. If the messengers meet with no delays in obtaining the responses, they should return by the day after tomorrow."

As he dipped the quill into the ink, he added, "I shall

pray that the preceptor's suspicions prove unfounded. It is hard to think that one of our brothers could be guilty."

When Bascot agreed with the sentiment, Emilius rubbed his hand over the sling on his withered arm and said, "During the battle when I received this wound, one of our Portuguese brothers lost his life to a Saracen arrow. We had been sent out into the countryside south of Almourol to try and find a band of Moors that had been ravaging villages in the area. We had been gone for some hours and had stopped to take a brief rest when the heathens attacked us, taking us by surprise. The brother who was killed had unbuckled the ventail over his chin and mouth to take a sup of water and an arrow took him in the cheek. It went deep and into his brain. He died almost at once."

The draper's eyes misted in sad remembrance. "Before we left Almourol to seek the Moors, that same knight had just completed his punishment for consorting with one of the Christian women in a village near the castle. She was a pretty thing, lushly formed as many of the women from Portugal are, and was unmarried and willing. The temptation was too great for him to resist, I suppose, and he bedded her. No one knew he had done so, but his conscience lay heavy on him and he went to our commander, confessed his sin and willingly paid penance. While I do not condone his breaking of his vow, I understand it. For brothers who are lusty, chastity is hard to bear."

He gestured towards the list of names. "If any of the men we are enquiring about has committed that same transgression, and has atoned, surely their wrongdoing could not spawn such hatred as these crimes suggest? Those of us who remain chaste are only too aware how hard it is to resist a woman's charms and would understand, and forgive, the sin of a brother who has strayed."

"Sometimes envy is just as great a spur as lust, Emilius," Bascot replied. "To watch another enjoy what you fervently desire can, in some men, foster a deep resentment which can turn to hatred."

The draper nodded. "You may be right," he admitted reluctantly. "It could be that one of our brothers has succumbed to what St. Paul called *mysterium iniquitatis*—the mystery of evil. But I hope it proves not to be a Templar that has either caused, or perpetrated these murders. The crimes are terrible ones for any man to commit, but for a Templar it is doubly so. He will not only have betrayed Christ and his brethren, but every man, woman and child in Christendom. The faith the populace have in the probity of those who belong to the Order will be severely tested."

Bascot nodded in commiseration. The purpose of the Order was to protect Christians; if it was found that one of its members had killed two Christian women, it would break a trust that should be inviolable. The doubting glances passersby had directed at Bascot on the day he had gone into town with Roget would become ones of loathing and disgust.

Emilius looked up, his face suddenly etched with determination. "As the preceptor said, we are at battle with this villain, Templar or not. The outcome shall be as God wills it. In that we must trust."

Ten

✠

LATER THAT AFTERNOON, AT D'ARDERON'S DIRECTION, BAScot went to the castle to speak to Gerard Camville. The Templar told Camville the departure of the contingent had been postponed and that the preceptor was taking steps to try and find any information that might uncover the identity of the murderer.

Camville had listened in silence while Bascot had been speaking, pacing back and forth on the hard-packed earth of the ward as he did so. Finally, he said, "And if the initiator of these crimes proves to be a Templar, will I be apprised of that fact?"

Bascot made no reply and the question hung unanswered in the air. After a few uncomfortable moments, the sheriff nodded, and said, "So be it. Since you will now be in the Lincoln enclave for the nonce, is d'Arderon still willing for you to give your assistance in the investigation?"

Bascot confirmed that the preceptor's sanction continued and, learning that Camville intended to send Roget into the town to question Adele's patrons, suggested he accompany the captain. The sheriff gave his assent and the two men, re-

lieved to be away from Camville's ill-humour, walked down
into the town through Bailgate, the massive arch that separated the upper portion of the town from the lower, and then
down the aptly named Steep Hill onto the main thoroughfare of Mikelgate.

The house where Adele Delorme had lived and subsequently been murdered was on Danesgate, a side street that
debouched into Mikelgate near the bottom of Steep Hill.
Roget had told the Templar of his finding of the thirty silver
coins but admitted that, in the confusion surrounding the
discovery of the body, he had not had time to search the
premises thoroughly. It was possible, they decided, that he
had missed some trace of the murderer's presence and so they
began their enquiry at Adele's house.

Danesgate curved in an arc down to Claxledgate on the
eastern side of the city. Bascot had been in this area once
before, when he had gone to view the bodies of four people
that had been found murdered in an alehouse. Adele's house
was not quite so far along the road as the alehouse, and was
a dwelling of modest size, two stories high, squeezed in
between two houses of more substantial proportions. The
location of Adele's house, Bascot noted, was not far from
the eastern wall of the town and a small gateway that led
out onto the path up to the preceptory. As d'Arderon had
pointed out, it would not have taken long for a man to come
into the town that way, enter the prostitute's house and murder her, and then make his escape outside the walls via the
same route. The thought that it might have been a Templar
brother that had done so filled him with dread.

As they stood in front of Adele's door, Roget told Bascot
that the prostitute's body had been removed to the char-
nel house of the nearby church of St. Cuthbert. "It was in

a terrible state, *mon ami*. The priest at St. Cuthbert uses the services of a couple of parish goodwives to prepare female corpses for burial. I have no doubt they will have spread reports throughout the town by nightfall of the butchery done to Adele's body."

They opened the door and went in. The entryway was small, with a floor of grey slate and a flight of stairs leading to the upper storey on one side. Climbing the stairs, they went into the bedroom where the harlot had been found. Apart from a small amount of blood that had dribbled from Adele's postmortem wounds onto a sheepskin rug that had been lying underneath her body, the room was hardly disturbed. A bed with a thick mattress was against one wall, a silken cover pushed back as though the occupant of the bed had risen hastily, and a small table set with a flagon of wine and pewter cups stood in one corner. The furnishings were of good quality. Beside the sheepskin rug, there were two chairs with arms and padded seats. A small tapestry hung on the wall near the bed. It depicted Jesus driving out the seven devils that had inhabited the body of Mary the Magdalene, a woman that many clerics claimed had been a prostitute.

They searched among the dead woman's personal possessions; a chest filled with clothes made from expensive materials, a small casket with a few items of jewellery, one or two set with semi-precious stones, and a small cupboard that held vials of perfume and pots of unguents. Both men felt a reluctance for the task, it was as though they were prying into the dead woman's intimate secrets. Underneath the clothes in the chest, they found a silk purse containing about five pounds in silver coins.

Finding nothing that gave them a clue to Adele's intruder, they went into an adjoining chamber, but it was empty except for some boxes containing more clothing and some household linen. In the corner was a trestle bed. On it was a rolled up straw mattress and a pile of rough woollen blankets. Roget had been told by the armourer who had found Adele's body that the servant employed by the prostitute had recently left and not been replaced. This would most likely have been the room a maidservant would use.

They went downstairs and into a small room that led off the entryway. It appeared to be a chamber that the harlot had used for a preliminary entertaining of her male guests before retiring to the bedchamber upstairs. Besides a table and two comfortable chairs, there was a brazier in one corner containing a few remnants of cold charcoal. On the table was an unstoppered jug of wine and a pewter cup filled to the brim. It was a handsomely appointed chamber, with wood panelling extending halfway up the walls and small tapestries hung above with depictions that were lascivious in nature. One featured a unicorn with an engorged phallus preparing to mount a snow white mare and the others were of scantily clad maidens posing in forest glades or reclining by secluded pools. Again there was no sign of a disturbance. If the murderer had been a patron of Adele's, it was likely she had offered him a cup of wine in here—which he had not drunk—and then taken him upstairs, and to her death.

The captain was glad that Bascot was with him. This investigation was not a task that Roget relished. More accustomed to using his fists or sword in direct confrontations with thieves and other petty miscreants, he was well aware that he had little skill in detecting the nuances that betrayed the identity of a murderer. The Templar, on the other hand, had a facility for searching out seemingly irrelevant inconsistencies and proving they were important. Roget did not know if Bascot's talent was due to the education he had received in a monastery during his youth or whether his years of imprisonment had made him more sensitive to his surroundings but, whatever the reason, the captain was more than willing to let the Templar take the lead in their search.

"Are there any buildings at the back of the premises?" Bascot asked, breaking in on Roget's reverie.

"Only a shed," the captain replied, leading the Templar out of the chamber and along a narrow passageway to a small enclosed yard.

There was little else and the two men were preparing to depart when the gate in the shoulder-high fence that surrounded the yard opened and a woman came through. She was about twenty-five years of age, demurely garbed in a plain grey gown and wore a white linen headdress. The rim of hair showing at the edge of her coif was dark brown. She was not uncomely, but neither was she handsome. Her most attractive feature was her eyes, which were a warm hazel colour and had a lively sparkle. Her glance flicked to the Templar badge Bascot wore on the shoulder of his tunic and then to Roget, dwelling on the copper rings that were threaded through his beard before she spoke to him.

"Are you the captain of the sheriff's town guard?" she asked in a voice that was soft and mellow.

"I am," Roget confirmed.

"I saw you both enter Adele's house from next door, which is where I live," she said. "My name is Constance Turner and I wanted to speak to you."

Looking behind her, she motioned to someone on the other side of the gate. A young serving maid crept through. She was a very small and skinny young girl, and looked to be no more than fifteen years old. Her bony little face was fearful and she was wringing her hands in distress.

"This is my maid, Agnes," Constance said. "I think she may have seen the man that murdered my neighbour."

"1 AM A PERFUME AND UNGUENT MAKER," MISTRESS TURNER said, "and, because goat's milk is kind to women's skin, I often use it in my preparations. I like to get it as fresh as possible and buy it from a neighbour just a few houses away who milks his goats early in the morning. Yesterday, I sent Agnes with a jug to get some and, as she was returning, she saw a man knocking at Adele's door."

Mistress Turner then added, without any seeming embarrassment for living in such close proximity to a prostitute, "All of us who live in the adjoining houses were well aware that Adele was a harlot and thought none the worse of her for it. She was a good neighbour, discreet and kindly spoken, and so we took no notice of the men who came to visit her on a regular basis. They, too, were circumspect and all of them are, or were, in the habit of coming in the evening, after dark. To see a man knocking on Adele's door at such an early hour drew Agnes's attention." She glanced at the maid and bid her relate what she had seen.

The maid was shy, but her confidence had been bolstered by her mistress's ease of manner. " 'Twas like Mistress Turner said, lords," she told them. "It were early, just after Prime. I was comin' back with the goat's milk when I saw this man walkin' ahead of me. I didn't take no notice 'til he stopped and rapped on Mistress Adele's door. After a minute or two, I saw her open it and speak to the man, and then she let him in."

"Did you see his face, *ma petite?*" Roget asked.

Agnes shook her head. "He had his back to me. I could only see that he were neither short nor tall, just middlin'."

"What about the colour of his hair, or the cut of his clothes?" Bascot asked.

Agnes flushed a deep red at being addressed directly by a man of knight's standing, and she answered hesitantly. "I couldn't see how he was dressed, or his face. He had a cloak on, a long one that reached the ground with a hood that was pulled up."

"That is why I thought the man Agnes saw must have been the one that strangled Adele," Constance Turner interjected, her voice trembling a little for the first time at mention of how her neighbour had died. "The spring weather is warm. Why would a man wear a cloak and hood on such a fine day unless he wished to mask his identity?"

She gave both men a direct glance before she went on. "It is possible, of course, that he merely did not wish to be recognised while visiting a prostitute, but it was very early in the morning for such an activity and, considering that my neighbour, from what I understand, was killed about the time that my maid saw the man at her door. . . ."

"You are probably correct, mistress," Bascot told her, "but without a description, it will be very difficult to identify him."

Constance nodded to Agnes. "Tell them the rest."

Again, Agnes blushed, but did as she was bid. "When the man lifted his hand to knock on the door, his cloak hitched up and I could see the clasp that were holdin' the edges together at the neck. I came nearer to him while he was talkin' to Mistress Adele and could see it plain."

She lifted eyes shining with awe. "It was a wondrous

clasp, masters, a circlet of gold bearing the image of St. Christopher! There were jewels on it, too, around the edge and on the saint's staff."

"Are you certain?" Bascot asked doubtfully, wondering if her youthful imagination had caused her to embellish the details of what she had witnessed. "You must have seen the clasp only fleetingly and from a distance."

But the little maid's insistence forced him to reject his misgivings. "I knows the blessed image of St. Christopher right well, lord," she said earnestly, "for I carries his likeness to keep me safe whenever I goes about the town for my mistress."

She reached inside the collar of her gown and pulled out a cheap pewter medal strung on a cord around her neck. It was etched with a crude picture of the saint reputed to protect travellers, a staff in his hand and a small child atop his shoulders. "The clasp the man wore had a picture on it just like this one," Agnes asserted, "and, like I said, I was near enough to see it plain. I knows it was St. Christopher."

Bascot and Roget looked at one another. This little bit of information could indeed be useful. Only a man of more than moderate means would be able to afford such an ornament and, to Bascot's private relief, was unlikely to have been worn by a Templar. The vow of poverty each brother took on entering the Order dictated that any wealth they possessed was to be given to a family member or donated as a charitable gift before they were accepted for initiation. It was possible there might be a brother who secretly retained some of his smaller valuables, but not probable. The evidence of the gold brooch decorated with precious stones, combined with two purses each containing thirty silver pennies that had been left by the murdered harlots' bodies, would suggest the killer was a man of considerable fortune. It was unlikely the retention of such wealth could have been kept privily in the closeness of the Templar communal routine. But while both men were grateful to the perfumer for offering her maid's testimony, the knowledge the two women possessed could put them in danger.

"We thank you for your help, and that of your maid," Bascot said to Constance. "But I would caution you both not to mention to anyone else that Agnes saw this man, or his clasp. If the early caller at Adele Delorme's door was indeed the murderer, he took great pains to ensure he would not be recognised. If he believes you possess even the smallest clue to his identity, your lives may be in peril."

The faces of both women blanched white and Agnes started to whimper. "As long as you keep silent, there should not be too great a risk," Bascot assured them. "And I am certain Captain Roget will assign one of the town guards to keep a constant watch over your house, just in case the man you saw should return."

"*Certainement*," Roget assured the perfumer. Despite the gravity of the situation, Bascot noticed that the former mercenary was favourably impressed with the appearance of Constance Turner. She was not the type of woman who usually attracted Roget; those that Bascot had seen him with during the time the Templar had spent in Lincoln castle had been more buxom and openly lusty in demeanour. But from the smile that lit the captain's face when he spoke to Constance, it was certain that he found her calm manner and soft brown eyes more than lightly appealing.

"There is just one more question I would like to ask you, mistress," Bascot said. "I am sure you will have heard that another prostitute was murdered before your neighbour and that her body was found in the Templar chapel of the Lincoln commandery. It has been said that her death was due to one of my Templar brethren having congress with a harlot. Since you said that you, along with others who live on this street, knew the identities of all the men that visited your neighbour, I must ask if, to your knowledge, any of them was a member of our Order."

Constance and Agnes both shook their heads. "All of Adele's patrons were men who live in the town," the perfumer replied. "As far as I am aware, you are the first Templar that has ever been seen at Adele's door."

Eleven

✦✦✦

IT WAS LATE IN THE AFTERNOON BY THE TIME ROGET RETURNED
to the castle bail. He and Bascot had spoken to all of Adele Delorme's patrons from a list Mistress Turner supplied and questioned them as to their whereabouts on the previous morning
about the time that Agnes had seen a cloaked and hooded
man enter the prostitute's house. Every one of them had witnesses to their presence elsewhere, most having been at home
with family members or household servants near at hand. A
couple had already been at work—one in the chandlery shop
he owned, the other in his premises in Parchmingate where he
stocked a selection of writing implements and supplies. The
assistants of both men vouched for their presence.

The captain knew that Camville would not be pleased
with their failure to discover any trace of the man and
dreaded giving the sheriff his report. Apart from knowledge
of the time the cloaked figure had entered the prostitute's
house, there was nothing else. When Roget left Bascot to
make his way back to the enclave, he saw the same look of
frustration on the Templar's face. There seemed to be nowhere else to search.

Gianni was in the ward when Roget came in through the castle gate and saw the dispiritedness in the captain's eyes. The time for the evening meal was over and the boy had been on his way to the barracks to sit down in a quiet corner and complete some mathematical exercises that Lambert had given him. Gianni was now in the final stages of completing the *Quadrivium*, lessons in arithmetic, geometry, astronomy and music. Since a clerk would have little use for knowledge of the stars and their movements or be involved in entertaining a patron with his skill on a musical instrument, Lambert, who was tutoring Gianni under John Blund's direction, had skimmed over both of these subjects and was concentrating instead on mathematics, for a good command of arithmetic was extremely important if the boy was to become a competent clerk.

Now, as Gianni watched Roget trudge up the steps of the forebuilding and into the keep, the lad felt a fleeting pang of nostalgia for the time before his master had left to rejoin the Order. In all of the previous investigations the Templar had carried out, it had been Gianni who had been by his side, often helping his master to find some important scrap of information that led to a successful outcome. He touched the pieces of much-scraped vellum on which Lambert had written the questions Gianni was to study. The lad knew that after Roget had made his report to Sir Gerard, he would, as was his habit, come and share a cup of ale or wine with Ernulf. It was also probable that the captain would tell the serjeant of the people they had spoken to that afternoon about the most recent murder and what results, if any, had been gained. Gianni decided that he would take his papers into Ernulf's cubicle and, as he had done earlier, listen to their conversation. He might not be able to accompany his former master and help him seek out the evil person who had killed those poor women, but hearing about the places the Templar had been and the information he had gleaned would go a little way to assuaging the exclusion Gianni felt.

IN THE PRECEPTORY, BASCOT TOLD D'ARDERON OF THE PAUCITY of evidence he and Roget had uncovered. The preceptor was a little heartened by the fact that the cloak clasp Agnes had seen was expensive.

"Even if it does not exonerate one of our brothers from having congress with these women, it does make it unlikely that it was a Templar who committed the crimes," d'Arderon said. "No brother is allowed to retain any of his personal wealth once he has joined the Order, although . . ." The preceptor gritted his teeth and did not finish what he had been about to say.

Bascot knew what d'Arderon's unspoken thought had been. It had been over eighty years since the Templar Order had been founded and, since that time, the number of brothers had grown from a sparse few to many hundreds scattered over all the lands of Christendom. With such an influx of initiates, and despite the Order's attempt to ensure that all applicants were free from the taint of worldly desires, it was impossible to ensure that every brother took his oath with complete sincerity. If an initiate found himself to be apprehensive of the abject state of poverty the Order required of its brethren, it would not be difficult to secrete some coins or small items of jewellery in a scrip or saddlebag as security against a time of need. And to any man with enough evil in his heart to commit secret murder, the retention of a few valuables would seem a paltry sin by comparison.

D'Arderon gave a heavy sigh. "I do not see what more we can do until the answers arrive from the northern preceptories," he said. "And, if the replies contain no report of any of the newly arrived men having been punished for consorting with prostitutes, we are at a standstill."

"Not necessarily, Preceptor," Bascot replied and gave voice to the thought that had occurred to him after he left Roget and was on his way back to the enclave. "It may be that we have been misled, deliberately or otherwise, away from the true provocation for these crimes."

"What do you mean?" d'Arderon asked in surprise.

"The occupation of both of the murdered women has led us to believe that the betrayal signified by the silver coins and the cross carved on Adele Delorme's torso is concerned with harlotry. But perhaps the victims were prostitutes because, by the very nature of the trade they ply, they are easy targets for violence. Harlots are accustomed to entertaining men who are strangers and would not be wary of being alone in the company of a man they do not know. If that is so, it might be that the murderer is not accusing the Templar brethren of lechery, but of a falsity of an entirely different nature."

Bascot paused for a moment before expanding on the notion that had come to him. "Have you, in recent months, had any disagreement with someone who is dependent on the Order for their livelihood? A supplier perhaps, whose goods have proved to be shoddy? Or someone who has protested the loss of part of an inheritance because a piece of property, or a sum of money, has been donated to the Order?"

The preceptor gave his full consideration to the question but, in the end, shook his head. "None that I can recall. There are always minor complaints from time to time—the cook declares that some of the vegetables lack freshness, or the wheelwright grouches that some of the wood we purchase from a timber yard in the town has not been properly seasoned. But these are all minor matters and usually resolved amicably."

"Has anyone recently deposited monies with you in exchange for a note of credit?" Bascot asked.

It was not uncommon for travellers, fearful of robbery while on their journey, to leave funds in the care of the Order in exchange for a receipt which, when they reached their destination, could be presented to a preceptory in the area for the stipulated sum. To cover the cost of handling the money, and to avoid the sin of usury, the amount declared was always lessened by a small percentage. It was just possible that someone who had undertaken one of these transactions now felt he had been betrayed, perhaps through loss of the receipt to provide authorization for release of the funds.

"There have only been one or two such requests in the two years I have been in Lincoln," d'Arderon replied. "And, as far as I am aware, neither gave cause for concern. If you wish, you may go through our records. It might be that something has escaped my memory but I am sure, if there was something that caused a heavy grievance, I would remember it."

"It may be an exercise in futility, Preceptor, but I think it should be undertaken."

D'Arderon nodded. "I will tell Emilius to make the records available to you after Prime tomorrow morning."

IN THE BARRACKS, GIANNI SAT QUIETLY IN THE CORNER AS, for the second time that day, he listened to the conversa-

tion between Roget and Ernulf. The two men paid the boy's
presence no mind, having become accustomed to him being privy to discussions relating to previous investigations
the Templar had undertaken. The captain told the serjeant
about all the conversations that had taken place with Adele
Delorme's patrons and then, leaning forward, said, "There
was one piece of information we uncovered that might be
useful. I only tell you because, although unlikely, it is possible that two women in the town may be in danger because
of it. If there is an alarm and I need the assistance of you or
some of your men, you need to be aware of the cause."

Ernulf rubbed a hand over his grizzled beard and both
men looked at Gianni. "You must keep to yourself what you
are about to hear, *mon brave*," Roget said to the boy. "The
Templar would not thank me if I put you, as well as the
women, in peril."

Gianni nodded and as Roget continued, listened with
full attention as the captain told how Constance Turner's
maid had seen a man going into the prostitute's house about
the time Adele had been killed, and of the cloak clasp he was
wearing. After Roget had finished the recounting, a fleeting
thought began to burgeon in Gianni's mind but, try as he
might, he failed to sustain it.

Twelve

❧ I ❧

Late the next morning, just before midday, one of the two men-at-arms that d'Arderon had sent with messages to the northern preceptories returned. The preceptor and Emilius were in the open space in the middle of the commandery when he arrived, sharing information about fortifications and conditions in Outremer and Portugal with the men of the contingent. With the exception of the knight that had been in the Holy Land on Crusade, only three of the others, brothers who had been in the Order for some years, had been overseas, but none to the Iberian Peninsula. Emilius was able to impart details of the castles at Tomar and Almourol and the terrain of the surrounding countryside that would enable them to be well prepared on their arrival.

Bascot was systematically going through the enclave's records in the chamber d'Arderon used as an office. The writing of the preceptor and Emilius was difficult to decipher. Both men had only a basic literacy and the words were a mixture of Norman French and Saxon English, and the spelling of some words varied in many places. It was not common for even highborn men to be skilled in the craft of reading and writing and, of the few that were, their scant training had usually been a few haphazard lessons given in their youth by a household priest or tutor. Bascot, not for the first time, realised how fortunate he had been that his father had placed him in a monastery during his formative years. The formal education he had received from the monks had stood him in good stead, not least because it had enabled him to pass his learning on to Gianni, who now was well on his way to becoming a clerk. The Templar wished the boy were beside him now, assisting him with his sharp eyes and quick intelligence, for poring over the often unintelligible writing with only the vision of one eye was making the task a cumbersome one.

When d'Arderon and Emilius came into the chamber with the missive from the preceptor of Temple Hirst, he pushed the sheets of parchment aside, and he and Emilius waited while d'Arderon scanned the letter. As they had expected, because of its closer proximity to Lincoln, the first reply had come from the preceptory at Temple Hirst. The information from this enclave was also the most important for, if a Templar brother was involved in the recent crimes, the commandery's nearness to Lincoln might have enabled a brother stationed there to become familiar with the town.

When the preceptor had made his laborious way through the contents of the message, he looked up at his companions, and said, "During their time at Temple Hirst, none of the four men now in the contingent had been punished for consorting with harlots." As Bascot and Emilius began to express their gratification, d'Arderon held up his hand. "As you are aware, we also asked for any background that was known about the newly come brothers. It seems that two of those previously stationed at Templar Hirst were born and bred close to, or in, Lincolnshire."

The preceptor went on to name the two men, one a man-at-arms, Thomas, who had been designated to look after the contingent's horses on their journey overseas, and the other the young lad, named Alan, who had been ill on the night Elfreda had been killed in the chapel.

"The Temple Hirst preceptor says he has no cause to doubt the horse-handler. Brother Thomas has been under his command for the last five years and has never given any reason for reprimand or an indication of dissatisfaction with the conduct of his other brethren. The preceptor cannot vouch for Brother Alan, because he is a recent initiate. But he does come from Barton, a village on the Lincolnshire side of the Humber estuary, and claims to be the youngest son of a man who weaves baskets and creels for fishermen in the area."

Bascot recalled the callow young lad that had so shame-facedly told him of the embarrassing effects of his bilious stomach. "He seems an unlikely candidate to be either visiting prostitutes or conspiring at women's deaths," he remarked.

"I agree," the preceptor replied. "He has a good ability with a bow—Hamo remarked on his skill and Alan told him that, as a boy, he used to practise regularly at the village butts—but other than that he seems a guileless youth. Beyond the odd fumble with a girl from his village, I doubt he has had any intimate contact with women at all, let alone a prostitute. And he certainly does not seem worldly enough to foster the deep hatred that seems to be inspiring this murderer."

The preceptor rubbed a hand over the short grey hairs of his beard. Relief was on his face, and also on Emilius's.

It did not seem probable that any of the Temple Hirst men were involved in the crimes. The other preceptories, at York and Penhill, were much farther north, and because of the distance from Lincoln, it was unlikely that any of the men from one of these enclaves could be implicated. They could not be certain of the latter supposition, however, until the responses from the preceptors of both the northern commanderies had been received.

THE SECOND MESSENGER RETURNED LATE THAT AFTERNOON, just as d'Arderon was sending Hamo to the castle with the purse of thirty silver coins that had been found with Elfreda's body. He had told the serjeant that the money was to be given to Nicolaa de la Haye, and had enclosed a request that the castellan take responsibility for ensuring the coins were used for the benefit of Ducette, Elfreda's little daughter, who was now, due to her mother's untimely death, an orphan.

"You may leave the purse in the care of Lady Nicolaa's steward, Hamo," d'Arderon instructed the serjeant. "I hope that by putting the silver to such a charitable use, it will remove the taint of contamination that is attached to it."

Just after Hamo left, the messenger that had been sent to the northern preceptories rode through the gate and delivered the pouch he carried into d'Arderon's hands. "I made good speed, Preceptor," the man-at-arms said. "Both of the commanders at York and Penhill wrote the replies with all haste, out of consideration for the gravity of the situation."

As d'Arderon was giving the soldier permission to stable his horse and take a well-earned rest, another rider came through the gate, a Templar cross emblazoned on the front of his tunic and riding a mount that was flecked with foam.

The new arrival slid from his mount and strode to where d'Arderon stood. His face was lined with grime and sweat trickled from beneath the conical helm he wore on his head. In his hand was one of the despatch bags used for communications within the Order. He handed the bag to d'Arderon. "I am come from London, Preceptor," he said in a voice tinged with weariness. "Master Berard bade me deliver this to you with all speed."

Calling to Emilius, d'Arderon took both messages with him into the chamber where Bascot had almost finished perusing the records of the enclave. None of the documents had revealed any trace of a situation that could have caused animosity towards the preceptory and he was just preparing to collect them all together when the two officers came in.

The letter from the northern preceptories was put to one side as d'Arderon broke the seal on the letter from Thomas Berard. Inside the rolled up parchment was another letter, also bearing the Templar seal. The preceptor scanned the London master's missive and tore open the other one, saying as he did so, "There is a letter from Master St. Maur enclosed with Berard's. I am bid to read it with all haste."

Amery St. Maur was Templar Master of England and, as such, a senior commander under the Grand Master of the Order, Philip of Plessiez. As the preceptor read through the letter, and Bascot and Emilius waited with barely restrained impatience to learn the contents, d'Arderon's face became sombre.

"Master St. Maur has recently returned from Paris where he was attending a meeting with our French Master, de Coulours, and other senior brethren. He was in the London enclave when my message arrived." D'Arderon looked at the two knights, his face wearing an expression of foreboding.

"While St. Maur was in Paris, de Coulours gave him some information that he feels may be pertinent to the murders."

The preceptor laid the letter on the table. "St. Maur says that de Coulours told him of an incident that took place in Acre a few months ago. A Christian man was killed in a brothel in a suburb of the town. The slain man was an Englishman, from Grimsby, and witnesses assert that he was killed by a Templar brother."

Thirteen

•┼•

Bascot and Emilius listened in shocked silence as d'Arderon told them what St. Maur had written. "The witnesses testified that not only is it a Templar who is responsible for the slaying of the Christian but that they are also certain he is, like the victim, an Englishman. Apparently, he and the dead man had been speaking together in the English tongue before an argument broke out between them. The squabble ended in a struggle between them with the Christian, whose name was Robert Scallion, dead on the floor. The Templar left before any attempt could be made to detain him. Scallion was, apparently, the owner of a sailing vessel, and traded mainly in onions that he purchased in the Holy Land and brought back to ports in France and England to sell. He was well-known in the brothel from previous visits to Acre and the other patrons in the stewe said he had just recently arrived in the port to lade his vessel with more stock."

"But the identity of the Templar is not known?" Bascot asked.

The preceptor shook his head. "St. Maur says not, only

that he is believed to be of knight's rank. But because he is thought to be an English Templar, de Coulours thought St. Maur should be apprised of the matter. As you know, any Templar brother found guilty of killing a Christian would merit expulsion from our Order. If his identity is discovered, that is what will happen and he will then be liable for prosecution by the Christian authorities in Acre. The commander of the Acre enclave is investigating the matter, trying to find out if the charge is true. St. Maur says he will inform me immediately if any further information reaches him, but you can see the connection between this death and the recent murders in Lincoln. . . ."

"Yes," Bascot replied, and Emilius nodded his head. "By now, such a terrible piece of news will not only have become known throughout Acre but also, no doubt, have been conveyed to the dead man's home port of Grimsby. If Scallion has family there and they have heard that their relative was slain by an unnamed Templar in a brothel, it is more than possible that one of them might feel a need to extract revenge for his death. If so, Lincoln is the closest enclave for the purpose."

"Such a motive would tally with the circumstances surrounding the murders of the two women," Emilius added with distaste. "Scallion's murder took place in a brothel, hence prostitutes were chosen as victims. And the coins implying betrayal—if it was truly one of our brethren who committed this deed, then he is indeed guilty of treachery—not only has he murdered a fellow Christian, he has also dishonoured his oath of chastity."

"Camville must be told of this news immediately," d'Arderon said, "especially as you will need his writ to question any of Scallion's relatives in Grimsby, de Marins. Since it is common knowledge in Acre, there is no need for the matter to be kept private within the Order."

"I will go to the castle straightaway, Preceptor," Bascot replied, rising from his seat. As he did so, Emilius asked the preceptor if he would now allow the contingent waiting in the enclave to depart. D'Arderon shook his head. "We do not yet have any surety that Scallion's death is the cause of these crimes. Until we do, the men stay here."

Bascot and Roget started out very early the next morning to ride to Grimsby, Camville's writ safely stowed in the captain's tunic. The port was nearly forty miles northeast of Lincoln and, if they kept their horses to a steady pace, they would reach it by mid-afternoon. Both men were riding mounts primarily used by messengers—Bascot's from the preceptory stable and Roget's from the castle—and capable of covering long distances at a steady speed.

The two men spoke little on the journey, stopping only to rest their horses occasionally and take a pull from the wine flask Roget had slung on his saddle along with a bite of the bread and cheese Bascot had brought from the preceptory kitchen. As they approached the port of Grimsby, situated on a narrow river called the Haven which emptied into the Humber estuary, the ground turned marshy. Grimsby had once been a small village but because of its sheltered position on the small tributary of the Haven—and hence the name of the little river—was fast becoming a thriving little town. Providing a safe harbour from the storms that often ravaged the North Sea, the port was used as a refuge for oceangoing vessels. That advantage, along with the copious quantities of fish its inhabitants were able to catch in their

small boats, had swelled its importance to the realm and
King John had granted the town a charter in 1201, allowing
its inhabitants to enjoy certain privileges that were denied
to hamlets less fortunately situated.

As they rode the last few miles, the salty smell of the sea
filled the air. There were no walls encircling the port for the
wide expanse of marshy ground surrounding the town provided ample defence against any attack by an enemy force.
The rippling ground of the flatland was covered in clumps
of couch and marram grass on either side of the road, in-
terspersed here and there with wildflowers, the most pre-
dominant of which was yellow-wort, the flowers of which
were used to make dye. The air was filled with the noise of
the birds that proliferated in the marshland, mainly ringed
plover and curlews, and they passed several small groups of
men and boys reaping a harvest from snares that had been
set to trap the fowl. Above them, the strident calls of terns
wheeling in the clear blue sky added to the cacophony.

Soon, the port lay ahead of them and, beyond the rooftops
of the houses gathered along the few streets of the town, the
masts of several ships riding at anchor in the swelling tide
could be seen. When they reached a small stone shed set
alongside the approach to the main street, they asked the
guard inside for directions to the house of the town bailiff,
Peter Thorson. The bailiff was known to Gerard Camville
and the sheriff had told them to ask for his assistance.

The guard nodded and pointed towards the harbour.
"Thorson's house is the one that overlooks the port," he said.
"Two stories high and has three scallop shells on the door."

The two men rode down the main street. The town was
small, not much more than a village, but seemed orderly.
As they dismounted in front of the house that had been de-

scribed to them, the smell of the ocean and its overlying odour of fish was strong.

Roget wrinkled his nose. "*Faugh*, what a stench. I hope our journey here has not been wasted, *mon ami*. I have never liked being near the sea, it reminds me of too many battles fought on shipboard along the coast of Outremer when I was in the army that followed King Richard on Crusade. I cannot swim and think the only reason I survived was because I was more fearful of drowning than being skewered by an enemy sword."

Bascot laughed. "I doubt there will be any need for you to board a ship here, Roget. If there are any suspects to be had in Grimsby, it is most likely they will be found on dry land."

"And for that, *mon ami*, I will be truly thankful."

As THE TEMPLAR AND ROGET WERE COMMENCING THEIR EN-quiries in Grimsby, Gianni was sitting at one of the lecterns in the scriptorium of Lincoln castle. His attention to his work was distracted as he tried to capture the fleeting thought that had so elusively slipped from his grasp the day before while he had been listening to the conversation between Ernulf and Roget. The exercise had cost him a sleepless night on his pallet in the barracks and, as he copied out various records of tenant fees paid into the Haye coffers, continued to elude him.

The bulk of his work entailed making copies for the archives of the many documents that passed through the hands of John Blund and Lambert. It was tedious work but Gianni enjoyed it. Not only were his writing skills improving with the exercise, but his Latin vocabulary was being greatly enhanced by the formal wording of many of the official papers. He was, as well, gaining a good knowledge of the vast properties that comprised the demesne Nicolaa de la Haye had inherited from her father. Pursuant to Lady Nicolaa's instructions, a duplicate was made of every record and stored in a chamber in another part of the keep. John Blund had explained to him that the reason for doing so was because, in the castellan's younger years, a carelessly tended candle had caused a small fire in the scriptorium and resulted in the loss of quite a few important documents. Thereafter, Nicolaa's father, Richard de la Haye, had instructed that a copy be made of every record and retained elsewhere. His daughter now followed the practise he had inaugurated.

As Gianni pulled forward another sheet of paper, a deed of transfer, onto the shelf of the lectern and placed a piece of second-grade vellum in front of him, he suddenly remembered what it was that he had been trying to remember. A few weeks before, he had been copying another such deed, a record of a Haye tenant requesting Lady Nicolaa's permission to change the name of the heir from an older son to a younger. The bequest entailed a property of a few arpents located not too many miles distant from the bulk of the estate. The reason for the alteration had been that the older son had now decided to "dedicate the rest of his mortal life to the service of Christ" and had entered holy orders. It had not been the contents of the document that had lodged in Gianni's mind—there were many such requests made to Lady Nicolaa who, because she held her lands directly from the king, was required to approve any changes in tenancy— but because there had been two different spellings of the older son's name and it had prompted Gianni to enquire of Lambert if he should make them conform and, if so, which spelling he should use.

Lambert had authorised the amendment, instructing him which form of the name was correct and then gone on to add a comment about the individual concerned in the document. "I do not expect the Roulan family will be sorry to see this son gone from their family home," he had said. "Lady Nicolaa's bailiff at Brattleby told me that he has a penchant for consorting with immoral women and that, before his father died, this inclination caused his sire much grief."

Lambert had tapped his ink-stained fingers on the document, his prominent jaw thrust out in disapproval as he said, "While the property was under this son's care, he lived there alone with some servants, supposedly preparing himself for the day when he would inherit it, but the bailiff told me there were rumours that prostitutes were often seen on the premises, sometimes staying for as long as two or three days at a time." The clerk had sniffed. "I would like to think that his sudden desire to join a monastery is due to repentance for his sinful ways, but I think it is most probably because his father threatened to cast him out of the family home if he did not make reparation for his sins. So the Brattleby bailiff gave me to understand, anyway."

The reason the connection of Lambert's comments and Roget's recounting had occurred to him, Gianni realised, was because of the mention of monks and prostitutes. The document did not state which order the errant son had joined, but it could just as easily have been the Templars as the Benedictines or Cistercians. Could there be a link between this man and the murder of the two harlots? From helping his former master with previous murder investigations, Gianni was well aware that while there could be many reasons for a person to commit murder, one of the more common compulsions was lust. A lover threatened, or scorned, or a woman left to face the birth of an illegitimate child, could foster a terrible need for revenge on the person responsible. Had this Jacques Roulan, the son who had so disappointed his father, committed such a sin and fled to the seclusion of a religious order to escape the consequences? Could the hatred of the person he had wronged become so all consuming that they were now wreaking vengeance on the Order he had joined and the fallen women he had fraternised with? There was only the slimmest chance that such speculations would prove true, but the boy remembered how often, in the past, it had been some seemingly innocuous scrap of information that had proved vital. How he wished the Templar was still in the castle and he could convey his suspicions to his former master. But that was not possible. The Templar was in the preceptory and youngsters, even male ones, were not allowed inside its walls.

Since Gianni had been in the scriptorium the previous day when the Templar had come to the castle to tell Gerard Camville of the information sent by Amery St. Maur, the boy did not know that there was now hope of one or more possible suspects for the crime to be found in Grimsby, and his desire to help his former master remained with him for the rest of the day like an itch he could not scratch. Finally, deciding that his conclusions must be brought to the Templar's attention in some way, he decided to write out the details of the document where Jacques Roulan was mentioned, along with how he thought it was possible there was a connection to the murders. He would then ask John Blund if he would give it to Lady Nicolaa with a request that, if she thought it relevant, she would see that the information was given to Bascot.

This he did and, gesturing to Lambert his intention by

means of the gestures he and the clerk used to communicate, asked his help in explaining his purpose to Blund. When Gianni's information and conclusions were given to the secretary, he gave it his careful consideration for a few long and silent moments.

Finally, he nodded his head in assent. "I well know how much assistance you gave Sir Bascot when he delved into previous murders and so does milady. It would be remiss of me not to present your conjectures to her, even if they prove to be erroneous." He lifted up the piece of parchment. "I shall ensure this is given to her before the end of the day."

WHILE GIANNI WAS SECURING BLUND'S PROMISE TO INTERcede on his behalf with Nicolaa de la Haye, Ernulf, the serjeant of the castle garrison, was knocking on the door of the former prostitute, Terese. He had been sent by the castellan to give her the thirty silver pennies that Preceptor d'Arderon had sent to the castle the day before.

As Ernulf had ridden down through Lincoln, he had noticed that the women of the town were fearful. All the females he saw were travelling in groups of two or three as they went about their daily shopping in the markets and stalls. Even though the murderer's victims, thus far, had been prostitutes, there was no assurance that if the villain struck again, he would not choose a woman of good repute as a target. The serjeant damned the murderer under his breath and hoped that the Templar and Roget would have good fortune in Grimsby.

Fourteen

※I※

Bailiff Peter Thorson greeted Bascot and Roget warmly when a maidservant announced their presence. On being told they had come to Grimsby on behalf of the sheriff of Lincoln, he readily invited them into his home. The bailiff was a man of middle years with a stocky frame and a belly that was beginning to thicken with age. A thick shock of greying yellow hair topped a face that was weather beaten, with bushy eyebrows above a pair of piercing blue eyes.

"You are well come," he said genially. "Sir Gerard did our town a great favour a few years back by ridding the Lincoln road of outlaws that were plaguing some of the merchants leaving here with supplies. We are in his debt."

Thorson led them to the back of the house and into a room where he transacted the business of his office. A large table sat at one end with inkpot, quills and piles of parchment on it. On the wall behind it was a large chart penned with indecipherable symbols that seemed to denote the times of tides. His wand of office, a finely polished piece of ash wood topped with three small scallop shells, lay on a small table alongside a jug of wine and some cups.

Bidding his guests be seated, Thorson called for a servant to pour them all wine and asked how he could be of assistance.

The bailiff listened without interruption as Roget told him of the murder of the prostitutes and the fact that the Templar Order seemed to be involved in the motivation for the crimes. The captain then went on to explain that there was a possibility that the death of a man from Grimsby, Robert Scallion, might have some connection to the murders. He was about to relate the circumstances of Scallion's death when Thorson held up his hand to forestall him.

"I already know how Scallion died and that a Templar knight was accused of murdering him," the bailiff said. "Scallion's ship is in our harbour. It came into port three weeks ago; his crew sailed it back here from the Holy Land."

Thorson looked directly at the Templar. "And I now understand the reason for your presence here, Sir Bascot. News of the death of the first harlot in Lincoln had reached us, but only that she was slain in a church, not that it was the chapel of your preceptory. And the second killing is, of course, too recent for tidings of it to have travelled to Grimsby. I expect that because there might be a connection between these recent killings and the charge that Scallion was killed by one of your brethren, you, as well as Sheriff Camville, are searching for a likely suspect among his family and associates. Am I correct?"

"You are, Master Thorson," Bascot replied, relieved at the bailiff's quick understanding of the situation. "And now that Scallion's crew is also here, our investigation must be extended to include them."

Thorson nodded. "Robert had only one relative, a sister.

She is married to a local fisherman, Sven Grimson, and both are well respected hereabouts. I cannot believe she, or her husband, would be involved. Or even have the inclination to wish revenge for his slaying. She would not be surprised that he met his death in the manner that he did. The only wonder is that he was not killed in some such way long before now."

The bailiff leaned back in his chair and explained the reason for his observation. "Robert Scallion was not a man of good repute. He seldom sailed into our port and, when he did, respectable townspeople kept clear of his company. Not only was he prone to an excessive consumption of ale—during which times he would usually start a brawl in whichever alehouse he happened to be in—there were also rumours that he practised piracy during his trips. A cordwainer who came to pick up some leather goods Scallion had brought from Spain claimed some of it was part of a shipment stolen from a boat that was carrying merchandise belonging to a trader in Boston. He said it bore the mark of a manufacturer in Rouen and had been pirated. But the cordwainer had no means of proving his claim and the charge was never substantiated. Nonetheless, the honest folk in Grimsby pride themselves on honest trading, and the cordwainer's accusation did not sit well with them. When the king granted us a charter last year, many were reluctant to associate with a man possessing such a stained reputation. This taint, added to his uncertain temper and fondness for strong drink, made me think it unlikely he would live long enough to make old bones. And I suspect his sister felt the same."

"Then I am surprised that Scallion's men brought his ship back here," Bascot said. "They could easily have sailed the vessel to another port and sold it or, if they had truly been engaged in piracy with Scallion, used it to continue their thieving ways."

Thorson nodded his head. "And so they might have done, I think, were it not for the man who was Scallion's steersman. His name is Askil and he, like Scallion, is a Grimsby man. They grew up together and it is well-known that, at one time, Askil hoped to marry Scallion's sister, Joan. Even though she gave him no encouragement and married another, Askil retains his regard for her. Since Joan is her brother's only heir, I believe Askil brought the vessel home for her sake, and hers alone. He also sold the cargo—which was mostly perishable goods, a type of onion that grows in the Holy Land and has been the main staple of trade in Robert's family for a couple of generations—in one of the ports along the coast of France and gave her the proceeds."

"Is it possible that this Askil might be the one we seek?" Bascot asked. "Do you think he is likely to be so enraged by his friend's death that he would seek revenge, or perhaps because he thought it would console the woman for whom he has such affection?"

Thorson gave the question a few moments thought before answering. "I cannot judge his reactions with any certainty. To his credit, Askil was never involved in Robert's forays into the alehouses and the inevitable fights that broke out. He usually stayed on shipboard during their rare visits here, so I have not had enough contact with him during these last few years to judge his character." The bailiff shrugged. "It is possible, I suppose."

"Is he in Grimsby?" Bascot asked.

"I believe so. Joan's husband paid him to remain on board Scallion's ship after its return, and keep watch over its safety while a new crew was found to man her, since most of those who returned with Askil have left the area. I suspect they have gone to one of the larger ports where Scallion's reputation for piracy might not be so harshly regarded."

"We would like to speak to the steersman," Bascot said, "and also any remaining crew members that were in Acre when Scallion was killed. They may have details about his death that are unknown to us."

"I can arrange that, and gladly," Thorson replied.

"And even though you assure us that Scallion's sister is unlikely to have any involvement in the crimes, I think it would be worthwhile to speak to both her and her husband. Either of them might have knowledge that could help us determine whether Scallion's death is connected to the murders in Lincoln or if we are chasing a false trail."

THORSON SAID THAT THE HOUSE WHERE ROBERT SCALLION'S sister and her husband lived was within easy walking distance and suggested he have one of his servants stable their horses in a building behind his house.

"And, if it pleases you, I would also offer you an evening meal and a bed for the night. There is a roomy chamber upstairs occupied by the eldest of my three sons with more than enough space to spread two extra pallets."

Both Bascot and Roget were grateful for the invitation and said so, since they had expected to have to find lodgings in a local alehouse. While Thorson summoned a servant to take care of the horses, the Templar and the captain went outside to wait for the bailiff.

"We shall have to try and find out for certain whether this Askil, or any others from Scallion's crew, have been away from Grimsby over the last few days," Bascot said. "If the steersman was loyal enough to undertake the long journey from the Holy Land to bring back his vessel, and the proceeds of the cargo, it sounds as though Askil's attachment to the captain was a strong one. He could be the one we are seeking."

Roget nodded his agreement. "And even though Scallion had no male relatives, it does not exclude a woman from having hired the villain who murdered Elfreda and Adele. We must take a close look at the sister and her husband as well."

When the bailiff joined them, he took them down the main street of the town towards the harbour. The buildings on either side were mostly of timber infilled with wattle and daub, but a few were reinforced with bottom courses of stone and had tiled roofs instead of thatch. Some of them had shutters on the lower storey which were pulled up to display a shop front inside where clothing, leather goods and household implements were laid out for sale. Men carrying trays of bread, fish pies and lumps of pease pudding threaded through the people walking along the main thoroughfare, crying the excellence of their wares as they did so. There were at least three alehouses along the street, all with bunches of greenery hanging outside to proclaim that a new brew was ready for consumption.

"In the last few years our small town has thrived greatly," Thorson said with pride. He pointed towards the harbour where the mast of a large cog could be seen jutting up above the horizon. "That vessel is from Norway, hauling timber, and last week we had a ship from Spain in port. A heavy squall out in the open water shredded her sail and the captain put in here for repairs. Truly the name of our little river,

Haven, is apt, for us as well as those who sail on the open sea. Our safe harbour brings in much trade, and earns good silver from the fees that the shipowners pay to offload their cargos, as well as from the money they spend for supplies and in our alehouses and cookshops."

About halfway along the main road, the bailiff turned off into a side street. "It is just along here that Joan and Sven Grimson live," he explained, pointing to a house that was two stories in height. It had walls of stone and was set alongside others just as solidly built. "Sven has done well for himself these last few years. He has three fishing vessels—all of good size and sturdily constructed—and plies the local waters for herring and plaice. Now, with Robert's death, he will be able to add the cog to his fleet."

When the door was opened in answer to Thorson's knock, a maidservant quickly ushered them into a large hall with a fireplace at one end and a solid oak table and chairs in the centre. To one side was an open-fronted cupboard laid with dishes and cups of pewter. The maid scurried away to call her mistress and, in a few moments, Scallion's sister, Joan, came into the room.

She was a tall woman and large boned, with hair of deep auburn framed by the soft linen folds of a head-rail and se-cured over her brow with a broad strip of embroidered rib-bon in the old Saxon fashion. Her eyes, pale brown in colour, were wide and deep set. Had it not been for the heavy lines of discontent that scored each side of her mouth, she could have been called handsome. Her gown, though of plain dark blue, was of good wool and the belt from which the house-hold keys depended had been finely chased. All proclaimed her standing as the wife of a prosperous man.

She gave a greeting to Peter Thorson and the bailiff introduced his two companions, explaining the purpose of their visit in a succinct fashion, saying Bascot and Roget were looking for a connection between the death of her brother and two recent murders in Lincoln.

"There were indications in both instances that the purpose of the killings was in retaliation for an act of betrayal by the Templar Order," Thorson added. "Since it is alleged that your brother was slain by a Templar knight, Sir Bascot and Captain Roget are trying to find out if his death is connected to the murders."

Joan's cool gaze flicked over Roget and settled on Bascot. "So, Sir Knight, not only does one of your monks kill my brother, your Order now has the effrontery to accuse me of murder. Not the behaviour I would expect from men supposedly devoted to the service of Christ."

Bascot answered her shortly, but kept his tone even out of respect for her sorrow. "We have not come to accuse, mistress," he said, "merely to enquire whether there might be any valid reason to suspect your brother's death may be linked to the murder of these two women."

She kept her eyes on his face for a few moments, assessing him. When she spoke again, it was to Thorson. "I do not have any knowledge that would be pertinent to the sheriff's enquiry, Bailiff. If someone is taking revenge on the Templars for my brother's death, it is without my consent, or awareness."

"And your husband, mistress," Bascot asked, "does the same hold true for him?"

"I believe so, but if you wish to ask him yourself, you will find him down at the harbour. He is there with Askil, arranging for some minor repairs to the ship my brother owned."

Joan lifted her chin as she said these last words, and added, "If you do find the man who murdered these harlots, I have no doubt he will be hanged. I wish the same fate awaited the Templar who killed Robert."

Fifteen

✢

"By God, Thorson," Roget exploded once they had left Joan Grimson in her house and were walking in the direction of the harbour, "I do not know how you can say you do not believe that woman is responsible for the murders. Her hatred of the Templars flows from her like an ocean tide. If she were a man, I would have no doubt that she was guilty."

"That is because you do not know the history between her and her brother," the bailiff replied calmly. "When their mother died, Robert was very young and it was left to her to look after him. Their father was a rakehell, just like Robert, and fell dead after a surfeit of wine a couple of years later. Joan took her responsibility seriously and was always berating Robert for his scurrilous ways. The last time Robert was in Grimsby, on a warm day last summer, Joan found him down on the beach after a night's debauch, dishevelled and still in his cups. With him was a doxy from one of the brothels. Joan took Robert to task, lashing him with her tongue and threatening to disown him if he did not mend his ways. He left Grimsby later that very day. She did not, in fact, ever have the chance to speak to him again, not by her own choosing, but because of his death." Thorson's face was full of pity as he related the manner of the parting between brother and sister.

"It is more than probable that Joan now recalls her threat and is filled with remorse for her harsh words," he continued. "And it is that, not any desire for revenge, which is causing her anger. Her words do not alter my opinion. I still do not believe she is capable of sanctioning murder. She is upright and well respected, as is her husband. Besides being the owner of three fishing smacks, Grimson's father owns a thriving ship's chandlery, which Sven's younger brother helps his father run. The family is fairly wealthy, and has a good reputation. Why would they endanger all that, and the future security of their two children, by involving themselves in such terrible crimes?"

"You may be right, Bailiff," Bascot said, "but, nonetheless, she cannot be discounted as a suspect, even if it is only of authorising someone else to carry out the murders on her behalf. If Joan's husband, or the steersman, cannot account for their whereabouts when the two women in Lincoln were murdered, we must consider not only their involvement, but hers also."

As they had been speaking they had approached the shore. The ground was sandy underfoot, with clumps of marram grass thick along the track. From this vantage point, the Norwegian cog in the harbour could be seen more clearly. The ship's huge sail had just been rolled up and sailors were climbing the tall mast to check the rigging that anchored it into position while below, other seamen were doing the same with the shrouds that secured the mast fore and aft. The tide was half out, and a number of smaller vessels were either beached on the shore or bobbed at the receding water's edge. Small fishing boats, a couple of wherries used for ferrying people across the mouth of the Haven River, and some coracles were among them. On the shore, near a wooden quay, the morning's catch was being loaded into panniers on the backs of waiting donkeys for transport into the town. A few other fishermen were sitting up above the waterline mending nets and repairing shrimp pots. Overhead gulls swooped, some landing on the furled sails and railings of the cog, their calls raucous and feathers ruffling in the strong breeze. Farther out the large shapes of gannets could be seen as they made sudden plunging dives into the depths of the ocean in a search for food.

Sven Grimson was standing in conversation with another man, looking out to sea at a vessel anchored a little way out, a sturdy clinker-built ship with a sheltered cabin at the prow and a huge rudder fixed to the side of the craft. A pennant bearing three white scallop shells on a black background flew from the top of the mast, a replica of the image beside the door of Thorson's home and on the tip of his wand of office. The name *La Rodenef*—the Roving Ship—had been painted on the bow. The vessel sat lightly in the water, the hold below decks now obviously empty.

In appearance, if he was truly a descendant of Grim, the Danish fisherman who had given his name to what had been just a little village over three centuries before, Grimson lived up to his heritage. Taller than average height and slimly built, Sven's hair was pale blond in colour and his eyes a clear dark blue. He was dressed in a belted tunic of dark green with matching hose and had a light cloak thrown over his shoulders. Altogether, his appearance was a prosperous one, and there was a touch of haughtiness in his wide-legged stance.

The man with him was shorter and darker, with long brown hair tied back with a leather thong, and heavily muscled shoulders. His attitude to Sven Grimson seemed deferential as he stood patiently listening to the other man's words, but there was no trace of obsequiousness on a face that had been tanned by sun and wind to the texture and colour of leather. At his belt was a knife, the sheath made of some type of fish skin, and he fingered the haft in an absentminded fashion while he and Grimson spoke together. As Thorson led Bascot and Roget up to the two men, the bailiff said in an undertone that the shorter man was Robert Scallion's steersman, Askil. As the steersman turned his face towards them, the oddness in the colour of his eyes was immediately apparent. One was a clear pale blue, the other dark hazel, a striking difference that made his countenance seem strangely awry.

After introducing Bascot and Roget to the two men, Thorson repeated what he had told Joan as to the reason for the presence in Grimsby of a Templar knight and a soldier in the service of the sheriff of Lincoln. Both Grimson and Askil looked shocked when they heard the details of the two murders, and Grimson immediately denied, albeit in a less truculent manner than his wife's, of having any complicity in the crimes.

"I will admit," he said to Bascot in a straightforward fashion, "that I would like to see the Templar that killed Robert answer for his villainy, but I can see no purpose in murdering two women, or any other persons, for the sake of that animosity. Such deaths will not change what has happened or bring my wife's brother back to life."

Askil's denial was in the same vein. "Robert was my friend and I mourn him," he said simply, the vowels in his words flatter and harder than those usually heard in the local accent. "But I have no desire for revenge, nor have tried to take any."

"Were you in the brothel on the night Robert Scallion was killed?" Bascot asked the steersman. Only a few details about the actual murder of the boat owner had been included in Master St. Maur's letter and it was possible this man might have seen something or somebody that could help them confirm or refute whether Scallion's death was connected to the recent murders.

Askil shook his head. "The ship was loaded with cargo," he said, "and I stayed with it along with most of the crew. Robert went into Acre to see a spice merchant in one of the souks. He said that if he could get a good price, he had a mind to buy a small quantity of nutmeg and cinnamon to bring back with us to sell in one of the ports along the French coast. Whether he made a contract to buy some of the spices or not, I do not know, and neither did the crew member who accompanied him when he went into the town."

"And it was from this crew member that you learned of your captain's death?" Bascot asked.

"Aye," Askil replied. "Dunny came haring back to the ship in the early hours of the morning. Said Robert had gone into a brothel and got into a fight with another Englishman."

"And this Dunny, did he come back to Grimsby with you and, if so, is he still here?"

Askil nodded, then turned around and gave a piercing whistle in the direction of the men who were mending nets a little farther along the shore. When he had their attention, the steersman made a motion for one of them to come forward and, reluctantly, the man did so.

Some years younger than Askil, who looked to be in his

mid-thirties, Dunny was lean of build, with straggly hair hanging in greasy clumps on his shoulders and a face scarred by old craters of childhood pustules. Sparse hair grew on his chin and he rubbed at it nervously as he joined the group, avoiding eye contact with anyone but Askil.

"This is Sir Bascot and Captain Roget, Dunny," the steersman told him. "They have come to ask about the death of Captain Scallion. Repeat what you know about the fight in Acre that took his life."

Dunny shuffled his feet for a moment and Sven Grimson, his voice tinged with impatience, said, "Speak up, man. Just tell what you saw."

Faced with a direct command from Grimson, the young sailor began his tale, stumbling over his words at first, then growing more confident as he went on. "The cap'n took me with him that night, just in case there was a need for someone to carry whatever he might buy from the merchant in the souk. He didn't get anything, tho', said we had to come back the next day. Then he said we'd go to a brothel he knew of, 'cause it was time I had a taste of some foreign women."

Dunny looked up at that point in his narrative and spoke directly to Roget who, the sailor rightly assumed, was partial to the company of women and would be more understanding of the reason for a visit to a stewe. "I'd only ever worked on fishing boats from hereabouts 'til the cap'n took me on board his cog and I'd never before been to a brothel the likes of those they have in France or Spain. The cap'n said the ones in the Holy Land were even better."

When Thorson gave Dunny a censorious glance for declaring his enjoyment of such places, the young sailor dropped his eyes before continuing. "The brothel was not what I'd expected. They had young boys for hire there as well as women. Outright sodomists, some of them were, and they gave me some sort of drink that the cap'n said was the closest thing they had to English ale. I took only one swallow and left the rest. It tasted like cat's piss."

"Just get on to what happened to Robert," Grimson said with irritation. "We don't need to know all the sordid details."

"Aye, master," Dunny replied obediently. "There was a lot of men in the place, mostly heathens, all dickering over the women—and boys—on display, and the cap'n took a fancy to one of the girls, a right little darlin' she was, with long black hair and great big . . ." A glare from Grimson curtailed his description of the bawd and he gulped nervously before he continued. "I couldn't understand what the cap'n was sayin' to the stewe-holder 'cause they was speakin' in the language they all talk in those parts, but I think he had made an offer for her when another man came into the brothel. The newcomer was dressed in good clothes and had a beard, I remember, and he walked right up to where the cap'n was standin' and said somethin' to the stewe-keeper, then flashed a pile of silver coins he took from his purse. The stewe-keeper looked at the man who had just come in and nodded, then shrugged his shoulders at the cap'n as much as to say he was sorry, but the other man would be havin' the girl.

"The cap'n turned to the stranger—somehow I thought as how they knew each other, just by the way the cap'n looked at him—and told him to feck off. The other man pushed the cap'n in the shoulder, and told him, in English, to do the same and to find another girl 'cause he wasn't getting this one. 'Twas then the cap'n called him a Templar, sayin' as how he was breakin' his vows by being in the place at all, let alone payin' for the company of one of the women."

Dunny shrugged his shoulders. "That was when the other man and the cap'n started to fight. They traded a few blows and the cap'n fell on the floor. The cap'n was a right good brawler, but the man he was fightin' was more than a match for him. All the rest of the men in the brothel was yelling, but I couldn't understand what any of 'em was saying. The whoremaster was screamin', too, and started banging on a big drum he had beside him. I thought as how I should maybe help the cap'n in some way, but couldn't see what I could do. If the cap'n couldn't get the best of the other Englishman, there was no way I was going to be able to. I wouldn't have had a chance anyway, 'cause it was then that I saw a knife flash between the pair of 'em."

Tears came into Dunny's eyes and he faltered for a moment. Askil laid a hand on his shoulder and the young sailor swallowed a couple of times to smother his anguish and then finished the tale. "I don't rightly know which of 'em pulled the knife, whether it was the cap'n or the other Englishman, 'cause everyone was millin' around and I couldn't see right plain," he said. "Alls I knows is that blood started to gush and I saw the cap'n go still. The stranger got up from where the pair of 'em was lying and one of the heathen customers tried to grab ahold of him, but he knocked the man down and scarpered out of there like a flash of lightnin' just before two big infidels rushed in—I think they was men the stewe-keeper hired to keep peace in the place and had come when they heard the drum bangin'. I went over to where the cap'n was laying, but I could see he was dead. The blade had took him under the ribs; must have gone right through his heart, so I ran out of the place myself. I didn't want one of those heathen bastards grabbin' ahold of me, and I run as fast as I could back to the ship."

Bascot looked at Askil. "And then what happened?" he asked.

The steersman's face was full of grief as he finished the young seaman's tale. "An official from the port arrived almost on Dunny's heels. I went and identified Robert's body and was told that the man who killed him had not been caught. I offered the information that he was a Templar knight, but apparently the stewe-holder had already told them he belonged to the Order, but that he didn't know his name."

"How did you know he was a knight and not of man-at-arms rank?" Bascot asked.

"Dunny told me," Askil replied.

Bascot turned to the younger sailor with an interrogative look.

The young seaman answered the unspoken question readily enough. "He was wearin' clothes that was too fine for an ordinary soldier," he replied. "They was made of better stuff than any man-at-arms would own and his gloves were soft leather. And the way he spoke to the cap'n—even if he was angry and swearing—it was educated like. He was a knight, right enough. Anyone could see that."

Bascot accepted the explanation. There was a difference in the type of cloth used for garments in the ranks of the Templar Order. Those of knight's rank wore clothing made from finely spun wool or closely woven linen, while the material used for the serjeants' and men-at-arms' garments was a much rougher type of cloth. Bascot briefly wondered why the knight had been wearing gloves in such a hot climate but, thinking it was possible he had injured his hands in some way, gave it no more thought and asked Askil what had ensued after he had identified Scallion's corpse.

"The official who was questioning me asked where our cargo had been bought and who from, then I was given permission to take Robert's body on board our ship and leave the port. We waited until we were well away from the harbour and buried the captain at sea."

A silence fell over the little group at Askil's last words. Even though the recounting of Scallion's murder had been told in sketchy words by the young seaman, it was vivid, and Bascot could understand why Joan, Scallion's sister, had been so angry. That a Templar had not only broken his vow of chastity by frequenting a brothel, but also committed the sacrilege of killing a Christian and fellow countryman was enough to raise the ire of any who heard the tale, let alone that of a family member. Bascot, although well aware that there would always be men who broke solemn oaths—history recorded that even kings that done it in the past—was heartily sorry that such a one had apparently been a Templar brother. However, he also knew that the Order did all it could to prevent any applicant suspected of harbouring baseness in his soul from joining its ranks. The sins of this one man should not be allowed to taint the purity of the many brothers who served the cause of Christ with absolute fidelity.

He glanced at Sven Grimson's face. His features had remained impassive throughout the recounting but he had heard the tale before and it would have been easy for him to disguise his true feelings. Was he as innocent of wishing revenge for Scallion's death as he claimed? Or had he, along with his wife and Scallion's good friend, Askil, conspired to murder the two Lincoln prostitutes as a means of extracting retribution?

"We shall need an account of your whereabouts, Grimson, during all the hours of the day the first prostitute was killed eight days back," Bascot said. "And also for the time of the second murder, three days ago."

It took a moment for the purpose behind the Templar's instruction to register, but when it did, Grimson's face tightened into an angry scowl. "Are you accusing me of killing those bawds?" he demanded, his hand dropping to the knife he wore at his belt. "I have already told you I have no knowledge of their deaths. Do you insult my honour by implying I have lied?"

Bascot took up the challenge with one of his own. "An innocent man would not balk at giving proof of his claim. It is not I who insult your honour, but yourself, Grimson."

Seeing the anger that flashed in the glacial blue of the Templar's eye, Bailiff Thorson intervened. "Sir Bascot is right, Sven. If you are, as you say, not involved in these killings, then you have no reason not to answer. Tell us where you were on the days the two women were murdered."

Grimson's aspect turned surly, but he realised the futility of pitting his strength against that of a Templar knight, and answered the question. "About ten days ago, Joan and I took one of my boats and went up to Hull to look into the practicality of keeping Robert's vessel and becoming, as he was, a trader. I am a fisherman; I know nothing of transporting commodities overseas and wanted to speak to some of the merchants that Robert did business with there. Hull is a large port and the one where Robert took a lot of his cargo on board. We wanted to see if these merchants, now that Robert is dead, would continue to trade with me. If the venture did not seem to be viable, we thought we would sell the ship."

"How long were you and your wife in Hull?" Bascot asked.

"We did not return until yesterday," Grimson replied.

"Then you were both away from Grimsby during the times the murders took place," Bascot stated flatly. "Do you have witnesses in Hull to verify your claim of being there?"

"Yes," the boat owner replied angrily, "Askil and Dunny were with us as a skeleton crew on the journey and can verify our whereabouts. And the merchants we visited, they will tell you the same if you wish to go to Hull and speak to them."

Bascot saw the flash of apprehension, albeit quickly masked, in Askil's eyes, as Grimson went on. "We discovered it will require a considerable outlay of silver to hire a crew and pay a deposit of surety for any cargo entrusted to me, so we also made enquiries about anyone who would be willing to purchase the boat and for how much. If you contact these men they will confirm that I was there."

Hull was in the county of Yorkshire and some thirty miles to the northwest on the northern shore of the Humber estuary, so any journey there, except by boat, involved crossing the estuary on a ferry. It was a long way for Bascot and Roget to travel to verify Grimson's statement, especially since it would be necessary for them to return to Lincoln first so that Roget could get Camville's permission to continue the investigation beyond the borders of Lincolnshire, and into a county that was outside the sheriff's jurisdiction. Roget glanced at Bascot. Camville's writ authorised the arrest of any individual that was thought to be suspicious. Grimson, his wife, Askil and Dunny could be taken into custody and detained until proof of their presence in Hull over the ten-day period was obtained. That way, the onus would be on them, rather than on the sheriff, to supply witnesses that would attest to Sven's veracity, either in person or by signed documentation. If Grimson was telling the truth, there would be no choice but to accept his word that the steersman and young sailor had accompanied him and his wife. It was not likely that any of the Hull merchants would have knowledge of the identity of the men who had crewed the fisherman's boat.

Bascot gave Roget an almost imperceptible shake of his head. Until they had further reason to suspect Grimson and the others of the crimes, it would be precipitate to arrest them. The Templar, however, did not intend to let them believe that he and Roget found their story entirely credible. There had to be a reason for Grimson's reluctance to admit his whereabouts during the times the prostitutes had been murdered. Bascot was sure he was lying about something and until the truth of his tale was determined, he did not intend to allow the wealthy fisherman to believe his story had been accepted.

"For now, Grimson, I will advise Sheriff Camville that you and your wife do not seem to have any complicity in the crimes he is investigating," Bascot said. "But I am sure he will send a messenger to the bailiff in Hull with a request that steps be taken to confirm your claim. Until that is done, both you and your wife, along with Askil and Dunny, will remain in Grimsby and report each evening to Bailiff Thorson. If any of you fail to appear as instructed, you will be declared outlaw and all your goods and chattels confiscated."

Grimson's pale face mottled red with fury as Bascot was

speaking. "You cannot place such a restriction on me," he shouted in outrage. "You are not an officer of the king."

"Sir Bascot may not be, but I am," Roget interjected, his fearsome visage set in a merciless smile as he pulled Gerard Camville's writ from the inside of his tunic and held it up so the sheriff's seal could be seen dangling from the bottom. "You will do as the Templar says, or suffer the consequences."

Sixteen

✦-I-✦

LATER THAT EVENING, AFTER A FINE MEAL OF POACHED SALMON and vegetable pottage provided by Thorson's plump and amiable wife, Bascot and Roget sat with the bailiff in his office over a jug of excellent Spanish wine and discussed the probability of Sven and Joan Grimson, along with the two sailors, being responsible for the recent murders.

"I still don't believe that any of them, especially Sven or Joan, are capable of such grisly acts," Thorson said, leaning back in his chair and lacing his fingers over his swelling paunch as he mused. "On the other hand, if it was a Templar knight that had been murdered, and it was known he was the one that killed Robert Scallion, I might say differently. Such revenge would be understandable. But killing two harlots and carving one of them up—no, I do not think so."

"Well, if Grimson is telling the truth and they were all in Hull at the time the women were attacked," Roget said, tapping the list of names the boat owner had given them of the people he had called on in Hull, "then they are in the clear. Lincoln is a far piece and they could not have been in two places at once, especially as the two harlots were murdered four days apart."

Thorson looked down at his wine cup, and then said slowly, "Well, that's just it, you see, Captain, while Sven and Joan might not have been in Lincoln, it is possible that Askil and Dunny were."

"How so?" Bascot asked. "Surely Lincoln is too far from where they claim to be. Even if they obtained fast horses, it is still a long way from Hull."

"Ah, well, it would seem so to a landsman, but not to one who is accustomed to travel by water."

Thorson's words took the Templar and Roget by surprise, as did his explanation.

"When I was a young man," the bailiff began, "I worked on the fishing boats and spent a little time as one of the crew on the ferry that plies across the Humber estuary. It goes from Barton on the southern bank to Hessle on the north side and back again. Not too far from Barton is the mouth of the Ancholme River, which, with a small craft, is navigable as far as Bishopbridge. Now Bishopbridge is not too far from Lincoln—perhaps fifteen miles—and close to Ermine Street. Sven's boat is large enough to tow a small skiff, or even take one on board—they are often laden for use in times of emergency, such as when a leak is sprung. If Sven were to anchor his boat on the southern shore of the Humber, near Barton, he and Joan could have taken the ferry across to Hessle and hired horses to ride to Hull. It is a very short journey, not above five miles. Once there, they could have visited the people whose names Sven gave us while, at the same time, Askil and Dunny took the skiff and sailed down the Ancholme to Bishopbridge. The two sailors could then have easily walked to Ermine Street and into Lincoln. It would not have taken them long; both men are fit and able to cover the distance in a few hours."

Thorson paused for a moment to see that his listeners had understood the route he had described. To his gratification, the Templar and Roget grasped it quickly. Both knew the territory along the northern stretch of Ermine Street fairly well and that the village of Bishopbridge lay only a short distance from the main road.

Bascot nodded and expanded on what Thorson had suggested. "And, once the seamen had walked to Lincoln, they could have murdered the prostitute that was killed in our chapel and then stayed within the town until they took care of despatching the second harlot a few days later. It would then be a simple matter to return to Barton by the same route they had taken on the outward journey and wait for Sven and Joan's return. Grimson's story would still ring true, for he and his wife would, in fact, have visited the men he has named in Hull and there would be no witness to deny the two sailors were anywhere other than, as he said, on board his boat."

It was not difficult to see how such a plan as Thorson suggested would have worked. A landsman would never visualise such a route but to a sailor, familiar with the many rivers and small tributaries that flow in the coastal region of Lincolnshire, it would be a logical one.

Thorson was careful to add a reservation. "I do not say that the Grimsons contrived with Askil and Dunny to do what I have suggested, only that they *could* have done. The two seamen would have had to make haste back to Sven's ship after the second murder, which was only three days ago, but it is still possible. To sail from Grimsby to Hull, or vice versa, does not take long if the wind and tide are with you.

And Grimson admitted he did not return until yesterday morning when the incoming tide was at its peak," he added, gesturing at the tide table behind him. "I would suggest you try to find out where Sven docked his boat when he weighed anchor in the Humber estuary. While he could have gone directly to Hull and instructed Askil and Dunny to sail the skiff across the Humber to the Ancholme, it would be more expeditious for him to take his boat to the southern shore and he and Joan take the ferry to the main port. That way, there would not be any chance of the sailors being seen when they left Hull. There are many small craft that ply up and down the Ancholme; one more would have not been remarked upon and, when they returned, Grimson's boat would be waiting for them on the southern shore." He shook his head. "May God forgive me if I am casting suspicion where it is not warranted, but it is my duty to ensure that the sheriff is apprised of these facts."

"I understand, Bailiff," Bascot replied. "He will be grateful for your help."

"Do you think we should arrest Grimson and the others after all, de Marins?" Roget said. "Now that we know there is a possibility they may have committed the crimes, Sir Gerard may want to question them further."

Bascot shook his head. "No. It would be best if an attempt is made to verify Sven's story first even if, as Thorson says, it would only indicate that he and his wife were in Hull, and not the two sailors. We should also try and find out if either of the seamen was noticed in Lincoln over the days they claimed to be in the estuary. Askil's parti-coloured eyes are distinctive. I have seen the variance before, but usually in horses and cats. It is not common in humans and I am sure this rarity would be noticed by any who saw him, es-

pecially in the bawdy house where Elfreda worked. It might
be worthwhile checking with Verlain again, and the other
harlots in the stewe, as well as people in the neighbourhood
of the house where Adele Delorme lived."

There was another reason that Bascot wanted to delay the
arrest of Grimson and the sailors. Thorson had mentioned
that the ferry across the Humber went from the small town
of Barton, and that was the village where the newly initiated Templar man-at-arms that had professed to be ill on the
night of Elfie's murder came from. Also, the other brother,
Thomas, the horse-handler that had travelled from Temple
Hirst to the Lincoln enclave, would have made many trips
to the Humber estuary while carrying out his duty of taking the Order's mounts for transport overseas. The animals
were mainly loaded on vessels at Faxfleet, which was a town
at the western end of the estuary and not a far distance from
either Barton or Hull. It was quite possible that either of
these Templars, especially young Alan, had known Robert
Scallion, since the trader had used Hull as his main port of
lading. Bascot could not tell either Roget or Thorson about
his suspicions because the details about both Templar brothers would be considered information that was to be kept
within the Order. Before he recommended the arrest of Sven
and the others, he needed to obtain d'Arderon's sanction to
question Alan and Thomas and try to determine if there was
a possibility it was they, and not any of the Grimson party,
who were involved in the crimes.

Roget, voicing his agreement that a description of Askil
and Dunny be circulated in Lincoln town, interrupted Bascot's unspoken thoughts and pulled the Templar's mind
back to the conversation.

"But it will take some time for Sir Gerard to check on

Grimson's story; not only is Hull a far piece for a messenger to ride, there is also the time it will take the bailiff in the port to speak to each of the witnesses on Grimson's list. While Sven and his wife may comply with your order not to leave Grimsby, I have doubts about Askil and Dunny. Now that Scallion's boat has been brought home, they have no ties to keep them here. If they decide to leave the area, it would not be difficult for either of them to hire on as crew of an oceangoing vessel and soon be far away from England's shores."

"I will keep a careful eye on them," Thorson promised, "and a word from me will ensure that none of the boats putting into our harbour will take them on board, as crew or otherwise. If any of them, including Sven and Joan, do not report to me exactly as you directed, I will place the others under arrest and lock them up in the town gaol to await Sheriff Camville's pleasure."

THAT SAME AFTERNOON, SHORTLY BEFORE THE WORKING DAY in the scriptorium drew to a close, John Blund gave Gianni's note to Nicolaa de la Haye, as he had promised. The castellan had just finished dictating the last letter of the day and was about to dismiss Blund when he handed her the piece of parchment on which the boy had written his speculations about the son of one of her tenants.

"Young Gianni asked me to give you this, lady," the secretary said. "The boy feels there might be some connection between these recent murders and a person whose name was recorded in one of the documents he was copying."

Nicolaa scanned the paper and looked thoughtful. "Have you read this, John?" she asked.

"I have," Blund assured her. "The hypothesis may seem nebulous but, bearing in mind Gianni often observed facts that were of assistance to Sir Bascot when the Templar was investigating similar mysterious deaths, I thought it only right to bring his observations to your attention."

Nicolaa nodded. "And you were quite right to do so, John," she assured him. "As you say, his postulations are uncertain, and all of them would hinge on whether or not Roulan joined the Templars or some other monastic order. If it was, indeed, the Templars that he joined and, as my bailiff told Lambert, was forced by pressure from his family into taking holy orders over his licentious ways, it is quite possible, as Gianni suggests, that he left behind someone who was devastated by his leaving. A girl he had promised to marry, perhaps, and considered his desertion a betrayal. Especially if she was enceinte. The humiliation of bearing an unwanted child is a stigma that is not short-lived. It could easily foster hate in her heart, one that has festered, and is now directed both at the Templars for taking her lover away from her, and prostitutes for being the cause of his downfall."

She thought about the notion for a moment before speaking again. "The more I consider the suggestion, John, the more viable it seems. We have good cause to remember that it was a woman who was responsible for wreaking havoc in Lincoln once before and caused a number of deaths before de Marins discovered her identity. It could have been a female that enticed Elfreda to the Templar chapel and also knocked at Adele Delorme's door. Neither harlot would have been as wary of one of their own gender as they would have been of a man."

She looked down at the paper and studied it further. Finally, she made her decision. "It is best to wait for de Marins

and Roget to return from Grimsby before looking into the
background of Jacques Roulan. If their journey has been successful, it may prove unnecessary. But if they return empty-
handed, I will ensure Gianni's suggestion is conveyed to
the Templar as soon as possible. In the meantime, send an
instruction to my bailiff at Brattleby. Tell him to report to
me at once. It was from him that this rumour about Roulan
came; perhaps he knows more details about the matter. If
any are pertinent, I will add them to Gianni's message before I pass it along to de Marins."

As Blund prepared to leave, Nicolaa added, "And, John,
convey to Gianni my commendation for his initiative. The
boy has an intelligent and enquiring mind, we must do all
we can to foster its development."

Seventeen

❧

IT WAS LATE IN THE AFTERNOON OF THE NEXT DAY BEFORE Bascot and Roget returned to Lincoln. The Templar turned off the road just before they reached the gate into the town and took the track that led around the city walls to the preceptory, while the captain went directly to the castle to report to the sheriff.

It was almost the hour of Vespers when Bascot rode into the commandery. The brothers were beginning to gather in the compound, waiting for the small bell atop the chapel to ring and signal it was time to attend the late afternoon service. All eyes turned towards Bascot as he rode his horse to the stables and gave it into the care of a groom. He saw no disquiet on the faces of the men that formed the delayed contingent, only resignation mixed with a tiny glimmer of hope that he had at last discovered information that would exonerate them of culpability and allow them to leave.

Serjeant Hamo was standing near the blacksmith's forge. When Bascot entered the commandery, he gave the knight a brief nod and then strode across the training area and through the door at the rear of the refectory that led to d'Arderon's office. The serjeant was gone for only a few moments and, when he reappeared, walked over to Bascot and told him that the preceptor would be pleased to hear his report of what had transpired at Grimsby as soon as the service of Vespers was done.

The bell above the chapel began to chime and Bascot followed the others into the church. With so many extra men in the commandery, the small chapel was crowded, and each man brushed the shoulders of those standing next to him. As Brother John opened the service with the prayer of lauds for the dead, Bascot felt a deep sorrow rise within him. It was a familiar emotion, one that had occurred during every previous case of murder he had investigated. The wilful slaying of another human being reminded him of a poisonous creeping plant, spreading its miasma from the dead person to everyone associated with the victim. The murder of the prostitute in the chapel where he was now standing had left Elfie's little daughter, Ducette, an orphan. And whether or not Scallion's death was connected to the killings in Lincoln, his murder in a heathen brothel had brought deep grief to his sister, Joan, and his lifelong friend, the steersman Askil. Murder not only spawned death, but also grief in equal measures. The act was insidious.

When the service was over, Bascot went directly to d'Arderon's office. After the long ride from Grimsby, during which he and Roget had stopped only to partake of the provisions Thorson's wife had thoughtfully packed for them, Bascot was hungry, but he would have to wait until after he had spoken to d'Arderon to partake of the light evening meal that was being served in the refectory.

Emilius was with the preceptor when Bascot went into d'Arderon's office. Both men listened without speaking as they were told of the conversation Bascot and Roget had with Bailiff Thorson and their interviews with Joan Scallion and subsequently, her husband, Askil, and Dunny. He then went on to relate Thorson's suggestion that it was possible that one, or both, of the seamen could have reached Lincoln via the Ancholme River and committed the murders.

"We must fervently hope that the charge against our brother in Acre is false," d'Arderon said, "but whether it is or not, if the relatives and friends of the boat owner believe it to be true, it is conceivable that one of them is seeking revenge for his death. If that is what happened, then all of our brothers in the preceptory can be absolved of guilt."

Emilius immediately concurred, and Bascot could see the glimmer of hope on their faces. The rumour that it had been a Templar who had murdered a Christian in the Holy Land was a stigma on the Order, but Acre was far away and the truth about the incident may not be learned for many months, if at all; their first priority must be to absolve, if they could, the brothers stationed in the Lincoln commandery. It was with great reluctance that he dashed the two officers' burgeoning optimism as he explained that two of the men in the contingent, Alan of Barton and Thomas of Penhill, could quite easily have been friends, perhaps of long standing, of the dead boat owner.

"Scallion did most of the English end of his business with merchants in Hull," he told them. "He loaded commodities, mainly wool, from the Yorkshire area and, for a commission from local merchants, delivered them to ports in Flanders and Normandy. He would then, apparently, travel down the coast of the Iberian Peninsula, stopping at ports in Spain and Portugal and buying items such as wine, furs and even small loads of timber that would be easy to sell to merchants in the Holy Land. Once in Outremer, he made his regular purchase of the onions that had proved such a popular item, along with a small supply of spices and silk, and returned home, selling the cargo at ports along the way. Each voyage might take him a year or more, but he usually returned to Grimsby at the end of each trip to visit his sister before going to Hull to arrange his cargo for the next journey. Since this would necessitate spending some weeks in the Hull area, it is feasible he would have been known in Barton and quite probably Faxfleet, and could have come into contact with both Alan and Thomas."

The information slightly daunted the preceptor, but he took the time to reflect on what Bascot had told him. "That may be true of Alan," he said finally, "for he admits that he grew up in Barton, but not necessarily of Thomas. Delivering the preceptory's horses to Faxfleet would only bring him into contact with the captain and crew of a ship belonging to the Order. He would have no reason to mingle with crews of other vessels anchored along the estuary. It is quite possible he may never have heard of Scallion, let alone met him."

"I agree, Preceptor," Bascot said. "But I still think it would be prudent to question Thomas as well as Alan. We must be certain that neither man knew the trader before we can acquit them of any involvement in his death."

"If they are guilty, they will lie, and will be warned of our interest in them," Emilius said in a depressed manner.

"That may not be an undesirable outcome, Draper," Bascot replied. "If one, or both, is responsible for the harlots' deaths, knowing of our suspicion will prevent them from making an attempt on the life of another prostitute. That alone makes questioning them worthwhile."

Emilius reluctantly nodded and then said to d'Arderon,

"And the rest of the contingent, Preceptor, if they are now deemed clear of involvement, will you allow them to depart for Plymouth? All of them grow restless with the delay. Such a mood is not beneficial for morale."

"They will suffer far worse discomfort when they are forced to camp in the arid terrain of Portugal," d'Arderon growled. "The experience will teach them patience."

"As you command, Preceptor," Emilius replied constrainedly. "It is merely that with this aura of suspicion laying over all of us, I am concerned that the dedication of those who are recently initiated will suffer."

D'Arderon sighed and relented a little. He knew that the draper was trying to maintain a semblance of order. "You are right, of course, Emilius. We must encourage the men, especially those who have recently taken their vows. I will wait to see the outcome of Sheriff Camville's enquiries about Sven Grimson. After that is done, I will reassess the situation."

The preceptor spoke to Bascot. "It is too late in the day now, but in the morning we will question Alan and Thomas. Hopefully their answers will clear them of suspicion."

IN THE CASTLE, AFTER ROGET MADE HIS REPORT TO GERARD Camville, the sheriff directed John Blund to pen a message that was to be sent to the king's authorities in Hull. In it, the secretary was to write a request that enquiries be made of the men who Grimson had claimed would substantiate that the fisherman and his wife were in the port during the time the harlots were murdered. Camville also instructed the secretary to add a directive that if Grimson proved to be telling the truth, the port-reeves along the estuary were to be asked if any had knowledge of where he had anchored his vessel during his stay.

"Thorson states that if Grimson moored his craft on the southern shore of the Humber, it would have been much easier for the seamen to take a skiff to the mouth of the Ancholme River," Camville said, "so it is important that, if possible, the bailiff's supposition is verified. Ensure that requirement is made clear in the message, Blund, as is the need for haste."

The secretary dutifully wrote the letter, using words of his own composition. Although Gerard Camville was competent enough in numeracy, he had little skill with literacy, and once Blund finished the document he read aloud what he had written. The sheriff nodded and appended his signature to the document.

"Send one of the men-at-arms off with that at first light. With good fortune, we may have an answer within three or four days."

LATER THAT EVENING, NICOLAA DE LA HAYE SENT A MAN-servant to find Gianni and bid him attend her in the castle solar. Gianni was in the barracks when the manservant came with the message, sitting with some of the off-duty men-at-arms and listening to them challenge each other with simple riddles. The boy jumped up immediately when he learned that Lady Nicolaa wished to see him and hastily smoothed down his unruly mop of dark brown curls and gave a straightening tug to his tunic. Then he ran as fast as he could across the bail and into the keep. His heart was filled with trepidation as he sped up the stairs of the tower in the western corner of the fortress and to the room on the top storey where Nicolaa was wont to take her leisure after the evening meal. The castellan must have sent for him because of the letter he had given to Master Blund. Even though the secretary had relayed her commendation of his initiative, Gianni still feared the reason for her summons. She had always been kind to him, but she was a lady who held the reins of great power in her capable hands and one who would not look kindly on any action she perceived as insolent. Had she sent for him because even though she accepted the merit of his observations, she was angry that he, a lowly apprentice clerk, had dared to ask her to forward a message to his former master? Did she see his action as one that smacked of conceit? Was it possible he was about to be reprimanded, or even dismissed from his post? He tried to push his fears from his mind as he cautiously pushed open the door of the solar and looked about the large room for Lady Nicolaa.

The chamber was almost empty. It was used primarily by the castellan and it was here, when she had female guests, that she entertained them. There were a number of beautiful tapestries on the walls and comfortable settles placed about the room. The pleasant aroma of cloves emanated from a small brazier burning in one corner. Some of the senior members of her household retinue were also permitted to take a part of their leisure hours within the chamber and now, at the far end of the room, the mistress of the wardrobe sat with two of the castle sempstresses conversing quietly among themselves.

Lady Nicolaa's diminutive figure was seated in a comfortable chair at the opposite end of the chamber, in front of a fireplace heaped with lengths of wood but, due to the warmth of the weather, was unlit. Gianni didn't know whether to enter the room or wait until someone saw him but his dilemma was soon resolved when the castellan turned her head in his direction and beckoned him to come forward. When his reluctant steps brought him up beside her chair, she gave him a smile.

"I usually take a cup of hot cider at this time of the day," she said. "On the table over there you will find a newly filled jug. Pour me a cup and, if you would like to taste it, you may take a small measure for yourself."

With shaking hands, Gianni did as she had bid, almost spilling the fragrant apple drink as he carried it to where she was sitting. When he had poured a drop in one of the cups for himself, she motioned for him to be seated on a stool near her feet. He noticed some rolled up sheets of parchment lying on a small table beside her chair. They had been secured with a length of yellow ribbon.

"When Master Blund gave me the message you wish passed to Sir Bascot," she said, "I read with interest your comments about Jacques Roulan and the possibility that his entry into a monastic order may be connected to the recent murders."

Gianni held his breath. He was too nervous to take a sip of the steaming cider and the heat of it through the sides of the fragile pottery cup was burning his hand. With a thudding heart, he waited for Lady Nicolaa to continue.

"Your hypothesis hinges, of course, on whether or not it was the Templars that Roulan joined. Since I felt it would be wise to first ascertain whether that was so before I passed your message on to Sir Bascot, I sent for my bailiff at Brattleby, the one whose conversation with Lambert set your thoughts in motion."

Nicolaa paused for a moment and took a sip of cider. "I

spoke to my bailiff today and it seems that it was, in fact, the Templar Order that Jacques Roulan entered and that his reputation was every bit as licentious as the original remarks implied. Even though my husband is, at the moment, making enquiries that might lead in quite a different direction, they have not, as yet, proved conclusive and so I have decided that your suppositions might just possibly be relevant."

Nicolaa noticed that her assurances made the young lad relax. He had been fearful, she knew, that his request would seem impudent. But she had come to have a great regard for the Templar's intelligence during the two years he had been in her service and thought that this boy, whether the talent had been imparted by his former master or stemmed from his own abilities, showed promise of being cast in the same mould. She was also aware that the lack of Bascot's protection had made the boy insecure and it was her intention to try and bolster the boy's confidence. She had promised the Templar that she would oversee Gianni's welfare and had every intention of doing all she could to ensure her pledge was fulfilled.

Reaching out, she picked up the roll of papers. "To that end, and because the Templars may have information about Jacques Roulan that I, or my husband, are not privy to, it is best that Sir Bascot be told of your conjectures. I have here the notes you wrote and a covering letter detailing my conversation with my bailiff. In the morning you will take it to the Templar enclave and give it to your former master. When you do so, you can answer any questions he may have about the content."

Gianni's face went white with panic. Surely the castellan knew he was too young to be admitted to the preceptory. How could he ever complete the task she had set him?

Nicolaa smiled, well aware of the reason for the concern so obviously delineated on his face. "Gianni, although you do not know the exact year of your birth you must, by now, be about fourteen years old. Many of the squires in my husband's retinue are the same age," she told him in a mildly admonishing tone, "and are given a man's responsibilities. You even have the beginnings of down on your upper lip to prove you are past childhood. You will not be barred entry into the enclave."

Gianni's hand flew to his lip. He never had occasion to see his reflection except blurrily on the surface of the water into which he dipped his hands every morning to sluice his face. As he touched the narrow ridge of fine black hair, Nicolaa saw his shoulders unknowingly straighten and hid her amusement. She remembered how her son Richard, as a child, had longed to scrape his face with a blade in the way his father did and his delight when his beard began to grow.

She handed him the sheaves of rolled up parchment and Gianni tucked them into the breast of his tunic with great care. "Because of your inability to speak, Serjeant Ernulf will go with you to the preceptory tomorrow morning. He can explain your errand to the guard and so gain your admittance. While you are with the Templar, record any comments he may wish to convey to me on your wax tablet, and bring them to me when you return to the bail."

Gianni rose from his seat, carefully set down the cup of cider he had been holding and gave Nicolaa a solemn bob of his head. As he walked towards the door of the solar, the castellan fancied that his strides were much lengthier than those he had taken when he came in.

Eighteen

—✦—

OVERNIGHT THERE WAS A THUNDERSTORM. THE PRECEDING few days had become unseasonably warm and the air had become oppressive. Just after midnight, loud rumbles began in the heavens, followed by lightning that lit up the sky. The ensuing cloudburst was of short duration but intense. By the time dawn arrived the storm had moved off to the west, but the dusty earth of the ground was covered in a heavy moisture which ran in rivulets over the hard-packed dirt of the training ground in the commandery.

Immediately after the service at Prime, d'Arderon told Hamo to bring Alan of Barton to his office. When the young man-at-arms came in, he found Bascot and Emilius with the preceptor.

D'Arderon was seated behind the table he used for a desk, and bid the soldier stand on the other side, facing him. Bascot and Emilius were standing by the window. With an apprehensive glance at the two knights, Alan obeyed the preceptor's order and took up the position as directed. The young soldier was of middling height, with a ruddy face and sparse beard of a dirty brown colour. High on his cheek was a boil that looked ready to burst.

"Your record states that you hail from a village near Barton on Humberside," d'Arderon barked. "Is that correct?"

"Yes, Preceptor, it is," Alan replied.

"And your father's trade is that of creel and net maker?"

Again the young soldier answered in the affirmative.

"His customers—they are men who sail along the Humber, to the ports at Hull and Faxfleet?"

Alan nodded and said, "Yes, my father is a good tradesman. He has a lot of customers among the fishermen."

"Are most of his patrons known to you?"

With a puzzled look on his face, Alan nodded.

"Was a man named Robert Scallion among them?"

Although seemingly still confused at the reason for d'Arderon's question, Alan answered readily enough. "I know the name, Preceptor, but Scallion was a trader, not a fisherman. He would have no need of my father's wares."

"But you say you know his name. Did you know the man?"

Alan shook his head. "I saw him once, when I went across the Humber on the ferry to Hessle to deliver some of my father's baskets to a customer there. Scallion was speaking to some men on a boat alongside the one my father's customer owned and I heard one of the men say his name. I knew who he was, for most of the traders who travel across the ocean are well-known in the fishing community, but I have never spoken to him."

Bascot interjected with question of a different nature. "How did it come about that you felt a desire to join our Order? Was it at your father's urging, or that of some other relative?"

Alan's face relaxed. He was still filled with the zeal that had prompted him to make an application to be accepted into the Templar ranks and it showed on his youthful countenance. "'Twas our village priest who encouraged me and wrote the letter I took to the preceptor at Temple Hirst. Father William saw me practising at the butts in our village and said I was a fine archer and should use the talent God gave me to protect Christian pilgrims from the infidel. He prayed with me for some weeks, wanting to be sure I truly felt a calling. But as soon as Father William made the suggestion to me, I knew it was right for me to do so. I saw Our Blessed Lord in my dreams that very same night, beckoning me to come forth and do battle against His enemies."

There could be no doubt of the young man's sincerity. It radiated from him like a beacon. Emilius next posed a question of a more blunt nature.

"Do you find it difficult to keep your vow of chastity?"

Alan's florid face turned an even brighter red and he stumbled over his answer. "I've never lain with a woman, sir," he replied.

"That does not answer my question," Emilius pressed. "It would be understandable if you did. Sometimes a man's natural urges are overwhelming."

This time Alan's answer was more forthright, and he squared his shoulders before he replied. "My father is a pious man and explained to me, when I was a young boy, that it is sinful to lie with a woman outside of marriage. I will admit there were occasions when I had unclean thoughts about one of the girls in my village, but I went to our priest and confessed, and he gave me absolution. Once I decided to see if the Order would accept me, our Lord purged my soul of desire."

He turned and spoke directly to d'Arderon. "If I am suspected of causing the murder of those women, Preceptor, I swear to you by Christ's holy name that I am innocent."

So earnest was his reply that d'Arderon nodded his head and dismissed him. Once the young man-at-arms had left, the preceptor asked Bascot and Emilius if they thought he was telling the truth, not only about the harlots, but about knowing Robert Scallion.

"I would think so," Bascot said slowly. "He could easily have denied all knowledge of the trader. The fact that he didn't implies he is not lying. As for the murders, I think he is too ingenuous to have practised the deception required to kill them."

"And you, Emilius?" d'Arderon said. "What is your impression of him?"

"I agree with de Marins. And I must admit that the boy has restored my faith in the integrity of our brothers. He is young yet, and artless, but his devotion to our Lord is genuine. His faith will not be weakened by maturity, but strengthened, as it should be."

Hoping the draper's conviction proved to be a true one, d'Arderon sent for the other man-at-arms, Thomas of Penhill. This soldier was a seasoned Templar. Although he had never been posted to active duty in foreign lands, he had been in the Order for ten years and, besides his skill with horses, had shown on the training ground that he had more than a passing ability with a short sword. He was of average height, well-muscled in shoulder and arm, with hair of bright red that contrasted with the darkness of the neatly trimmed beard that covered his chin. He stood easily in front of the preceptor, his back erect and manner deferential.

His father had been a farrier who had sometimes been

called upon to help with shoeing the horses in the Penhill preceptory. Thomas had joined the Order in the year that King Richard had mounted his Crusade in the Holy Land, caught up in the fervour that had swept through Christendom at that time.

"I was five years at Penhill preceptory and was then ordered to join the enclave at Temple Hirst," he said. "When I first joined the Order I had hoped to be sent to Outremer, but it did not happen. But even though I have never been on active duty," he told them, "not a day has gone by when I regretted my decision to become a Templar. While I care for the mounts that go to our brethren in Outremer and Portugal, I know that Lord Jesus has blessed me with my skill so that I may ensure only those animals with the best of strength go to aid our men. When I was told that I was to be sent to Portugal, I rejoiced, for it seems a sign that God is pleased with my efforts and is rewarding me by sending me to a post where I can take an active part in defending our faith."

When asked about his trips to Faxfleet, Thomas answered readily, saying he had often gone there, not only with horses but sometimes with bales of wool that had been sheared from sheep on Templar properties in Yorkshire. The name of Robert Scallion meant nothing to him, he said, for the mounts were, without exception, put aboard galleys belonging to the Order and the wool was always taken by the same vessel, one belonging to a trader that had a contract with the Templars to deliver it to Flanders. That trader had not been Scallion.

The two officers and Bascot accepted his explanation and then asked if he had ever been to Lincoln in the days before he had joined the Order and, if so, had he visited any prostitutes within the town.

Thomas, a mature man, was not embarrassed by the nature of the second part of the question as the guileless young Alan had been. He told them he had never been to Lincoln before in his life and that his village, like the Penhill preceptory, was far from any town that was large enough to have a brothel.

"There was a girl in my village that I tumbled a couple of times when I was a young lad," he replied frankly, "but I've kept the vow I made on my initiation. I'll admit that at first I didn't find it easy, but 'tis like any other temptation—if you don't give in to it, the urge goes away in time."

After d'Arderon dismissed him, he looked questioningly at the draper and Bascot.

"I think that Thomas, like Alan, is also telling the truth," Emilius said. "I am sure that neither of these men is involved in the murders, either through an act of lechery, or a desire for revenge because of Scallion's death."

The preceptor and Bascot agreed, although privately Bascot knew that those responsible for the commission of secret murder usually possessed great deviousness and would find it easy to mislead others. He was not completely sure that both of the men-at-arms were innocent, especially Alan, who had admitted to being away from his pallet during the hours Elfreda was murdered. He could be masking his guilt behind a naive demeanour. Bascot was, therefore, relieved when d'Arderon did not change his decision to delay the departure of the contingent for another few days.

IN THE TOWN, ROGET BEGAN HIS ENQUIRY ABOUT A POSSIBLE sighting of Askil or Dunny within the confines of Lincoln. First he went to the brothel where Elfie had worked and asked Verlain and the other prostitutes if any of them had ever had a customer, or if Elfreda had ever mentioned meeting a man, that had eyes of different colours, one blue and the other brown. He also gave them a physical description of Dunny, describing his slim frame and manner of speaking. The stewe-keeper and all the prostitutes had shaken their heads, assuring the captain they would have remembered such a peculiarity as Askil's if they had ever seen or heard of such a rarity and, as far as they knew, none of their customers were seamen. From the bawdy house, Roget went to visit the childminder Terese and asked her the same. She, too, shook her head in negation.

Discouraged, Roget went to Danesgate and knocked at the door of the home belonging to the perfumer, Constance Turner.

Constance answered the door herself and seemed relieved by his appearance. "I am glad you are here, Captain," she said, inviting him inside. "I hope you have come to tell me the man who murdered my neighbour has been apprehended."

Reluctantly, Roget told her he had not. The perfumer's smile was as lovely as he remembered, and so was the warmth in her soft brown eyes. He knew that Constance was not a woman who would be interested in a casual dalliance and, for the first time in his lecherous life, found himself longing for the company of a female without considering whether or not she was beddable.

"No, mistress, I am afraid the villain who murdered Adele has not yet been found," Roget said. "But you must not be fearful; one of my guards has been on constant watch near your house, both during the day and at night. It would be impossible for him to get into your home."

"I know you have kept your promise, Captain," Constance replied. "I have seen your men outside, but it is not for myself that I am concerned, it is my maid Agnes. She will not leave the house, not at all, not even if I go with her. At night, and during the day, she bars the front door and the back entrance for fear the man she saw outside Adele's door will come in and kill her, just as he did my neighbour. I have been forced to go and get our bread and other food myself and, by the time I return, she is in a terrible state, shaking with fear and crying lest I have been murdered while I was gone. Not only am I concerned for her sanity, she is upsetting my customers with her weeping and wailing and, since you instructed me not to speak of what Agnes saw, it is most difficult to convince them she has not lost her senses. I do not know what I am going to do about her."

"Let me speak to the little one," Roget offered. "Perhaps I can allay her fears."

Constance led him upstairs to the chamber where she prepared her scents and sweet-smelling unguents. "Agnes will not leave the upper floor except to go down and bar the doors," Constance said as they went up the stairs. "She keeps herself either locked in her room or stays with me while I work."

The chamber they entered was crammed with pots and stoppered jars. Bunches of herbs and orrisroot hung from a beam in the ceiling. Some of the pots contained dried leaves or pieces of root that had been crushed with a pestle, others were filled with liquid, among them the goat's milk that Constance had said Agnes had gone to fetch early in the morning of the day that Adele had been strangled. The room had a heady fragrance that was almost overpowering and Roget recoiled slightly when they went in. Constance

noticed his reaction and went over to the larger of the two
casements and threw it open.

"I am sorry, Captain, for the strong aroma. I am so used
to it that I sometimes forget it can be cloying, especially to
men."

In a corner of the room Agnes was seated on a stool. She
was, as Constance had said, in a state of abject terror. Her
eyes were red from weeping and her hands were clenched
into fists on her bony knees. She was a girl of the utmost
plainness and her sorry state made her more unattractive,
but not even the most hard-hearted of men could have
failed to be touched by her plight. She was like a tiny rabbit
caught in a trap, fearfully waiting for its neck to be wrung.
Roget went over to her, and hunkering down in front of her,
spoke in soft tones, assuring her she had no need to be afraid.
"I promise you, *ma petite*, that you will come to no harm.
One of my guards will be outside your mistress's house every
hour of the day and night. This man who is frightening you
will not get in here, I assure you."

He took her hand in his and stroked it. Her fingers were
thin and the skin rough, the nails bitten down to the quick.
Roget continued to speak in the same vein until the girl
began to relax. Finally she gave him a tremulous smile and
when Roget asked her if she could summon up the courage
to answer some questions, she gave him a hesitant nod.

Constance had stood and watched the captain calm her
young maid and, when Roget stood up and turned to face
her, she gave him a grateful smile, her eyes alight with appreciation of his kindness. The captain felt a stirring in the
region of his heart and tried to ignore it. He had long ago
promised himself that he would never get seriously involved
with any woman, but realised he was perilously close to feel-

ing more for this lovely perfumer than simple lust. Trying to disguise his emotion from both himself and Constance, he asked if either of the women had seen men answering the description of Askil and Dunny.

"They are both sailors; Askil is the older of the pair and has eyes of unusual colour—one is brown and the other blue. Dunny is young, very slim and has pitted skin on his face. Have you noticed any men who look like that outside in the street, or entering Adele's house?"

Constance and Agnes both shook their heads and suddenly the little maid burst into tears. "But I didn't see the man's face, Captain," she wailed. "He could have had eyes like you said, or a scarred face, and I wouldn't have noticed. What if he did and thinks I saw him? He'll be sure to come after me."

This time it was Constance who calmed her maid. In an even voice she said, "Then the guard outside will catch him, Agnes, and your travail will be over. Come now, pour the captain a cup of cordial. We must show our appreciation for the care he is taking to protect us. It is not every woman in the town who has a guard on their door day and night. You must compose yourself and be brave."

Her words seemed to penetrate the fog of fear that surrounded Agnes and she went to the corner and poured some liquid into a cup for Roget. It was thin stuff and scented with some sort of flower essence, but he drank it down as though it were ambrosia. To remain in the company of the attractive perfumer he would have drunk stagnant water and believed it to be the finest of wines.

Nineteen

⊹

ABOUT AN HOUR AFTER PRIME, GIANNI AND ERNULF LEFT THE castle bail and walked across the grounds of the Minster and through the gate in the eastern wall of the city. As they travelled along the path that led to the enclave, the boy felt his anxiety return. That morning he had looked at his reflection in the piece of polished metal that Ernulf used for shaving. In its wavy surface he could see the fine line of down on his upper lip and, initially, it had swelled his confidence. Now, however, apprehension filled him with a desire to run back to the castle.

As they approached the preceptory, Gianni distracted himself by remembering what Bascot had told him about the Lincoln enclave. The Templar had said it was a small one, similar to other provincial preceptories that were subordinate to commanderies in large cities like London and Paris. Some of these were huge, Bascot had said, especially in lands where there was need to protect pilgrims from infidel attack and the brothers were often engaged in battle with Saracen forces. The larger ones usually had a castle as their base and many more officers in the chain of command, such as a seneschal and a marshal. Nonetheless, when they neared the squat twin towers that guarded the entrance, Gianni's heart began to pound. What if the Templar on the gate refused to admit a boy of his small stature? Had Lady Nicolaa been right in saying he was old enough to go inside or had she been mistaken? He was glad he had the stocky bulk of Ernulf by his side. The serjeant would ensure, at least, that the message Gianni carried would be given to his former master.

The boy's fear was not realised. After Ernulf told the guard of the purpose of the visit, the Templar man-at-arms made no demur at Gianni's presence and bid them come in, calling to one of the soldiers inside the compound to tell Sir Bascot there was a message for him from the castle.

After they walked through the solid archway of stone, Gianni was surprised to see that the interior of the enclave, although smaller, was not much different in arrangement from the castle bail. To one side was a long low building housing the stables, there were storehouses and a forge and, instead of a keep, a two-storied building where the Templars ate and took their rest. Only the round chapel marked a strangeness that Gianni was not accustomed to; that and the absence of women. The latter radiated an aura of maleness that was almost palpable. Here were men carrying out tasks that, in the bail, were the lot of female servants—in one corner a man with a humped back was washing clothes in a huge tub of water and, nearby, another was emptying vegetable slops from the kitchen onto a midden. The air rang with the sounds and smells of masculinity—the clashing of the blacksmith's hammer on his anvil, the acrid tang of sweat and the pungent aroma of leather and metal. It was an atmosphere that Gianni breathed in eagerly, consciously relishing his emerging manhood.

Bascot was among a few pairs of men exercising their military skills in the middle of the training ground. Facing him was a younger man that also wore the three-foot-long sword wielded by those of knight's rank. The other knight was young and, since Gianni knew there were only the preceptor, the draper and his former master of knight's rank stationed in the commandery, judged that the younger knight must be one of the men forming the contingent whose departure had been delayed. Bascot was instructing the knight in how to use his shield as a defensive weapon. Both men had kite-shaped shields painted with a Templar cross slung from their shoulders and were holding flails—short-handled weapons to which a length of chain was attached. At the end of the chain was an iron ball fitted with wicked looking spikes. On the ones they were holding, these spikes had been blunted but when they were used in battle, they would be honed to needlepoint sharpness. As Gianni watched, Bascot and his opponent hefted their shields in front of them and began to strike at each other with the flails. In one quick movement, Bascot hooked the edge of the other knight's shield with the iron ball, pulled it out of his opponent's grasp and then struck at his exposed body with his own buckler, giving him a hefty blow in the chest. The knight fell back but Bascot did not press his advantage. Instead he began to instruct the man in how he should have moved to defend himself.

Gianni was well aware that if they had been engaged in real battle, Bascot's shield would have struck more solidly and his flail would have come down in a deadly stroke that would have incapacitated, or even killed, the other man. The boy's narrow chest swelled with pride. Even though he now thought it unlikely that a Templar had killed the prostitutes, the danger to the man he held in such high regard was always at the back of his mind. Watching Bascot give the young knight instruction had reminded Gianni of the Templar's skill with arms and went a little way to relieving his concern for his former master's safety.

The man-at-arms sent by the guard on the gate waited until Bascot had finished instructing the young knight before interrupting to tell of his visitors. As he did so, the Templar looked up and saw Gianni and Ernulf. With a broad grin, he walked around the other pairs of men in the training ground and towards where they were standing. Gianni was so glad to see his master that it took a great effort not to run forward in greeting as he had been accustomed to do when they had been staying in Lincoln castle. Now, conscious of the immaturity of such an action, he merely stood still and returned Bascot's smile with one of his own.

Ernulf explained why they had come and Bascot took them into the refectory. The eating hall was empty now and, unlike the hall in the castle keep, the long tables of oak had not been pushed to one side but remained in place in rows down the middle of the chamber with benches set alongside. Explaining that they could speak in here privily, the Templar laid his hand on Gianni's shoulder in a light touch of welcome, and bade him and Ernulf be seated at one of the tables while he read the message Gianni had brought.

When he had finished, he looked up, the icy blue of his eye startlingly bright in the gloom inside the refectory. "Your postulation is of great interest, Gianni. We had never considered that the murderer might be a woman, but now that you have suggested it, I can see no reason why a female could not have committed the crimes, or perhaps acted as an accomplice. A woman of reasonable strength would have no difficulty overcoming another of her own sex and garrotting is a relatively simple method of killing if the victim is taken by surprise. Or she could have approached both of the women and introduced a male confederate. I will convey your suspicion to the preceptor. I have no doubt he will wish me to investigate the background of Jacques Roulan. I, along with Lady Nicolaa, commend you for your perception."

Gianni flushed with gratification as Bascot spoke to Ernulf. "In her covering note, Lady Nicolaa suggests that I go with Roget to the Roulan manor house at Ingham and question Jacques' relatives," he said, "and try to ascertain if there was any liaison Jacques might have formed that could be a basis for these crimes. Please tell her I will be ready to ride there tomorrow morning and will meet Roget at Newport Arch just after Prime."

Bascot walked back to the gate with his visitors. As they passed the huge storage shed, he asked them to wait for a moment and, going inside, soon returned carrying a small leather sack. It contained over a dozen of the boiled-sugar lumps that were sent to England from Templar properties in the Holy Land, and were made from sweet canes that grew in parts of Outremer. The Arabs called them *al-Kandiq*, but in England they were known simply as *candi*, and were one of the items the Templars used in trade to raise funds for the upkeep of the Order.

"Here," he said to Gianni, handing him the sack. "You deserve a reward for your discernment." The boy's face lit up with a wide grin. He was very fond of the sweets.

As they made their way back to the castle, Gianni and Ernulf each munched on one of the *candi*, relishing both the taste of the confection and the success of their errand.

* * *

After Gianni and Ernulf left, Bascot went to the journal that recorded the entrance of initiates into the Order to determine if it had been at the Lincoln commandery that Jacques Roulan had been initiated into the Templars. Gianni's note had said that the document recording the transfer of property had been dated a year before, so he started at that time and went backwards, presuming the transfer would not have been made until after the original heir had left. He soon found it, some six months before the date Gianni had given. The entry stated that Roulan had been granted admission by the draper who had held the post before Emilius, on a date when d'Arderon would have gone on his annual trip to London to meet with Thomas Berard and preceptors from other English commanderies for a general accounting of the lands they managed for the Order. The record also stated that Roulan had subsequently been posted to the commandery at Qaqun, a small town located near Mount Nablus. Qaqun was not far south of Acre.

Bascot pondered the information. Again, the city of Acre and its environs had popped up in this enquiry, for it was in the suburbs of Acre that Robert Scallion had reportedly been killed by a Templar knight. But Acre was a large port and many Templars were stationed there, as well as in fortresses in other cities and towns in the area. Dismissing the coincidence as having no relevance, Bascot went to find d'Arderon to tell him of Gianni's hypothesis. Both the preceptor and Emilius would be relieved to learn there might be others beside the people close to Robert Scallion that could be involved in the recent murders. Although the slaying of the prostitutes was still obviously connected to the Templar Order, this latest information provided additional reason to hope that the perpetrator had not been one of their brethren.

Twenty

✦❖✦

THE NEXT MORNING, AS ARRANGED, BASCOT WENT TO MEET
Roget at Newport Arch. The captain was waiting for him
and, as the Templar came up to where the former mercenary
sat on his horse, he noticed that Roget looked weary; the old
scar on his face had a whitish tinge and even the copper rings
threaded through his beard seemed dull.

"I am afraid, *mon ami*, that our trip to Ingham must be
delayed," Roget said. "Another woman was attacked in town
last night. She is not dead, thanks be to God, but it was a
near thing."

Bascot felt a cold chill settle over him. "Another prostitute?" he asked.

Roget shook his head. "She was a harlot once, but not
anymore. It was Terese, the woman who looks after Elfie's
little daughter."

The captain turned his horse back towards the arch,
threading it through a few carts laden with produce that
were wending their way north on Ermine Street to exit the
city. "I spoke to her briefly last night about the man who
attacked her, but she was very shaken and concerned for the

children in her care. I left one of my guards with her and told her I would be back this morning. The sheriff told me to ask if you would accompany me."

"Of course," Bascot replied. "Did her assailant enter her home?"

"No." Roget ran a tired hand over the ragged scar on his face. "She was in the street near her house when the attack took place." He gave the Templar an inquisitorial look. "You have been told that Preceptor d'Arderon asked Lady Nicolaa to give Terese the money that was found with Elfie?"

When Bascot nodded, Roget went on. "Terese had lodged the money with Verlain at the stewe. She was fearful it would be stolen if she kept it at home and paid Verlain a small fee to keep it safe for her in the chest where he stores the bawds' earnings. The stewe is not far from where Terese lives and so is near enough to be convenient for her to get a few coins when she needs them. Last night, she went to the stewe to get a small sum to pay for food over the next few days, leaving the tinker that lives in her house to watch over the children. It was as she was returning that she was attacked. Fortunately, she was carrying a knife—she said she has been doing so ever since Elfie was killed—and managed to stick the *bâtard* with it. Then she screamed her head off and the ruffian Verlain hires to keep order in the stewe came running but, by the time he got to her, her assailant had run away."

Roget gave an admiring chuckle. "She is a woman *formidable*, that Terese. Even after Verlain summoned one of my guards, she did not cry one tear, just begged that she be escorted to her home straightaway, for she did not want to leave the little ones for too long a time."

"Did she see the man who attacked her?"

"She says not, but now that she has had time to reflect,

she may remember something that will help us catch this *chien*."

As they reached Bailgate and descended Steep Hill into the town, Roget told Bascot of another happening that had taken place the night before. Bailiff Thorson had arrived at the castle in the early evening with the news that he, along with Sven Grimson, his wife, and the two seamen, had come to Lincoln and taken lodgings in the town.

"Thorson said Sven and Joan had insisted on coming to Lincoln to speak to the sheriff personally, as they had further information that would allow Sir Gerard to lift the restriction that had been placed on them. They asked that they be granted a meeting with him today."

"We only came back from Grimsby two days ago," Bascot said in astonishment. "How did they miraculously come by 'further information' in such a short time?" He shook his head in disbelief. "It would appear we were right to suspect they were lying. Does Thorson know what it is they have to tell?"

"No. He said only that Sven and Joan came to him the morning after we left and insisted they must speak to Sir Gerard themselves, that what they had to tell could not be passed through another's agency. Because the bailiff had taken responsibility for ensuring they would not flee, he decided that he could not countenance them setting off unaccompanied, so he came with them."

"And how did Camville react to this news?"

Roget gave an evil grin. "He lost his temper. I was not there, but Ernulf told me that although he did not rail at Thorson, he told the bailiff he would see the Grimsons at his leisure and they could consider themselves fortunate he did not throw all four of them in the castle gaol."

Roget urged his horse into a trot as they approached Butwerk and the hovel where Terese lived. "I think he plans to talk to Sven and the others this afternoon, which is another reason why we cannot go to Ingham today. Sir Gerard would like you to be present when he hears what it is they have to say."

One of the town guards under Roget's command was on duty outside Terese's door when they arrived. The captain asked him if all had been well during the rest of the night and, when the soldier nodded, they knocked on the door.

When Terese opened it, it was obvious she had managed to get little sleep. Her erect figure was slightly stooped and lines of weariness etched her face. She bid both of them come in and gently shooed the band of little girls, who were gathered behind her clutching at her skirt, to the far side of the room, urging them to sit quietly while she spoke to their visitors.

"They do not know what has happened, but are aware that something is wrong," Terese said. "It would be best if we spoke about this matter in quiet tones, so they are not alarmed any further."

"If you will allow me, mistress, I can think of a way to distract them," Roget said and strode to the door. Giving the guard a couple of pennies from the purse at his belt, the captain told the soldier to go to the nearest baker and buy two loaves of fresh bread. "And some honey or conserve to spread on it. And don't dally, or else you will feel the sole of my boot on your backside."

The guard sped off and Terese smiled. "You are not quite so fearsome as you seem, Captain," she said.

"Women of all ages should be cherished, not frightened," Roget responded gallantly.

While they waited for the guard, the captain poured them all a cup of wine from the flask he kept hanging from his saddle and, as soon as the soldier returned and the bread and honey had been distributed among the children—whose eyes all stretched wide at the rare treat—and they were sitting quietly, Roget asked Terese to tell Bascot of her frightening experience the night before.

"I was only a few steps from the stewe," she said in soft tones, "and just passing the mouth of an alleyway that leads to a midden at the back of the houses. I saw a movement out of the corner of my eye and suddenly I felt something—a cord or a piece of rope—go around my neck and begin to tighten. I barely had time to pull out the knife I have been carrying since Elfie was killed before the garrotte cut off my breath entirely. I am fortunate I had a weapon on me."

She pulled a small blade about five or six inches long from a small battered sheath strung on a cord around her waist. Although the knife was not very big, Bascot and Roget saw that it had been honed to a fine sharpness on both sides of the blade. The edges glinted wickedly in the narrow shaft of sunlight that came through the small casement beside the front door. "It is the knife I use to cut up vegetables. I had the tinker sharpen it for me," she explained. "It has served me well."

"And then, mistress," Bascot prompted as her eyes began to darken with remembered terror.

Terese recovered her composure and continued, "My cloak must have hampered my attacker from tightening the cord further and, as he moved close behind me to get a better grip, I stabbed out with my little blade." She demonstrated the action she had used, holding her arm stiffly down at her side and driving the knife backwards.

Her lips drew into a small smile of satisfaction. "I felt it cut into that pig's flesh, the top of his leg I think, and so I pulled it out and struck again. He gave a grunt of pain and I felt the noose go slack. Then I screamed and the door to the stewe flew open and Verlain's guard came rushing out. But before he could grab ahold of my attacker, the coward had turned and run back down the alleyway. The guard searched the area, as did two of your constables, Captain, after Verlain rang the alarm bell at the end of the street to summon them, but they could not find him."

"You showed remarkable courage, mistress," Bascot said to her.

"Not courage, lord, but desperation. My life may not be worth much, but it is mine, and I do not intend to give it up to any but the Good Lord above when He decides it is time."

Both men agreed wholeheartedly with her sentiment and Bascot asked if she had seen the face of her attacker.

"No, I did not," she answered with a dissatisfied grimace. "The moon is in a dark phase so there was not much light in the street, only a small glimmer from the torch outside Verlain's stewe. And the villain had a cloak on with a hood which shadowed his face. I am sorry, lords, I have been wracking my poor brain all night to try and think of something that may help you identify him, but I cannot. It all happened so fast, and it was very dark."

"What makes you think it is Elfie's killer that attacked you, mistress?" Bascot asked. "Might it not have been someone who was merely intent on stealing the money you had just collected from Verlain?"

Terese shook her head. "If it had been a thief, he could have simply struck me over the head to knock me senseless and then robbed me of the little bit of silver I was carrying. This man was intent on killing me. That is why I think it is the same one that murdered poor Elfie and Adele Delorme. In the gloom, it would have been easy for him to have mistaken me for one of the bawds from Verlain's stewe, for the darkness would have hidden the age lines on my face. And it was in Verlain's brothel that he found easy prey once before, when he took poor Elfie to your Templar chapel and killed her. No, he was not a thief."

Bascot put his next question with seeming mildness so as not to influence Terese's answer in any way. "There is a slim possibility that it might be a woman who is responsible for these crimes. Did you notice anything about your attacker that might indicate whether this could be so?"

After a fleeting glance of surprise, the former harlot gave the question careful consideration. Finally she said that she could not be certain. "I only saw his figure after he—or she—ran back down the alley." She concentrated for a moment longer as she thought carefully over the attack before reluctantly shaking her head. "I could feel my assailant's body close against my back, but was not aware of any breasts pressing into me. It could have been a woman who is not buxom but, I am sorry, lord, I cannot be sure."

"But, whoever it was, you are certain you wounded him?" Bascot pressed.

"Oh, yes, of that I am most positive. My little knife was bloodied to the haft." Terese gave a grim smile of satisfaction. "And he was limping as he ran away."

Twenty-one

AFTER LEAVING TERESE, BASCOT AND ROGET RODE BACK TO
the castle. As they did so, the captain remarked that he was
going to ask Gerard Camville to second some of the castle's
men-at-arms to the town guard.

"I have a dozen men," the captain added. "Two are needed
to guard the perfumer's house—one during the day and another at night—and now another two to keep watch at Terese's home. That will leave me with only eight men, four
for the day shifts and four for nights, to patrol the town.
It is not enough to maintain security, especially with this
mad dog of a murderer on the loose. It is unfortunate that
Terese did not catch a glimpse of the face of the person who
attacked her. That would have been most helpful."

"Even though she did not, Roget," Bascot replied, "she
marked him with her knife and said he was limping from
the effect of the wound. We must take particular notice of
any man, or woman, who is favouring one leg."

He paused for a moment and then added, "Terese said,
like the man Mistress Turner's maid saw, that her assailant
was of average height. It might be worthwhile to take note

of the stance of those in the Grimson party, since they were all in Lincoln last night. Sven is too tall, but Askil would fit the description, and so might Dunny, even if he is perhaps a little short of stature. And if a female is responsible, Joan is the right height and also a strongly built woman."

"I believe Peter Thorson and the constable he brought with him watched over them all in the lodgings where they stayed last night," Roget told him. "The bailiff is not a man to shirk his duty. I would be surprised if any of them would have been able to escape his vigilance."

"Perhaps so, but it can be difficult for a man to oversee a woman all night long unless he is her husband. With Sven's connivance, Joan could easily have slipped out without Thorson being aware of it."

Roget gave a chuckle. "For a chaste Templar, your knowledge of a woman's ways sometimes surprises me."

Bascot returned his smile. "In the years of my youth, before I joined the Order, I was often tempted by the charms of a willing female. And I did not always resist."

AFTER LEAVING THEIR HORSES IN THE CASTLE STABLES, THE pair went into the keep, where trestle tables were being set up for the midday meal. The Haye steward, Eudo, met them at the door and told Bascot he was to convey an invitation from the sheriff that the Templar stay and eat with the household so that he would be present when Thorson brought the Grimson party to the hall after the meal was over.

While Roget went to sit with Ernulf and the men of the garrison near the back of the hall, Bascot took the seat he had been accustomed to use while he had been staying in the castle, at a table used by the household knights set just below the dais. In the centre of the table was a huge salt cellar that marked the division of those of highborn status from ones of lower station. Bascot's regular seat had been at the lower edge of the line of demarcation and, as he slid into place, the knights in Camville's retinue all gave him a warm greeting. A few moments later, Gianni came into the hall with John Blund and Lambert. As one of the higher ranking household staff, the secretary took his seat just below the salt and expressed his pleasure at being in Bascot's company. Both Gianni and Lambert, as Blund's assistants, were allowed to sit beside the secretary, and Lambert did so, but Gianni immediately came around behind the Templar and filled his wine cup. The lad then began to lade Bascot's trencher with viands from a huge platter in the middle of the table, just as he had done every day for the two years he had been the Templar's servant.

John Blund looked on with a nod of approval and Lambert gave a smile of commendation. Bascot felt a warm glow in his heart and, when Gianni had piled his trencher high, thanked the lad and gave him permission to take his own seat. The boy's actions were a nice gesture of courtesy, and betokened well for the character of the man he was on the verge of becoming.

Once the meal was over, Gerard Camville, seated on the dais, sent a page to where Bascot was sitting with an invitation to share a cup of wine at the high table while they waited for the Grimsons and the two seamen to appear. The Templar joined the sheriff and Lady Nicolaa while the detritus of food was removed and the tables taken down and stacked against the walls and then, as Camville had instructed, the hall was cleared of servants. When the expected party arrived in the company of Bailiff Thorson and his constable, the huge chamber was empty except for Bascot, the sheriff, Nicolaa de la Haye and Roget. The steward, Eudo, had remained at the door only long enough to usher Thorson and his constable, with the Grimson party trailing behind, into the hall before exiting himself.

The bailiff and his constable went to stand beside Roget, leaving Sven and Joan standing below the dais, Askil and Dunny behind them. All were dressed in a sober manner. Joan was clad in a gown of dark grey topped with an old-fashioned Saxon head rail similar to the one she had worn on the day Bascot and Roget had first met her in Grimsby, this time of a heavier material that almost completely covered her hair and was fastened in place about her forehead by a plain band of dark blue. Sven's tunic was of good quality material and of a red so dark it was almost black, while the two seamen wore hose and tunics of russet brown that had been patched in places. This time not only Askil's hair, but also Dunny's, was tied back with a leather thong and the younger sailor's previously greasy locks appeared to have been recently washed. Camville let them wait for a moment before he spoke.

"Bailiff Thorson informs me that you told Captain Roget and Sir Bascot a pack of lies when they were in Grimsby. You have until I drink this cup of wine to explain yourselves to my satisfaction. If you do not, you will be taken to the castle gaol and stay there at my pleasure."

Sven flinched at the sheriff's threat, but his wife did not show any fear. She stepped forward a pace and spoke in the icy tones Bascot remembered so well from the day he and Roget had questioned her in her home.

"The only lie my husband told was of our purpose in going to Hull," she said steadily, her hands loosely clasped in front of her and her demeanour showing no sign of agitation. "We were, as Sven said, absent from Grimsby for some ten days but none of us have any involvement in the murder of the prostitutes."

Placing her hand on the sheriff's arm to forestall further speech, Nicolaa de la Haye now leaned forward and spoke in measured tones to Sven's wife. It was a tactic she often employed when Camville's choler was rising, her own calm authority a perfect foil to her husband's irascibility. And it was deceptive, for Nicolaa was just as implacable as her husband when it came to the pursuit of justice. "And why were you unwilling to tell my husband's officer the true reason you went to the port?"

A brief frisson of relief, quickly masked, crossed Joan's features as she turned to speak to the seemingly mild-mannered castellan. "It was because of the Templar's presence, lady." She gestured behind her at the two sailors. "Dunny, one of the seamen my brother Robert employed, did not tell all that he knew of the night my brother was killed in Acre. Before the fight began between Robert and the knight who stabbed him, they stood for a little time in conversation and mention was made that they had previously been in each other's company in Hull, and that the knight was from Lincolnshire. My husband and I did go to the port to speak to some of Robert's customers but Sven also went to some of the alehouses my brother patronised to see if anyone knew the name of the knight. We thought that if we could find out who he was . . ."

Camville's temper snapped at the glib recital. Rising from his seat he strode down from the dais and went to stand in front of Joan. "And what would it profit you to know the name of this knight?"

Joan recoiled slightly at the suddenness of the sheriff's attack but managed to answer steadily. "Then, lord sheriff, we would have reported it to you. As far as we know, the knight who killed Robert has not been apprehended, but even if he is, he would merely be expelled from the Templar Order, not hung as he deserves. If he returned to Lincolnshire after his expulsion, he could resume his former life with ease and none would be the wiser. But, if you knew of it, you could charge him with the crime and see that he paid the full penalty. The reason we did not want Sir Bascot to learn of our purpose is because it is well-known how Templars support each other, and we feared he might give my brother's murderer warning."

"And if this knight—whose name you do not know— does not return to England, but has stayed in Outremer, what then?" Camville demanded.

"It was implied by the conversation Dunny overheard that the man who killed my brother is a knight of Lincolnshire. If so, he will have family here." Joan's voice rang with resolution as she gave vent to outrage that had been too long suppressed. "Even if he does not return, if we learn his identity then we can publically denounce him. Let his relatives suffer, as I have done, for his evil act. It will not compensate my grief, but it will go a long way to alleviate it."

Bascot noticed that Askil was watching Joan with undisguised admiration in his eyes. There could be no doubt that the sailor, as Thorson had judged, was in love with her. How far would such devotion drive a man? Would Askil commit murder if Joan asked it of him? The Templar thought it entirely possible. Sven, too, seemed in thrall to his handsome wife. It was evident that this scheme of discovering the identity of her brother's murderer was of her making. Both her husband and Askil were merely following her direction, taking Dunny along in their wake.

Bascot switched his gaze to Joan and tried to assess the truth of her words. She had merely glanced at him as she had made her accusation against the Templar Order and her words had been charged with seeming sincerity. But, once again, he had the feeling she was masking her true purpose. He leaned forward and asked a question of his own.

"Now that you have made Sheriff Camville cognizant of your intent, mistress, you have no need to fear any complicity on my part in aiding the man who killed your brother. Tell us, did either you or your husband discover the name of the guilty knight?"

"No, we did not," she replied coolly. "Our journey was in vain."

"As is the reason for holding this meeting," Camville said heatedly. "I am trying to find out who murdered two women and attacked another last night in the town. Your futile search is a distraction and wasting time that I, and my men, could put to better use. You will stay in Lincoln until I receive an answer to the message I sent to Hull. I will allow you to remain in the lodgings you have secured, but Bailiff Thorson will keep watch over all of you."

With that, Camville strode to the back of the hall and called loudly for Eudo. When the steward appeared, the sheriff gave him an order to have some wine sent up to his private chamber and left the hall. Lady Nicolaa rose from her chair and Bascot did the same.

"You have heard my husband's judgement," the castellan said to Sven and Joan Grimson. "If you are wise, you will obey his command and not cause him further irritation."

As the pair departed, the two seamen trailing behind

them in a disconsolate fashion, Bascot took care to notice the manner in which each of them walked. If their story was a cover for a more nefarious purpose, they could still be guilty of the murder of the two prostitutes and the attack on Terese. A glance at Roget told the Templar that the captain was also watching all of the party, including Joan, carefully. But there was no hesitation in the steps of any. Sven paced the length of the hall without a falter in his long-legged stride, and Joan glided over the rushes on the floor of the hall with her head held high. The two sailors followed them with the swaying gait common to seamen. Whatever any of them might be guilty of, it seemed it had not been one of them that had attacked the former prostitute in the street outside Verlain's bawdy house.

Twenty-two

B̲ASCOT AND R̲OGET DECIDED THAT IT WAS STILL EARLY ENOUGH
for them to make the trip to the Roulan property at Ingham.
The village was situated just a little over eight miles northwest of Lincoln, a distance that would take them barely an
hour on horseback. As they rode out of the bail, Roget asked
Bascot what he thought of Joan Grimson's story about the
reason she and her husband had gone to Hull.

"It seems to me," Bascot said, "that she is lying by omis-
sion. Just as we were not told all the facts in the first tale
Sven gave us, there are still some details that have been left
out."

Roget snorted his agreement. "I do not believe that if
they had discovered the name of the Templar that killed
her brother, she would have meekly told the sheriff about
him. If the knight has returned to Lincolnshire, she would
have ensured he was dead before she denounced him. She is
a determined woman, that one, and does not intend to be
thwarted."

Bascot nodded. The Templar remembered the besotted
look on Askil's face as Joan had courageously faced Gerard

Camville's threat of imprisonment. The steersman would do anything to please her, Bascot was sure, even commit murder.

As the pair rode out onto Ermine Street and headed north, they passed many other travellers. Some were on foot—tinkers with packs slung on their shoulders, charcoal burners carrying sacks secured by a heavy band around their forehead, and the occasional tradesman walking alone, carrying a sack of tools. There was wheeled traffic too, a few small carts and a couple of men pushing barrows, along with a small number of affluent merchants on horseback. As they exited Lincoln through Newport Arch, they found a large dray laden high with sacks of grain in front of them. The iron shod wheels on the cart must have been new, for the metal glistened in the early summer sun but, as the wagon began its journey up the dusty road, grime began to film the shiny circles and within a few moments, their brightness started to become tarnished. The rhythmic glitter of the turning wheel was hypnotic and Bascot found his attention drawn to it as they overtook the wagon and passed it.

It was not long before they came to the turnoff for Ingham. As they slowed to ride onto the track, Roget gestured to the east, where the rolling terrain stretched northeast towards the Humber estuary. "If, as Bailiff Thorson suggested, Grimson's two seamen did come down the Ancholme in a small skiff, we are not far from where their journey would have ended at Bishopbridge."

Bascot turned his head so his sighted eye had a better view of the landscape. Sheep were scattered over the grassland, some partially hidden by the occasional clump of trees or bushes. There were many small villages in the area, and tracks would lead from all of them to join up with the high-

way, including Bishopbridge. It would not have taken the
seamen many hours to walk to Lincoln, just as Thorson had
said.

The path to Ingham was a dusty trail that led west towards the Trent River. Urging their horses into a trot, they
rode down the track and through a small village. Beyond the
hamlet the road ended, its terminus the large manor house
owned by the Roulan family.

THE RESIDENCE WAS A SOLID STRUCTURE OF TWO STORIES EN-
circled by a stout fence of wooden palings. Nicolaa de la
Haye had told them that after Jacques left to join the Templars, his father had died, and the eldest brother, Gilbert,
had inherited the estate.

"The property mentioned in the document that Gianni
was given to copy is not far from Ingham, near a village
called Marton. It was part of the dower Gilbert's mother
brought to her husband on their marriage day," Nicolaa had
told them before they left. "Both Ingham and Marton are
part of the demesne I inherited from my father, and held in
fee, but it is the property at Ingham that brings in most of
their revenue, mainly from sheep. Originally, Jacques was
named as beneficiary of the Marton property in his mother's
will, but when he left to join the Templars, she changed the
document and named the youngest brother, Hervé, as the
son that will inherit Marton after her death. Besides Gilbert
and Hervé, there is also a sister. I seem to recall her name
is Julia."

Nearly all of the Roulan family were inside the capacious hall of the manor house when Bascot and Roget were
shown in by a manservant. The eldest brother, Gilbert, a

man of about forty years of age with greying hair and weary
eyes, was seated with two women at a large oak table in
the middle of the room. Slumped in a chair beside an unlit
fireplace was a younger man, the aquiline curve of his nose
and set of his jaw enough like Gilbert's to proclaim that he
was the youngest brother, Hervé. At his feet was a wine jug
and in his hand a full cup. His mulish expression and slack
jaw suggested he had been drinking for some time. Leaning
against the far wall, alongside an open casement, was a man
of an age somewhere between that of the two Roulan brothers. He, too, possessed the same beak of a nose as Gilbert
and Hervé, but the rest of his features were more softly cast.
He stood with arms folded and a solemn expression on his
countenance. The top half of his face was tanned to a copper
hue, but the flesh about his mouth and chin was much paler,
as though he had recently shaved off a beard. There were no
servants present in the room and a faint aura of tension hung
in the air, giving the impression that a heated argument had
been in progress, which the arrival of Bascot and Roget had
interrupted. When the servant announced the name of the
visitors, Gilbert rose from his chair and came forward to
greet them.

"The sheriff has sent us to ask you a few questions concerning the recent murders that have taken place in Lincoln
town," Roget told Gilbert when he enquired the reason for
their presence.

A wary look came into Gilbert's eyes, but he bade them
be seated and directed the elder of the two women, who
he introduced as his wife, Margaret, to bring wine for their
guests. She was a few years younger than her husband and
had a wan comeliness in her pale blue eyes and small shapely
mouth. A few tendrils of blond hair showed at the rim of a

linen coif which covered her head in a haphazard fashion, as though she had donned it hastily. Bringing cups from an open-faced cupboard at the end of the room, she poured a full measure in each and then set them before the two visitors.

The other woman, much younger and with the same dark hair and hazel eyes as Gilbert and Hervé, but without the unfortunate prominence of the family nose, also rose from her seat and went to stand beside the man standing by the window. Her figure was plump, and the set of her shoulders seemed defiant.

"My sister, Julia," Gilbert said as she moved away from the table. He then gestured to the man seated by the fireplace. "And that is Hervé, my younger brother."

"And this," Hervé proclaimed in a slurred voice and throwing his arm up and pointing to the man beside his sister, "is Savaric. He is also a relative, a half brother, a baseborn offspring of my father's lechery, but a member of our family all the same."

A look of disgust crossed Julia's face. "Have another cup of wine, Hervé. Perhaps it will make you incapable of speech, for which we will all be truly thankful."

"Enough, both of you," Gilbert said and turned to Bascot and Roget with a look of apology on his face. "I am sorry if we seem inhospitable. A private matter we were discussing has caused some dissension between us but"—here he gave a stern glance at his siblings—"it will be put aside for now."

Returning his attention to his visitors, Gilbert said, "We have heard about the murder of two prostitutes in Lincoln. But I do not understand why you have come to ask us questions about these crimes. I can assure you that neither Hervé nor I are in the habit of frequenting brothels, so we could not have seen or heard anything that would be pertinent."

Although it had been Roget who had related the purpose of their coming to Ingham, it was to Bascot that Gilbert, who held the status of knight, made his response, addressing him as a man of equal rank.

"The reason we have come is that the motivation for both of these murders seems to be dual in nature. The manner in which they were carried out suggests not only a hatred for harlots but also for the Templar Order," Bascot replied. "We are therefore looking for some trace of a connection between the two. It could be, for instance, that a Templar brother was in the habit of consorting with prostitutes before he joined our ranks and, because of that indulgence, has incurred a grievous enmity in a person who is seeking revenge. We have been told that your brother, Jacques, often sought out the company of such women. . . ."

A bark of drunken laughter came from Hervé. "Often! That is an understatement. The only time Jacques wasn't rutting was when he was sleeping. And even then, more often than not, he kept a bawd in bed beside him to be handy for when he woke up."

Everyone was, momentarily, shocked into silence by Hervé's outburst. Julia broke it by striding across the room and slapping her brother firmly across the face. "You pig! Have you no compassion for our brother? I wish it was you who suffered—"

Gilbert cut his sister's outburst short. "I said that is enough, Julia. Be quiet!"

As his sister, her face flaming with anger, clamped her full lips shut and walked defiantly back to stand beside Savaric, Gilbert once again apologised for his family's rude display of emotion. "We were recently told that Jacques is dead and are all sorely grieved. I fear that sorrow has overtaken my sister's sensibility."

Gilbert's pronouncement surprised Bascot and he asked how they had learned of their brother's demise. It was usual for the Order to send a message to the preceptory nearest to the family of any brother who had met his end while serving in their ranks, in order that the dead Templar's relatives could be informed. None such had come to the Lincoln enclave.

"Savaric came with the news two weeks ago," Gilbert replied, waving a hand in the direction of his baseborn half brother. "When Jacques joined the Order, Savaric went with him as his squire. After my brother was taken from his earthly life, Savaric returned here as quickly as he could and told us what had happened. I am sure a report of his death will soon reach your preceptor."

Bascot focussed his attention on the man by the casement. Savaric's grave expression had not altered throughout the exchange between the Templar and Gilbert, nor had he moved when Julia had leapt forward and slapped Hervé's face. If Savaric had returned to Lincoln after Jacques' death, it meant he had reneged on his oath to serve in the Templar ranks. It was not a common occurrence for a squire to leave the Order when the lord he followed died, but it was not unknown. Such a sad event usually strengthened a man's devotion, but there were a few occasions when it eradicated it. Now the darkness of the skin on the upper half of his face was explained. When he had shaved off the beard that was required to be worn by every Templar brother, the newly exposed flesh was much paler than the rest from lack of exposure to the harsh glare of the sun in Outremer.

"How did Jacques die?" Bascot asked the squire. The Templar recalled that the records in the preceptory had stated that Jacques Roulan had been stationed at Qaqun, near Acre. There were often confrontations with the Saracens in the area and, if the knight had died in battle, the report of Jacques' death would have been sent quite quickly, for a notation of it would have been included in the details that were sent of any clash with Saracen forces to Templar headquarters in London or Paris. But if Jacques had been stricken with one of the many illnesses that afflicted men in the harsh climes of the Holy Land, it was quite possible the news had been delayed, waiting for inclusion in the next regular report that was sent every few months to London from commanderies in Outremer.

"Sir Jacques' horse bit him in the shoulder and the wound suppurated," Savaric replied in a harsh monotone. "He withstood the infection for a time, but a fever took him in the end."

The Templar nodded. Destriers could be fractious and often struck out with teeth or hooves and even if the wound was small, it could easily become putrid. The Templar offered Gilbert condolences for the family's loss and then returned to the reason he and Roget had come.

"Even though your brother is dead, it does not change the possibility that the indulgence of his carnal appetites may have spawned a reason for the murders. We are considering the likelihood that it may be a woman who is responsible and that the passage of time has deepened her hatred. Are you aware of any paramour that Jacques had, highborn or otherwise, that may have been left distraught, or in humiliating circumstances, by his desertion?

Hervé, far from being discountenanced by his sister's attack, now lurched to his feet. "If you mean, Sir Bascot, did my brother leave a pregnant female behind him when he went overseas, the answer can only be one of uncertainty. Jacques roamed far and wide to take his pleasure. He could have scattered bastards from Nottingham to York for all we know."

Now it was Gilbert who became angry with his brother and, rising, he went over and pushed the drunken man back in his chair. "If you cannot speak of Jacques with respect, then speak not at all, Hervé. If you open your mouth again, you will feel the weight of my fist."

Gilbert returned to his chair and once again expressed his regret for one of his sibling's unseemly behaviour. "All of our family are under great pressure at the moment," he said tightly. "It is not so long since my father died and then Savaric brought the news about Jacques . . . Hervé seeks solace in a wine cup, while our mother lies upstairs on her bed and refuses to rise. It is a difficult time."

He motioned for his wife to refill his wine cup before he continued. "To answer your question in a sensible fashion, Sir Bascot, I do not know of any woman that Jacques may have treated in the fashion you suggest. There had been no marriage arranged for him, nor had he professed any interest in a woman of suitable rank. As for any . . . other females he consorted with, of them I have no knowledge. To put it less crudely than Hervé, not only was Jacques of a licentious nature, he was also fickle with it."

"Did he visit any brothels in Lincoln?" Bascot asked. Even though Jacques Roulan had left Lincoln well over a year ago there might have been a prostitute who, like dead Elfie, had borne a child and believed him to be the father. The Templar remembered the bitterness with which Terese had spoken of the ways of men. A woman struggling to raise an infant may well have felt hatred for the man who impregnated her and focussed her rage on the Order he had joined. If so, other women in her profession would be an easy target, for none would expect violence from one of their own.

"He may have done, and most probably did," Gilbert replied. "He visited stewes in most of the towns throughout Lincolnshire."

The eldest Roulan brother raised his tired eyes to Bascot. "Jacques' immoral behaviour caused my father much distress. While it is understandable for a man to visit a brothel on occasion, there was no excuse for my brother to neglect his duties on our demesne so he could spend his days in a constant bout of drinking and whoring. He was never here, and not often at the Marton property that would one day be his and which Father had given into his charge. Finally, my sire issued an ultimatum and told Jacques that if he did not mend his ways, he would disown him. At first, my brother paid no mind and continued with his profligacy, but when Father ordered all of Jacques' belongings packed into a coffer and told him to leave, my brother finally realised our sire's threat had not been an idle one.

"It was then that my father entreated Jacques to take holy orders and join a monastery. He reminded my brother that his sins were many—not only did he need to atone for his inordinate lust but also for his dilatoriness towards his responsibilities. Such monumental disregard was an offence to God and only a life of abstinence would give proof of his repentance."

Gilbert took another swallow of his wine and said that it had been Jacques' own idea to join the Templar Order. "He felt that the monotony of life as an ordinary monk would not suit one of his restless disposition and that the military aspect of the Templars would be more to his taste. Within a short time, Jacques was as ardent to become a celibate soldier in the service of Christ as he had once been in the pursuit of female company. My brother, Sir Bascot, was a man of deep passions but, unfortunately, they were often quixotic."

Bascot considered the implications of what he had been told and the attitudes of the various members of the dead knight's family. It seemed that Jacques had not been the only Roulan possessed of strong emotions. Both Hervé and Julia displayed a tendency to let impulse rule their actions. Not so with Gilbert and Savaric, although the Templar suspected their inner feelings were just as unruly, but held in check by necessity. Gilbert because, now he was head of this turbulent family, he needed to try and control them as his unfortunate father had attempted to do and Savaric, due to his baseborn status, had probably learned to present a bland face to his legitimate relatives at a very young age. Any one of them could be responsible for the murder of the prostitutes, with the possible exception of Hervé, who did not seem to have felt much love for his dead brother. Could it be that one of the people in this room had become so enraged by the news of Jacques' death that they were seeking an outlet for their grief by murdering the women they perceived as having led him astray?

The Templar glanced at Roget, who looked back with a quizzical raise of his heavy black brows. Bascot gave a nod and the captain spoke to Gilbert, asking him, and the others, for an account of their whereabouts during the times the two prostitutes were killed and also on the evening of the previous day.

At the inclusion of the last, Gilbert's head snapped up.

"Why yesterday night? Has another prostitute been killed so recently?"

"A former harlot was attacked but fortunately she did not die," Bascot replied.

At his response there was an audible hiss of indrawn breath from Julia, and Gilbert's wife, Margaret, stifled a sob. Gilbert shook his head wearily and answered Roget's question.

"We have all been here at Ingham during every one of those times," he declared. "On the first occasion, Savaric had barely returned with his sad news and it took all of us, and our energies, to cope with my mother, who was in a hysterical state. Since then, except for duties about the estate, we have all been here at Ingham. Our servants can verify this, not only my steward but also the men who care for our sheep. They will attest to the truth of my words."

Bascot knew that questioning the servants would most likely prove futile. Any servant would lie to protect a master on whom his livelihood depended. He did not, however, voice this opinion, and merely said that steps would be taken to do so. He and Roget rose from their seats and, with a sigh of weary resignation, Gilbert Roulan accompanied them to the door.

Twenty-three

✠

"MA FOI, WHAT A TRIBE!" ROGET EXCLAIMED AS THEY RODE down the track leading to Ermine Street. "My mother was a harridan and my father a toper, but compared to that lot, they seem like angels." He gave Bascot a sidelong glance. "Do you think one of them is the person we are seeking?"

"I would rule out Gilbert and his wife as suspect," Bascot replied. "The eldest brother is a dutiful man and might murder to protect one of kin, but I do not believe he would jeopardise the safety of his wife, and his holdings, to take revenge for a fate that Jacques brought on himself. And Hervé, too, I think, is not culpable. Unless his professed dislike of his dead brother is a pretence—which I think a drunken man would find hard to simulate so convincingly—I do not believe he is responsible. That is not to say," Bascot added, "that they are not protecting another member of their family who is guilty."

"If the murderer is a woman, I do not think it can be Gilbert's wife," Roget said. "And if the person who attacked Terese is the same one who killed the harlots, Margaret is too short to fit the description Terese gave us."

"And of too frail and timid a nature, I suspect," Bascot replied in agreement. "That leaves Julia—who is tall enough and, from the way she struck her brother, of sufficient strength—and the baseborn half brother, Savaric."

"I will ask about the town to see if anyone noticed either of them during the times the two prostitutes, and Terese, were attacked," Roget replied, and then grimaced. "That means my knuckles will once again become bruised from knocking on doors." Almost as the words left his mouth, his aspect brightened. "I will go first to question the perfumer, Constance, and her maid. That task, at least, will be a pleasure."

Bascot smiled at his friend's bewitchment with Mistress Turner. It was not often Roget took an interest in a respectable woman. He wondered if the captain, after so many years of protesting he would never take a wife, had finally succumbed to the charms of a female.

"It might also be advisable to ask Lady Nicolaa if her bailiff, or some other person on her household staff at Brattleby, can speak to the servants on the Roulan property. Servants will be less reluctant to tell another menial the truth about Gilbert's claim that none of his family left his demesne during the times in question. They might not be so forthright with either of us."

"A good thought, *mon ami*," Roget replied. "I will suggest it to Sir Gerard as soon as we return to the keep."

THE NEXT TWO DAYS PASSED UNEVENTFULLY. IN THE PRECEPtory Bascot, having given a report of all that had passed with the Grimson party and the Roulan family to d'Arderon, joined the other men in the enclave in the regular regime of attending religious services throughout the day and taking part in daily exercise in the training ground. The tempers of all of the men were growing short. The men of the contingent were eager to be gone and found the delay frustrating, while the regular soldiers based in the Lincoln enclave grew testy from sharing the overcrowded quarters. Even the servant with the crooked back, normally cheerful, wore a scowl on his face as he cleaned the midden and strewed flea-deterring herbs on sleeping pallets.

As Bascot went about his duties, he went over and over in his mind the small amount of information that was known about the murderer. The only hints to his, or her, identity were the limited description that Terese had given and the gold cloak clasp Agnes had seen. He tried to fit them in with the suspects they had—Joan and Sven Grimson, the two seamen they employed, and Savaric and Julia Roulan. There were also the two Templar men-at-arms, Thomas and Alan. Although the description might fit all of them, it was unlikely that either Askil or Dunny would possess such a valuable item as the clasp, or Savaric who, as a baseborn relative, would not have access to the wealth of the Roulan family. With respect to the two Templars, even if they had not given up all of the valuables they possessed at the time they joined the Order, both came from impoverished backgrounds and were unlikely to have ever owned such an expensive piece of jewellery.

Bascot felt as though he were trying to reconstruct a shattered pottery jar from only half the pieces. There was something that dragged at the edge of his consciousness—a half-remembered phrase or a detail that had seemed of little importance at the time—but now would not come to the surface. Doggedly he threw himself into training the two unseasoned knights that had come from York. Once before a bout of strenuous exercise had loosened the knots that hampered his thoughts, he hoped it would happen again.

IN THE CASTLE, NICOLAA DE LA HAYE SENT INSTRUCTIONS TO her bailiff at Brattleby to try and find out if all of the Roulan family had, as they said, remained at Ingham over the last two weeks. Such information could not be obtained quickly. It would take time for the bailiff to approach those who lived at the Roulan manor house in such a way as to engage in casual conversation. While she waited, the castellan chafed at the delay.

Roget embarked on his rounds of knocking on doors in the town enquiring about the Roulan family. As he had told Bascot was his intention, he began with the home of the perfumer, Constance Turner. He was given a warm welcome and invited in to partake of a cup of wine and pleased to find that, this time, it was one of good Spanish red which Constance had bought for him especially. As the captain sat in a little parlour enjoying both the wine and Constance's lovely smile, he was surprised to hear that the perfumer's little maid, Agnes, had been perversely relieved when she heard of the attack on Terese.

"Agnes now reasons that the murderer is not aware that she saw him," Constance told Roget with a mischievous glint in her eye, "for, she said, if he had, he would have come after her and not attacked another woman. I do not follow her logic, but am thankful that she thinks thus, for she is now willing to go about her duties as formerly and I can at last give my full attention to my work."

Roget spent a pleasant hour in Constance's parlour before

he reluctantly left to resume his task of trying to discover whether any of the Roulan family had been seen in Lincoln. Before he left, however, he obtained a promise from the perfumer that he could come back and spend an evening in her company.

"I will cook you a meal," Constance said with an inviting smile, "and may even get another bottle of Spanish wine to accompany it."

"It will be my pleasure, *ma belle,* to provide the wine," the captain replied.

When Roget left, both he and Constance were well satisfied with the arrangement.

Twenty-four

✦┿✦

"GRIMSON IS A LYING COWSON!" CAMVILLE GROWLED TO BAS-
cot the following morning. "He anchored his vessel on the
southern side of the estuary, just as Thorson said he might
have done."

The sheriff gestured at the message he had received the
day before from the town official in Hull, which now lay un-
furled on a table in Camville's private chamber. The sheriff
was pacing the room in exasperation as he spoke. Nicolaa
de la Haye was also present and it was she who related the
details of the message.

"Although the men on Sven's list all confirmed he had
been in contact with them on the days he stated, the Hull
bailiff couldn't find anyone who saw Grimson's vessel in the
port," she said. "Since my husband had asked that a check
be made on that detail, the bailiff sent one of his constables
across to Barton to question the man that operates the ferry
across the Humber. The ferryman remembered seeing Sven's
boat at anchor in the harbour and also stated that he took
both Sven and his wife across to Hull, but he swears the two
sailors weren't with them. As Bailiff Thorson said, it would

have been an easy matter, during the time Grimson's boat was at Barton, for the seamen to have sailed a skiff down the Ancholme to Bishopbridge, and then walked to Lincoln and killed both of the prostitutes before returning the way they had come."

"And despite Thorson keeping watch over the Grimson party while they are here in Lincoln," Camville added, "it could be that one of them is responsible for the attack on the harlots' childminder. I should have thrown them all in the castle gaol when they first came."

Bascot considered the conclusion Camville had reached. The Templar had always felt that the Grimson faction was not telling the complete truth but, as he had said to Roget, he did not think they were lying in a direct fashion, only omitting certain facts for their own purposes. He mentally reviewed the tale that Dunny had told them and Joan Grimson's later claim that the knight who had killed her brother was from Lincolnshire. The remarks Thorson had made about Scallion's unsavoury reputation came to his mind and then Roget's mention of Bishopbridge as he and Bascot had ridden up Ermine Street and approached the turnoff to the Roulan manor house. Suddenly, the Grimsons' purpose became clear.

"I do not believe the seamen killed the prostitutes, lord," he said to Camville, "although I think, as Thorson suggested, that they did make the journey down the Ancholme. But it was not Lincoln that was their destination."

Camville spun around in surprise and Nicolaa raised her eyebrows in query. "Where else could they have been going?" she asked.

"Ingham," Bascot replied.

* * *

An hour later Sven and Joan Grimson and the two seamen stood once again in the hall of the castle, facing Gerard
Camville, Lady Nicolaa and Bascot, who were all seated on
the dais. As before, Roget stood to one side in the company
of Peter Thorson.

Camville let silence reign for a few moments and then he
rose from his seat and came down onto the floor of the hall,
coming to a stop a few paces in front of Sven, his hand on
the hilt of the sword at his belt. "You have been lying to me,
Grimson, and I have no patience with prevarication, or the
men who practise it."

Sven Grimson blanched. Although taller by a good hand's
span than the sheriff, Camville's massive bulk, and his authority, seemed to tower over the boat owner.

"Lord, I have not told you an untruth, I swear," he stuttered. "I went to Hull, just as I said, to enquire if anyone
knew the name of a knight Joan's brother had fraternised
with in the town. We thought it might be that he was the
one who killed Robert. . . ."

"And you sent the two seamen who work for you to seek
him also, did you not?" Camville demanded.

Grimson shook his head in confusion. "They went with
me to Hull. . . ." he began to protest.

"To Barton, you mean," the sheriff barked.

"We anchored at Barton, it is true," Sven said nervously,
"but we went to Hull, as we said, to try and find out the
identity of . . ."

"Enough," Camville roared. "You already knew the name
of the knight that killed your brother-by-marriage. It is
Jacques Roulan. And you sent the two seamen to Ingham to
see if he had returned home. If you do not admit the truth, I

will charge you all with bearing false witness to an officer of the king." The sheriff's rage was palpable.

Joan Grimson laid a hand on her husband's arm. "What you say is true, Sir Gerard. We did know that it was Jacques Roulan who killed Robert, and that was the main reason Sven and I went to Hull. But we found no one who had seen him recently and neither did Askil and Dunny when they went to Ingham."

Camville turned his venom on the wife. "That, mistress, is because he is dead!"

Now it was Joan's turn to step back in shock. "But he cannot be," she said haltingly, her composure finally slipping. "Dunny saw him run away, after he had killed Robert. He was not injured in the fight between them. . . ."

"A man can die many ways, mistress," Camville replied, "and it was months ago that Roulan took your brother's life. Much can happen in such a space of time."

Nicolaa's cool voice interjected from where she sat on the dais. "I suggest, Master Grimson, that you and your wife now tell us exactly what you know of the night your brother died in Acre, and of your actions since you learned of it."

And so the whole story came out. As Bascot had suspected, Dunny had, all along, been aware of the identity of the knight who had killed Robert Scallion. He had heard his employer call Jacques by name and had relayed the information to Askil who, having been a lifelong friend and companion of the boat owner, knew the Roulan brother from the days before the knight had joined the Templars and had, on one or two occasions, been present when Scallion and Jacques had shared a debauched drinking spree in the alehouses and brothels of Hull. When Askil had brought

her brother's vessel home, Joan had reasoned that if Roulan
had been expelled from the Templar Order for murdering
a Christian, it was probable he would have returned home
to Ingham. She had insisted they make an attempt to find
him.

Still Joan persisted in her claim that neither she nor her
husband had any intention of harming Roulan if they found
him, claiming that their purpose had merely been to denounce him to the sheriff and hope that some repercussions
would fall on the family, if not on Jacques himself. Since it
would be easy for Askil and Dunny to pose as itinerant seamen looking for work, it had been Joan's idea to send them
to the village near the manor house and see if they could
discover if Jacques had returned, while she and Sven went to
Hull and looked for the knight in the alehouses and brothels
where he and her brother had been so fond of carousing.
The two sailors went to the hamlet and took lodgings in
the local alehouse, telling the ale keeper they were on their
way to Torksey and hoped to find work on the barges that
carry goods up and down the River Trent. That night, they
sat in the alehouse and got into conversation with some of
the villagers over a few rounds of ale, encouraging them to
talk about the local nobility. Eventually the name of Roulan
was mentioned, and that one of the family had joined the
Templar Order. Many tales were told of his rakehell ways
before he became a monk, but no mention was made that he
had come back to England or of his having been seen in the
neighbourhood. Not aware that Savaric had only recently
returned with the report of Jacques' demise and that this
news had not yet reached the villagers, Askil and Dunny decided their journey had been in vain and returned to Bishopbridge. They then went back to Barton as they had come, via

the Ancholme, and rejoined Joan and Sven. After discussing the matter and deciding that Jacques must still be in the Holy Land, they had all sailed back to Grimsby.

"And, so, mistress, for this capricious whim to avenge your brother, you have wasted my time and that of Bailiff Thorson," Camville said.

For once Joan was contrite. "I apologise for that, lord," she said. "I admit my grief overwhelmed my good sense."

"So it did, mistress, so it did," Camville replied, returning to his seat on the dais and picking up his wine cup. "And you shall pay for that error. Before you return home, you and your husband will sign a pledge to submit a fine of twenty pounds for the inconvenience you have caused me, and you will also give Bailiff Thorson a sum of five pounds for the cost of his time and trouble in escorting you to Lincoln."

Sven Grimson gasped at the amount. "But, lord, that is more silver than I can earn in many weeks with my fishing boats. . . ."

Camville leaned forward and glowered. "Would you rather spend six months in Lincoln's town gaol?"

The boat owner shook his head and, accompanied by his wife and the two sailors, Roget and Thorson escorted them out of the hall.

Camville grunted in disgust as they left and took another swallow of wine. Nicolaa commended Bascot on his insight in realising that Scallion and Roulan's similar penchant for whoring and drinking could have easily thrown them into each other's company in Hull, and then connecting that with the fact that Bishopbridge was close to the Roulan manor house at Ingham and could quite conceivably have been the sailors' destination instead of Lincoln. With hindsight, it was an obvious link, but one that had not been so beforehand. The Templar shook his head in denial of the compliment.

"Exposure of the Grimsons' lies has brought us no closer to discovering the identity of the murderer. And unless we can garner some new information, or uncover a pertinent detail that has been missed, I fear we shall get no further."

The Templar's heart sank as he thought of telling Preceptor d'Arderon that the Grimson party was now cleared of suspicion. The elimination of their culpability took the investigation back to where it had been at the beginning and the need to once again face the unpleasant prospect that it might be a Templar brother who was guilty of the crimes.

As Bascot drained his wine cup and prepared to return to the enclave, the Haye bailiff from Brattleby came into the hall, requesting an audience with Nicolaa. Although not apparent at the time, the bailiff's report would eventually provide the means of unearthing the evidence the Templar was so desperate to find.

Twenty-five

✦✛✦

Bascot returned to the preceptory in a dispirited mood. The Haye bailiff had confirmed what Gilbert Roulan had told them; that, to the Ingham servants' knowledge, none of the family had gone to Lincoln during the days in question, nor left the property at all except to travel to their holding at Marton on a few occasions. As Lady Nicolaa had told him to be thorough, the bailiff had then gone to Marton to ensure the proclaimed reason for their absences had been a true one.

The property at Marton was about eight miles southeast of Ingham and close to the Trent River. It was small, its income mainly derived from a herd of pigs that was raised there and fed mainly on mast that fell from a large stand of oaks growing on the perimeter of the property. Under the guise of making a routine inspection for Lady Nicolaa, the bailiff had spoken to the swineherd who lived there and looked after the pigs.

"In answer to my question about whether any of the Roulans had lately visited the property," the bailiff reported, "the swineherd confirmed what the servants at Ingham had said, that some of them had been there recently. He said that none of them had used to come very much in the past, but lately Savaric had been there at least three times that he knew of, although Sir Gilbert and Sir Hervé had only come once, accompanied by Lady Julia. It appears the reason they went is that they are intending to make Savaric the steward of the place and there is need to sanction repairs he has suggested be made to the small dilapidated manor house on the property. At any rate, lady, they did go to Marton just as the servants at Ingham told me and aside from the times they went there, have gone nowhere else."

After Nicolaa thanked her bailiff and dismissed him, she, Camville and Bascot had discussed what, if any, direction the investigation into the harlots' murder should take.

"Roget has made enquiries in the town to see if anyone has lately seen Julia Roulan or Savaric about the streets of Lincoln," Camville declared. "A couple of merchants—a cutler who supplies the Roulan household with spoons and other household utensils, and a draper from whom they buy cloth for bed linen—recall Julia, in the company of Gilbert's wife, Margaret, making purchases last autumn, but none since then. It is the same with Savaric. Before he left to join the Templars with Jacques, he would, on occasion, carry out errands for Gilbert's father in Lincoln, but no one remembers seeing him since he returned from Outremer."

The sheriff shifted his restless frame in his chair as he went on. "As far as I can see, if neither the Grimsons nor the Roulans are involved in these crimes, there is nowhere to look for this murderer except in the Templar preceptory."

He had looked directly at Bascot as he spoke and the Templar felt compelled to give a response. "Preceptor d'Arderon has investigated all of the men that are in the enclave, lord, and, as far as we can determine, none are guilty, either of giving cause for the murderer's enmity, or of committing the crimes."

Camville nodded his acceptance of the statement and added, "Then, de Marins, much as it grieves me to say so, I fear we must accept that we may not find this miscreant."

When he returned to the preceptory, Bascot told d'Arderon what had passed and then resumed his regular duties, but his mind was not on his tasks as he went to check on his destrier and, afterwards, join the men at practise on the training ground. By the time Compline had passed, he was more than ready to retire but found, when he lay down on his pallet, that sleep took a long time in coming. When it finally did, it was filled with fragmented dreams of his childhood, and of the years he had spent with the monks in the monastery to which he had been given as an oblate—a gift to God—before his sire removed him to fill the place of an older brother of Bascot's who had died.

He tossed and turned on his pallet, trying not to disturb the men who were sleeping alongside him on two long rows of pallets in the dormitory. Even though he was accustomed to the rush lights that were kept burning all night long in the chamber, their glimmer disturbed his peace and he flung his arm over his sighted eye to block the light. Eventually he fell into a doze but his rest was soon invaded by a vivid dream involving the elderly monk who had taught reading and writing to the novices in the monastery. He could see the monk's face clearly. Above his former tutor's head was a halo and around him, whirling so fast they were almost a blur, were spinning discs of light. The sensation made Bascot feel as though he were falling even though he was lying flat on his back and he woke with a start. As he opened his eye, the dream receded but, as it did so, the sound of the monk's voice instructing him in a lesson echoed in his mind—"and you will conjugate the verb in Latin and French."

He knew that the tutor's words had not been spoken in his dream, but came from some deep well in his memory of the actual days he and the other novices had been sitting at their lessons. But the words had been extremely clear, just as though the monk was sitting at his bedside. The intense reality of the experience left him fully awake and he knew that it would be useless to again seek rest, so he quietly pulled on his boots and, leaving the dormitory, went outside into the open air.

There had only been a few brief showers over the preceding days and the hard-packed earth of the training ground was dry and dusty. Above him stars wheeled in the sky, pinpricks of light that formed a bright background for a half-full moon. As he walked from the dormitory out into the open space in front of him, the guard on the gate did not hear his steps and he realised how easy it would have been for Elfreda and her killer to have stolen through the shadows around the perimeter of the walls and gone into the chapel. The duty of the sentry was to keep out intruders, and his attention would be focussed outward, beyond the walls, not towards the inhabitants of the preceptory.

He judged it was now just about an hour before dawn and the service of Matins. Feeling a need to find a quiet place to think, he walked across the training ground to the smithy. The door of the small building housing the forge was usually left open unless it was raining, and was now pinned back by a wooden wedge. Bascot went inside and sat down on a large block of wood. Beside him was a wheel that needed the iron rim repaired and he rested one elbow on its edge and let his gaze roam around the interior.

The forge was built on a stone standing, its fire banked down low so as to be ready for morning with bellows ready to hand. The smith's tools were neatly arrayed with the smaller ones—tongs, hammers, rasps and files—hanging from large nails on the walls, while anvils ranging in size from small to large stood on the floor, the largest one next to a barrel of water that the smith used for cooling the red hot metal. Atop the anvil lay a pair of heavy gloves and the leather apron the smith wore while he was at work. From the fire in the forge came a comfortable warmth which removed the chill from the night air, and the tangy smell of metal filled his nostrils in a comforting fashion.

As Bascot sat on the block, he thought back over the dream that had been the cause of his wakefulness. Aware that it was common for a dreaming mind to throw up bizarre images of objects and happenings experienced while awake, he made an attempt to clarify the ones that had appeared in his dream in case they should have some relation to the mystery he was trying to solve. The whirling orbs reminded him of something, but of what he could not discern. And why had his old tutor had a halo above his head? A kindly man he had been, most certainly, but not a candidate for sainthood. And, if the instruction that had come into his mind as he had awoken did, in fact, bear some relation to recent events, what verb was he meant to conjugate? Although the dream had been a powerful one, nighttime illusions were often capricious. It could simply be that the image of his tutor had been caused by recent thoughts of Gianni and the lessons the boy was learning. He wished Gianni were with him now,

the lad's recent studies might give him some insight into
the echo of scholastic instruction he remembered from his
childhood.

The Templar returned his mind to yet another review of
the scant evidence they had managed to obtain, and recalled
Agnes's description of the cloak clasp worn by the man she
had seen knocking on Adele Delorme's door. On it had been
a picture of St. Christopher. Was this the saint to which his
dream referred? But, if so, how was the saint linked to the
circles of light whirling around the figure of the monk?

Suddenly, Bascot held his breath and retuned his gaze to
the wheel, recalling how he had been attracted by the motion of the rolling wheels on the dray that he and Roget had
passed on their journey to Ingham. The turning discs in his
dream had been very like wheels, spinning in the brightness
of the sun as the driver urged the horses to a faster pace on
the stretch of road. The Latin word for wheel was *rota*; the
French, *rouet.* But these were nouns, the directive had been
to conjugate a verb. Mentally he ran through verbs describing
the spinning motion of a wheel. In Latin—*versare, volvo . . . ,*
in French *tourner, rouler . . .* He stopped. If he conjugated
rouler—to roll—he came to *ils roulent*—they roll, which was
almost identical phonetically to the name of the family to
which Julia and Savaric belonged—Roulan.

He held his breath as he let the essence of the dream carry
him to further suppositions. Many people's names indicated
their appearance, but often it was a habit or possession, or
their family's role in society. His own name—de Marins—
denoted, in French, a maritime connection because his family had always held a castle protecting the seashore. Robert
Scallion's name was derived from the onions in which his sire
and grandsire, and Robert himself, had traded. Was it the

same for the Roulans? Had the wanderlust that seemed an integral part of Jacques' character been inherited from forbears whose inclination to rove had earned them their name? It could be so—rolling wheels meant travelling and that was certainly what Jacques had done. Hervé had said his brother had "roamed far and wide to take his pleasure." And the patron saint of travellers was St. Christopher, the very image Agnes had seen. It would be an obvious saint for a family with such a cognomen to adopt. Were these the connections that the dream had been attempting to convey?

If he accepted the validity of the thought, he must reconsider Julia and Savaric as suspects even though they had not been seen in Lincoln during the pertinent times. Sitting completely still and silent in the dark, that is what he did. Was it possible that one, or both of these two people, had embarked on a horrific plan of extracting revenge for the death of Jacques in the Holy Land? Mentally, he shook his head in negation. The idea was implausible. Jacques had not been killed by either a harlot or a Templar brother. He had not even died in battle, but simply from a wound inflicted by his horse, an injury that could happen to a man in any walk of life, and had no connection with either prostitutes or the Templar Order. Why would either of them, if they felt the need to expunge their grief, commit these murders as a means of doing it? But he could not dismiss the idea, it was the only lead he had. Doggedly he carried on, thinking carefully back over Dunny's description of the dead knight.

He recalled the sailor describing Jacques' apparel and the conversation with Robert Scallion that had evolved into an argument with such deadly consequences for the boat owner. He then reviewed the visit he and Roget had made to the Roulan manor house and what had been said by the members of Jacques' family. One of the most memorable instances was how Julia had reacted when the drunken Hervé had slighted his brother's character. What had she said? "Have you no compassion for our brother? I wish it was you who suffered——" Gilbert had cut his sister off at that point, interrupting her flow of speech. In retrospect, Bascot thought she seemed to speak of Jacques as though he was still alive, but both Savaric and Gilbert had said he was dead. Had they been telling the truth? Had Jacques, as Joan Grimson believed, escaped retribution for the crime of killing Robert Scallion and returned to England? Was he even now hidden somewhere at Ingham, or in the deserted building the Haye bailiff had spoken of at Marton, shielded from the outside world by the rest of his family? If so, it was a plan doomed to failure. He could not stay hidden indefinitely. Sooner or later he would be seen, if only by a servant, and the news would spread. When that happened, and because of Joan Grimson's accusation, he would eventually either be brought to answer for his crime or, at the very least, shunned by everyone who knew him.

But the Roulan grief had appeared too intense for it to be false. There had been real sorrow mixed with the anger in Julia's voice as she had castigated Hervé. It could not be doubted that, as his family asserted, Jacques was dead.

Bascot leaned back against the wall behind the wooden block on which he sat, trying to find a comfortable position that might help compose his leaping thoughts. As he did so, his hand fell on the blacksmith's gloves and apron that lay on top of the anvil beside him. Almost simultaneously, he dislodged some wooden planks that had been laid to rest vertically between two nails hammered into the wall. They fell with a loud cracking noise onto the stone of the floor, reminding Bascot of a sound he had heard recently. The small incident caused his thoughts to coalesce and, with a simplicity that now seemed devastatingly obvious, the last piece of the puzzle surrounding the murders fell into place.

He stood up quickly, ignoring the sentry who had been alerted by the noise of the falling wood and was coming across the training ground to investigate. With haste, the Templar retraced his steps to the dormitory, intent on rousing d'Arderon.

Twenty-six
✛

BARELY AN HOUR LATER, BASCOT AND EMILIUS WERE CROSS-ing the Fossdyke and riding to Torksey, beyond which lay the Roulan property at Marton. After Preceptor d'Arderon had listened to Bascot's conclusion of who had murdered the harlots, and why, he had readily given permission for the Templar to prove his theory. D'Arderon had, however, sent for the draper, insisting Bascot take Emilius with him.

"If what you propose is true, the responsibility lies with us, as Templars, to arrest this man, and you will need another brother with you to bear witness," d'Arderon had said.

Emilius was more than willing to go. "It is, as you say, Preceptor, our duty, for even though this man is no longer a brother, it must be publically shown that the Order would never have conspired to shield him from punishment for his evil actions."

Bascot had then stressed the need for haste. "We must leave straightaway, Preceptor," he said. "It may be that because Roget and I went to Ingham yesterday, the family has been alerted. If so, they may take steps to ensure he is gone from Lincoln. The quicker we get to Marton, the better. It may already be too late, but if we get there before anyone is astir, we may just be in time."

D'Arderon nodded. "Go now. I will send a message to Camville immediately. It should not be too long before he sends some of his men-at-arms to follow you."

Not a quarter of an hour later, Bascot and Emilius were astride mounts and riding through the gates of the enclave. They had taken only a scant few moments to arm themselves and don conical helms. To have taken the time to garb themselves in hauberks and hoods of mail would have used up precious minutes that Bascot was not sure they could afford. The preceptor's final words rang in their ears as they put spurs to their mounts. "May God strengthen your purpose," he said. Both Templar brothers fervently hoped his prayer would be heard.

Dawn had already broken and the sun had started on its skyward path by the time they reached Torksey. Marton lay only a couple of miles to the northeast and, as they approached the Roulan property, they dismounted in a stand of oak and beech trees a small distance from the rundown building that Nicolaa's bailiff had mentioned. The smell and sound of pigs reached them as they secured the reins of their mounts to a tree and walked quietly through the small wood to where the animals were penned.

The swineherd was in the process of feeding his charges when he heard the approach of the two knights. Dropping the leather swill bucket he held, he backed up a few paces in alarm and Bascot quickly put his finger to his lips to ensure quietness and then beckoned the swineherd to come forward. The pig man, a stoop-shouldered individual of about fifty years of age, and wearing clothes that were smeared with pig muck, crept hesitantly to where Bascot and Emilius stood.

"Is there anyone in the main building?" Bascot asked in low tones.

The swineherd nodded. "Master Savaric came yesterday. He must still be in there, sleepin'."

"No one else?" Bascot pressed.

The pig man nervously shrugged his shoulders. "Not so's I seen, but I goes to bed early, 'cause I've got to be up at dawn to feed the swine. Someone could 'ave come after that, I suppose, but if they did, I never heard 'em."

"Is there a back entrance to the building?"

"Aye, lord, it goes to the privy, but 'tis usually barred. Until Master Savaric needs to use it, it'll most like stay that way."

"Do you ever have occasion to go inside the house?"

An expression of shock crossed the swineherd's dirty face and he grimaced, revealing a mouth that held only one or two snaggled teeth. "Me, lord? I'se been told not to go near there and whatever I'se told to do, I do. Be more than my job is worth to do aught else."

Bascot nodded and told the swineherd to put some distance between himself and the main building. The pig man needed no other direction. Without a sound he sped off into the woods and did not look back.

Bascot and Emilius scrutinised the building that stood a few score yards from the sty. It was, as the bailiff had said, in need of repair. The walls were sturdy enough, made of stout timber, but the tiles on the roof were old and some missing in places. There were two casement windows at the front, one on either side of the door, and both had shutters firmly secured in place. A small wing was attached to the western side of the building, probably once intended as sleeping quarters for guests. It appeared to have been, in years past, a substantial, if modest, property and the size and plumpness of the pigs in the sty suggested that they still provided a lucrative source of income.

"I will circle around the back, Emilius, and make sure the door is closed," Bascot said quietly to his companion. "Watch for any signs of movement until I return."

Emilius gave a quick nod of his head and crouched down beside the sty, wrinkling his nose at the malodorous smell as he did so. The pigs grunted curiously at his approach but were too interested in feeding on the mash the swineherd had brought to give him more than cursory attention.

Bascot stole along the edge of the sty and moved quickly around some small outbuildings that stood near the edge of the trees. One of them, he guessed, was the hut where the swineherd lived, for the clumsily nailed planks that formed a shield for the door stood ajar and he could see a cracked wooden plate and mug set on a roughly hewn table inside. Moving along the back of a small woodshed next door to the hut, Bascot had a good view of the rear of the main building. As the swineherd had said, there was only one door, a small one leading to a privy a few feet away. As far as he could see, the door appeared to be firmly closed. From the shelter of an open-sided stable on the other side of the main building, the whicker of a horse sounded softly.

He went back to where Emilius waited. "It does not appear that anyone is astir inside. The front entrance is probably barred as well, but the door does not look as though it is a sturdy one. Be prepared to put your shoulder to it, if needs be."

The two Templars walked up to the entrance, watching for any movement at the casements. Pushing against the main door, Bascot was surprised to find it unlocked and swung open under a gentle pressure from his hand. The movement of the door prompted a sudden rustling from inside and Bascot drew his sword while Emilius took a firm grip on the mace he carried as they stepped inside.

The room seemed dark after the brightness of the daylight outside and the figure that rose from a pallet on the floor on the other side of the room was at first indistinct. As their eyes adjusted to the gloom, they saw in the illumination of a small taper alongside the pallet that the person they had disturbed was Savaric. He was in the act of getting dressed and was about to pull on his boots.

"Sir Bascot!" the baseborn Roulan brother said, his impassive features registering surprise. "What do you here?"

"We have come to take Jacques into custody," Bascot replied. "We know he is the one who murdered the harlots."

Savaric faltered for a moment, and then set his mouth in the stern lines that Bascot remembered from his visit to Ingham. "As I told you, my half brother is dead. Your purpose here is pointless."

"A leper may be considered dead to society, but is not truly so until he has been buried," Bascot replied sternly. "Where is he?"

Savaric reeled back a step and glanced at the short sword that lay in its sheath beside his bed.

"Do not be foolish," Bascot warned. "You and the rest of your family can no longer protect him. He must answer for his crimes."

"It is not his fault," Savaric protested. "His brain—it has been turned by the disease. He does not know . . ."

His words were cut off as the inner door that led to the wing on the end of the building crashed open. Through it leapt a figure swinging a double-headed flail. So abrupt was his entrance that all of them were caught off guard. Emilius was nearest and, as he turned and raised his mace in a defensive movement, the chain of the flail caught the draper about the head, one of the wickedly spiked balls smashing into his cheek, the other catching him in the neck, just above the rim of the leather gambeson he wore. Blood spurted like water from a geyser and he dropped to his knees. His attacker pulled the flail free and charged at Bascot, swinging the weapon over his head.

"Filthy whoremongers!" he yelled. "You don't deserve to live!"

Bascot leapt to the side, bringing up his sword and dodging out of the way of the needle-sharp spikes. There could be no doubt that this was Jacques Roulan. Although his eyes were wild and staring above his unkempt beard, he had the same beaklike nose that the Templar had seen on Gilbert and Hervé's visages. Bascot's glance flicked to the handle of the flail, which Jacques was gripping with both hands. He must have chosen the weapon because it was easier to control with fingers that had lost the sense of feeling. But it was just as deadly an instrument as a sword, especially in the hands of a man who had been trained to its use, as Jacques would have been.

As Jacques' wild charge carried him past, Bascot noticed a rough bandage wrapped about the thigh of the leper's right leg and guessed that this was where Terese had stabbed him with her knife. The Templar aimed his sword at the same spot and felt the blade bite into muscle just above the strips of linen. The Templar did not want to kill the diseased man if he could help it; if at all possible, he should be taken into custody alive and pay the ultimate penalty of being hanged for his crimes.

Jacques stumbled on his injured leg and blood poured from the fresh wound. Bascot glanced in Savaric's direction to see if he intended to come to his half brother's aid, but the former squire was kneeling on the floor by Emilius, trying to bind the draper's terrible injury with a piece of old blanket.

Once again, Jacques charged at Bascot, and even though his gait was lopsided still managed to land a blow on the circular helm the Templar wore, causing sparks to fly. Only the nasal bar stopped it from catching Bascot in the face. Without a shield, a double-headed flail was a difficult weapon to defend oneself against. The possible loss of the sight in his remaining eye lessened the Templar's resolve to try and take Jacques alive. Even if it meant killing the leprous knight, he had to be disarmed.

Jacques spun around, using his sound leg as a pivot, and once again lifted the flail, swinging it above his head with furious intent. Stepping forward, Bascot thrust underneath the upraised arms, seeking the vulnerable point below the chest bone. The point of his sword struck true, plunging deep into vital organs and Jacques fell back onto the stone flags of the floor, the flail landing on the floor with a metallic clatter as it dropped from his hands.

Bascot picked the weapon up and, after ensuring that Jacques' wound was severe enough to incapacitate him, ran to Emilius and dropped to his knees. Savaric, with a stifled sob, backed away from the stricken Templar and went to crouch beside his half brother. With one glance, Bascot realised that the draper's wounds were mortal. The flesh of one cheek had been torn away and hung in a flap, the bone beneath it crushed. One of the spikes in the ball of the flail had sliced a deep gash across the side of Emilius's throat, severing the main arteries. Blood from the wound had formed a large puddle on the floor beneath the draper, but the pulsating flow was ebbing as the life essence became depleted. Emilius would not live for much longer than a few more minutes.

Gently removing the draper's helm, Bascot lifted the dying man's head and rested it in the crook of his arm. Emilius's eyelids fluttered as he did so, but it was plain his vision was beginning to dim. The draper muttered something faintly and Bascot leaned close to hear. He only caught the last few words before Emilius, with a sigh, expelled his final breath, but Bascot knew well what the draper had said. *"Non nobis, Domine, non nobis, sed Tuo Nomini da gloriam."* Not to us, O Lord, not to us, but to Thy Name give the glory. It was the battle cry of the Templar Order.

Twenty-seven

✦

With great care Bascot laid Emilius's head back on the floor, and then rose and strode over to where Savaric was slumped on his knees by his half brother. Hauling the squire to his feet, the Templar shoved him roughly back against the wall and told him to stay there. Then, sword in hand, he knelt beside the rogue Templar. A quick glance told him the man responsible for so many deaths was now, himself, dead.

Bascot scanned the features of the leper, taking in his visage more closely than he had been able to when Jacques had come charging through the doorway. The knight had once been a handsome man; white even teeth, dark curling hair and a generous curve to the mouth beneath the hereditary aquiline nose. In life, it was easy to imagine his head thrown back with laughter and a rakish glint in his eye. There was no doubt women would have found him attractive. But now the disease had taken hold. Patches of scaly skin could be seen in small bare patches beneath the curls of his beard and on the lobes of his ears and, when Bascot lifted with the point of his sword the cuff of one of the heavy gloves Jacques wore, a dark circle of lesions around the wrist was revealed.

No doubt other parts of his body, underneath his clothing, were scarred in a similar fashion.

From across the room, Savaric spoke, his attitude no longer impassive, but wrought with emotion. "Jacques was not always an evil man, Sir Bascot," he sobbed. "The disease—it turned his brain. Once he knew he had leprosy, he became a man completely unlike his former self."

"Whatever the reason, four people are now dead because of it," Bascot replied bluntly.

Motioning for Savaric to go outside, the Templar followed him out of the building and told him to sit on the ground. Using a length of rope hanging from the gate of the pigsty, he bound the squire's hands behind him. By now, Gerard Camville would have responded to the message sent to him by d'Arderon and it would not be long before the sheriff's men-at-arms arrived.

As they waited, Bascot tried to stem the tide of angry sorrow that threatened to engulf him. Emilius's murmuring of the battle cry had been a correct judgement although when he and Bascot had left the preceptory they had not expected to engage in a confrontation with the leper. If they had, they would have taken the time to don complete armour, along with mailed hoods, and Emilius's neck would have been protected from the spikes of the flail. But both Bascot and d'Arderon had surmised there would be no more than token resistance from a fatally ill man who had, so far, attacked only helpless women. How wrong they had been. And Emilius lay dead because of that error.

Bascot knew he would have to give a recounting to the sheriff of the unrelated events that had led to his assumption that the murderer was Jacques Roulan. To calm himself, he ran through them in his mind. They were many and, for a time, had seemed to bear no relation to each other. Master St. Maur's advice that the death of Robert Scallion in Acre might be involved in the slaying of the two harlots; the sighting of the image on the cloak clasp by Constance Turner's maid, and how later, through Bascot recalling the meaning of the Roulan name, it seemed likely that one of the family would wear such a piece of jewellery. Then there was the involvement of the Grimsons and last, but not least, the moment when the blacksmith's gloves in the preceptory's forge had reminded him that Dunny had mentioned how the knight who killed the boat owner had, in the intense heat of the Holy Land, been wearing gloves.

This last had been one of the final pieces of the puzzle. While it was usual to wear heavy gauntlets in battle, gloves were only otherwise necessary when there was need to protect the hands from cold or while performing an abrasive task. In the hot lands of Outremer, and in a brothel, they served no purpose. When Dunny had first mentioned them, Bascot should have recognised their importance, that gloves were a strange item of apparel to wear on such an occasion, but he had not. It was only later that he realised they were hiding the telltale scarring of leprosy.

It had been when he tried to envision, without success, either Savaric or Julia as the guilty party that he recalled Nicolaa de la Haye's bailiff mentioning that all of the brothers and their sister had made a visit to the property at Marton. Why had Julia gone there? It would be within Gilbert or Hervé's province to authorise repairs, not hers. Why would she go with them to inspect a rundown building? Then he had begun to wonder if Joan Grimson's suspicion that Jacques had returned to Lincoln was true and the disgraced Templar was living there in secret. But if so, why? He had no reason to hide. The murder had taken place in a distant land; Joan's threat of exposing him was not a serious one. It was more than probable that the sheriff would have no interest in arresting a man for the commission of a crime that had taken place so far away. As for the Order, any Templar brother could leave their ranks if he wished. To break one's oath in such a fashion might imperil a man's immortal soul, but it was not a crime. And, besides, the whole of the Roulan family had claimed he was dead. If he was alive, what was the purpose of such a terrible lie?

Julia's outburst had provided the answer, for she had spoken of her deceased brother as though he still suffered mortal agony. How could he be dead and at the same time still in pain? There was only one answer to that. He was a leper.

His conclusion had been strengthened by Jacques' reputation for insatiable lechery. It was commonly believed that leprosy was most often contracted through sexual congress. The truth of that opinion had not yet been proved, but it was more than probable that Jacques, like most people, believed it. If he had discovered that his body was fatally diseased, he could easily have conceived a deep hatred for the type of woman who had given it to him. And a man with his lack of conscience would have blamed a prostitute for his condition rather than his own lust. That conclusion could easily foster an unreasonable craving for revenge.

Bascot looked down at Savaric. Emilius's death had left Bascot bereft of compassion, not only for Jacques but for the rest of the Roulan family. If they all, especially Savaric, had not aided their diseased brother, the two prostitutes and the draper would still be alive. But there was one point that still puzzled him.

"There are Templar lazar houses in Outremer that care for

brothers afflicted with leprosy," Bascot said harshly. "Why did your half brother not enter one of them?"

Savaric gazed at the man standing over him with more than a little trepidation. The one-eyed knight was so angry that his face could have been carved from stone. The icy blueness of his sighted eye seemed as though it would freeze Savaric's soul if he did not tell the truth. There was nothing left to gain by lying anyway, he thought. Deception had been Jacques' tool and Savaric had always been reluctant to use it.

"He left it too late," Savaric answered flatly. "Once Jacques had killed Scallion, he knew he would be expelled from the Order and a place in a Templar lazar house would be denied to him. And if he was taken by the authorities for murder, he would be hanged. There was nothing else he could do but get away from Acre before he was caught."

There was a tremor in Savaric's voice as he went on. "He pleaded with me to bring him back to Lincoln. He was my close kin and had always treated me as an equal, even though I was baseborn. I could not deny his wish to die at home."

Savaric's mouth twisted into a bitter smile as he added, "Had it not been for Scallion's death, Jacques would have remained in Acre and never returned to England. But the ironic part of it all is that when my half brother got involved in that fight with the boat owner, he was not trying to harm him but was, instead, making an attempt to prevent him from being infected with leprosy."

The squire glanced up at the Templar. Savaric did not expect clemency for himself, but felt he had to try and justify the actions of his dead relative. At a curt nod from Bascot, he went on.

"Jacques had been to that brothel before, just a short time after we arrived in the Holy Land. He found chastity very hard to bear, but he had an honest desire to atone and managed to stay celibate while we were in Qaqun, where there are not many brothels. But we were only at Qaqun a few weeks before we were sent to Acre, and the port has a stewe on almost every corner. The temptation became too great for Jacques. One night he stole out of the enclave and spent an hour in the bawdy house where he later met Scallion. For a time, his lust was sated but, a few months later, he realised that the harlot had given him a disease. At first, when his man's parts swelled, he thought it was the pox, but then a rash appeared on his hindquarters and back and he knew he had been infected with leprosy. I had never seen him so distraught. From that moment, he began to change and became not the brother I had once known, but a stranger.

"I tried to dissuade him from going back to the brothel but he would not listen to me. He insisted he must denounce the girl to prevent her infecting others, but I feared he meant to kill her. Thinking I might forestall him from doing so, I insisted he let me accompany him. When we got there, I stayed outdoors to keep watch on the guards that were standing a little way along the street. It wasn't until later he told me that when he went in, the boat owner was inside. They were old friends; they had whored and got drunk many a time in the brothels and alehouses in Hull. But the girl that infected Jacques had taken Scallion's fancy. Jacques tried to dissuade him from laying with her, and even offered the whoremaster a huge sum to keep her away from Scallion, but the boat owner was drunk—he had been drinking some of that filthy liquor made from fermented dates they have in Outremer—and was in a vile temper. He threatened to report Jacques to the Templar commander in Acre and began to taunt him for breaking his vow of chastity."

The former squire gave a heartfelt sigh. "It was then that they began to fight and somehow Scallion got ahold of the knife at Jacques' belt and, in the struggle, it ended up in the boat owner's chest." Savaric shrugged. "That is what Jacques told me happened. I cannot vouch for the truth of it, but he had no reason to lie."

"And, when the hue and cry was raised to find Jacques, you helped him get away?" Bascot asked. Although he felt no compassion for the man he held captive, he began to understand the depth of the squire's quandary. It would not have been easy to deny aid to a much loved brother, even if he was gravely at fault. And love his legitimate brother Savaric must have done, for not only had he followed the immoral knight to the Holy Land, but he had also stood by Jacques when he had committed murder. There was courage there, too—not many would risk exposure to leprosy for another's sake, no matter how closely they were related. But Savaric's loyalty had been misplaced, and he had known it to be so. For that Bascot could not forgive him.

Savaric nodded. "When Jacques came tearing out of the stewe, we got away from the area as fast as we could. After we felt we were safe from discovery, he told me what had happened. Jacques had a couple of rings and a gold chain in his scrip. We waited on the outskirts of Acre until morning, and then exchanged some of the jewellery for a couple of mounts from an Arab horse trader. Then we rode southward down the coast towards Haifa. There we hired a boat to take us to Cyprus, and sold the horses and the rest of the jewellery to pay for passage home. The rest you know."

"So your brother not only broke his vow of chastity but, by keeping valuable items in his possession after he entered the Order, also the one of poverty. And neither he nor you gave any thought to the infection he was spreading among the people you came into contact with on the journey back to England." Bascot's fury resurged and, with it, disgust. "The silver coins that Jacques left beside the bodies of each of the prostitutes he killed. Were they also part of his secret hoard?"

"He left some silver coins and jewellery buried here, at Marton, when he went to join the Templars," Savaric admitted shamefacedly. "None of us knew he had done so. I only got the truth out of him last night."

"I cannot condone your actions," Bascot replied, "but in a small part I can understand them, at least until you brought your brother safely back to England. What I fail to comprehend is why, once you had returned to Lincoln, your family did not ensure that Jacques entered a lazar house?"

"Gilbert wanted him to go to the one in Pottergate," Savaric said, "but Jacques begged to be allowed to stay at Marton, which is where I brought him when we first returned. I smuggled him in at night while the pig man was sleeping and then went to Ingham and told the family what had happened. Gilbert, Hervé and Julia rode here the next morning and tried to persuade him to go to the lazar house but he pleaded with them to leave him here, promising he would let no one see him or come into contact with him. He said his only wish was to die at home on the family demesne. Julia took his part and said that after all Jacques had gone through to return home, it would be cruel to lock him away at the end of his journey."

Savaric glanced at the Templar. "My half brother could be very persuasive, Sir Bascot, especially with women. His mother and Julia idolized him. When his dam heard what had happened, she collapsed and we feared she would not recover. Julia told Gilbert that if he did not want to be the cause of their mother's death, he would do as Jacques asked. Since I had been in his company for so many months and might have already contracted the disease, I offered to bring him food and keep him company when he wished it. Gilbert finally, and reluctantly, gave in, although Hervé advised against it. They all—Gilbert, Julia and Hervé—came to see him just that one time, for Jacques insisted they stay away after that, for their own safety's sake."

"And after he garrotted the harlot in our chapel," Bascot said in a hard voice, "was the love all of you felt for this degenerate brother so strong that you also condoned his sin of murder?"

"No, Sir Bascot, it was not," Savaric replied, his words exploding from him with a brief flare of defiance. "We didn't know, at the time, that he had killed her, or that he murdered the other one a few days later. It was not until the day that you and Captain Roget came to Ingham that we found out he was responsible. I only spent the odd night or two at Marton and none of us knew Jacques had gone into Lincoln, or that he was responsible for those terrible crimes. I had gone early that same morning, before you came, to take him some food and wine. I arrived before he was out of bed and saw the strips of cloth he had wrapped around the wound on his leg. When I asked him how he had come by the injury, he blustered at first, saying he had stumbled on one of the broken boards in the house and the shattered end had pierced his leg. I looked at the wound and could tell it had been made by a knife. When I challenged him with his lie, he finally told me the truth. But although he admitted he killed the two harlots, he did not tell me he had attacked another woman the night before. We did not learn of that until you came to the manor house later that day.

"His brain had been turned by the disease," Savaric continued sadly. "He said he wanted to kill as many harlots as he could because they were the cause of all his troubles. It was because of them, he said, that he had been forced to join the Templars. If he hadn't done so, he would never have lain with the prostitute that infected him."

"But why did he implicate our Order?" Bascot demanded. "Surely Jacques could not blame the brethren for his downfall."

"As I said, his thinking was deranged. He said the Templars were hypocrites; that they all lusted after women and bedded them whenever they had an opportunity to do so. Because he had visited a brothel and not been caught, he was convinced there were many others that did the same. He said that if the leprosy had been sent by God to chastise him for breaking his vow of chastity, it was a punishment that was not warranted, for he was but one of many."

Savaric gave Bascot an earnest look. "I tried to tell him he was wrong, that there were very few Templars who dishonoured their vow, but he would not listen. He just raged at me and said it could not be so, that it was not natural for a man to live like a eunuch. He said that before he died, he intended to make the brothers' rampant fornication known to all of Christendom, and expose them to the contempt they so rightly deserved. His reasoning made no sense, but I did not try to dissuade him. It was too late. The women were already dead. Nothing I could say would bring them back."

The former squire shook his head sadly as he continued, "After he finished raving, I locked him in the sleeping chamber here at Marton and went to tell Gilbert what had happened. It was that discussion you and Captain Roget interrupted when you arrived at Ingham. It was a shock to learn that he had attempted to kill another woman."

"How did he get into Lincoln? Did you leave him a mount?"

"No, I did not, for there was no reason for him to have need of one," Savaric replied. "He told me that he walked into Torksey after the swineherd was abed—the pig man drinks his fill of ale in the village alehouse every afternoon and then comes home to sleep like a stone until morning— and hired a horse from a stable there."

"And the women he killed, how did he entice them into his company?"

The former squire looked shamed as he repeated what Jacques had told him. "He said he went to the brothel where the first girl worked and asked her to aid him in winning a wager that a woman could not be smuggled into the chapel at the preceptory. She came willingly when he offered to pay her handsomely for her help."

Savaric's voice diminished to almost a whisper as he described how Jacques had gained entry to Adele Delorme's house. "The second harlot was known to him from before he entered the Order. He had been friends with her paramour, a knight who lives in Newark, and had helped to persuade her lover to pay her handsomely to leave the town before he got married. When he called at her house, she recognised him as an old friend and had no suspicion that his intention was anything other than harmless."

The Templar felt a tide of loathing flood him at the recounting of such flagrant evil. "And, knowing all this, your family still did not give him up to Captain Roget's authority when we came to Ingham," Bascot spat out. "How many more women did he have to kill before you would have done so?"

"There would have been no more!" Savaric responded heatedly, his sorrowful demeanour vanishing. "I came back to Marton after you left the manor house and stayed to keep guard over Jacques. We knew he could not last much longer; that it was only a matter of time before he became too weak to be a threat to anyone. He was starting to lose the feeling in his fingers and his toes had begun to waste. And, more than once, he had been taken with a wracking fever that I thought would be the end of him. We planned to take him to a shepherd's hut at the edge of the pasture lands at Ingham that is isolated and not used anymore. I was going to send the pig man away on some errand and take Jacques there today. If you had not come to Marton this morning, I would have cared for him until the end and he would have spent whatever time was left to him with his family nearby. . . ."

"He was a foul murderer and deserved no such consideration," Bascot said brutally. "His death was too quick to serve justice; he should have swung at the end of a rope and had a taste of the terror he inflicted on the women he attacked. And the rest of you should suffer a like fate for enabling him to commit his vicious crimes."

Bascot's reply was deliberately pitiless. He had seen the body of poor Elfie and heard Roget's description of Adele Delorme's corpse. Had she not been fortunate, Terese would have died in a similarly cruel manner. And if that had happened, little Ducette, Elfie's young daughter, would have been twice bereft, not only of her mother, but of the only other person in the world who cared for her.

Savaric made no reply and they sat in silence until Roget and half a dozen men-at-arms rode up the track towards them. Bascot explained to Roget as succinctly as he could what had happened and suggested that Jacques' body be secured in the building where it lay and left there until someone from the lazar house in Pottergate could come and fetch it.

"The baseborn brother may be infected. He can ride his own horse back to Lincoln under escort by your men," Bascot added. "Once you reach the castle he should be put in a cell on his own until a leech has examined him to see if he has contracted leprosy. Then the sheriff can do with him, and the rest of his cursed family, as he will."

In a hard voice he added, "Tell your men that if Savaric tries to escape, they are to cut him down. He should not be shown any mercy, for he deserves none."

Roget nodded and watched with concerned eyes as his friend went into the ramshackle building and emerged a few moments later with the body of Emilius cradled in his arms. Going over to the horse the draper had ridden on their journey to Marton, Bascot laid the dead Templar across the saddle, covered him with his cloak and tied him securely in place. Then Bascot mounted his own steed and, taking up the reins of Emilius's horse, rode off down the track. Roget's heart went out to his friend and the rest of the brothers in the Lincoln enclave. The draper had died at the hands of one of their own, a corrupt brother who had kept neither the vows he had sworn nor upheld their honour. Their grief would be inconsolable.

Twenty-eight
✛

AFTER ROGET LOCKED SAVARIC IN A HOLDING CELL AND WENT
to relate to Gerard Camville what he had been told by Bascot, the captain was sent to Ingham to arrest Gilbert, Hervé
and Julia Roulan. Gilbert's wife, Margaret, was left at the
manor house to manage the supervision of the servants and
to care for their grief-stricken mother. The two brothers and
sister were locked in a separate holding cell from that of
Savaric and, at Nicolaa's suggestion, a request was sent to
Brother Jehan, the elderly infirmarian at the Priory of All
Saints, asking him if he would come to the castle gaol and
examine the prisoners for signs of leprosy. Jehan was an extremely able herbalist who had, in his long lifetime, treated
most of the ailments that plagued mankind. Both Nicolaa
and Gerard trusted his judgement in the matter.

After spending some time with Savaric, and a brief visit
with the other Roulan siblings, Jehan returned to the hall
and said that, as far as he could tell, all four of them were
free of the disease.

"With regard to the three legitimate members of the
family," the monk told them in his slow sonorous voice, "I

am assured, both by them and the baseborn son, that they had no close contact with the leper. They did not even, at his request, embrace him, so it is unlikely they have been infected. With regard to the illegitimate son, however, I would ask you to bear in mind that I cannot be certain he has not contracted the disease. Although there is no rash with the distinctive scales that the word *lepra* implies, he had been exposed to the noxious breath and touch of a leper and may yet contract it. While many of the monks that attend the lazar house below Pottergate do not become infected with the disease, there is usually one or two who catch it in the fullness of time."

For a moment Jehan's gaze became unfocussed as he pondered on the affliction. Finally, he said, "I asked the baseborn son some questions about the leper who was slain by Sir Bascot and I would be very surprised if he contracted the disease in Outremer. I think it most likely he was already infected before he went to the Holy Land."

At the looks of astonishment on the faces of Nicolaa and the sheriff, the infirmarian explained his reasoning. "I base that judgement on studies I have conducted among the monks who have served in the lazar house in Pottergate and eventually fall prey to the disease. The monks do not, of course, have carnal liaisons with the women there, but are in close contact with all of the lepers on a daily basis while they tend their needs. I have never seen any of the monks become infected before at least a year of service and, even then, the telltale rash develops slowly. From what I was told about the advanced state of the leprous brother's symptoms, it would seem he may have been infected long before he lay with the heathen prostitute and probably some time before he left England."

"Then he was already ill before he joined the Order," Nicolaa exclaimed. "His judgement of the Templars was entirely misplaced."

Jehan nodded. "I could be in error, of course. God has yet to reveal to mankind any certainty of the manner in which the infection is spread, or why some escape the disease and others do not. I also suspect that there are often cases which are deemed to be leprosy but are, in fact, a different ailment entirely, for I have noticed that the flesh of many marked by an unsightly rash does not waste with the passage of years." He sighed with frustration at his inability to be of more help to those infected with the disease and finally added, "I do not think the dead man would have lived for very long, in any case. Many lepers' lives are taken prematurely by a secondary infection that proves fatal in their weakened state, while others live to a great age even though they are terribly deformed. It sounds as though his volatile nature made him susceptible to minor ailments, any of which could have killed him."

The monk stood up, his reflections done. "I fear that all I can assure you, at the moment, is that none of the prisoners appear to be suffering from the disease."

Nicolaa thanked the infirmarian for his assistance and, after he left, she and Gerard decided that it would be best to keep Savaric in solitary confinement until they could be certain he carried no taint. In the meantime, there remained the question of what charges were to be brought against him and the other members of Jacques Roulan's family.

"If what de Marins was told by the baseborn brother is true, then they did not truly give their aid to Jacques when he murdered the prostitutes," Nicolaa said to her husband. "But by shielding him, they made the crimes possible, and should be brought to answer for that action."

Camville's eyes glinted with anger. "Do not fear, Wife. I will ensure they pay for their complicity," he said. "Had they not harboured their murderous brother in the first instance, neither of the prostitutes would have been killed. Nor would a Templar knight have been slain. I will take great pleasure in bringing charges against them when I preside over the next sheriff's court."

BY EARLY AFTERNOON, THE WHOLE CASTLE HAD HEARD OF what had passed and the news had spread down into the town. The reaction it provoked was one of commiseration. Many of the women shed a tear for the Templar who had been slain and the men gathered in alehouses about the town discussed the matter with grave expressions on their faces. In the scriptorium, Gianni listened with horror as Master Blund told of the details he had learned when summoned by Nicolaa to write down a record of the events for subsequent presentation in Camville's court.

For Gianni, the worst part of Blund's recounting was the manner in which the Templar knight had died. The lad was appalled by the thought that it could so easily have been his former master who had been fatally struck by the spikes of the flail. Gianni had always been aware, since the day that Bascot had rejoined the ranks of the Templars, that the knight would most likely face death many times while he was on active duty in some war-torn land, but this recent close brush with death suddenly made that nebulous possibility now a frightening reality. It was with a heavy heart that the lad left the scriptorium at the end of his work day and wandered out into the bail.

In front of the barracks he saw Roget and Ernulf standing with pots of ale in their hands. The faces of both men were downcast and their conversation, usually bantering, was desultory. The events of the morning had cast a pall over the entire castle as servants tended to their tasks in a dispirited fashion, and occasional baleful glances were directed towards the holding cells where the family of Jacques Roulan was imprisoned.

Gianni did not feel like partaking of the meal that was being laid out in the hall, nor did he wish the company of others, so he turned his steps towards the old stone tower that stood in the southwest corner of the bail. This building had once been the keep and main residence of the sheriff and his wife but with the erection of a taller, and much more capacious, fortress a few years before, now housed only the armoury on the bottom storey and a few empty chambers above that were used to accommodate visitors to the castle. The tower was three stories high and, at the top, was the small room that Bascot and Gianni had been given when they arrived in Lincoln in the winter of 1199. The lad entered the building and slowly mounted the stairs to the upper storey, remembering how it had been difficult for his former master to climb them when they first arrived because of an injury he had sustained to his ankle while escaping from the Saracens. It had only been due to Bascot's acquisition of a new pair of boots skilfully fitted with strengthening pads by a Lincoln cobbler that the Templar had finally been able to climb them with ease.

Gianni came to the door of the room they had occupied for two long years and slowly pushed the door open. It was as bare as he remembered it, with a stone shelf on one side where the Templar had slept on a straw-stuffed mattress. Gianni's bed had been laid on the floor, his covering an old cloak Bascot had provided. The straw pallets were still there, rolled up and piled in a corner for use by the next guest, and the small brazier that had dispensed their only warmth in the cold days of winter stood in a corner, piled high with unlit charcoal. Gone, of course, were their meagre personal effects—the trunk with their few items of clothing and the little box in which Gianni had kept the scribing instruments with which the Templar had taught his young servant to read and write.

Gianni went over to the stone shelf that Bascot had used for a bed and knelt beside it. This was where he and the Templar had been accustomed to saying their prayers and that is what he did now, sending up heartfelt thanks to God for keeping Bascot free from harm. He then added an earnest plea that Brother Emilius be greeted with favour in heaven. Once this was done, he took the straw pallet that the Templar had used, spread it on the stone shelf and lay down. Nicolaa de la Haye had said he was now a man but, at this moment, he still felt like the young orphan that the Templar had rescued from certain starvation in Palermo. He knew his insecurity would pass with time and that once the Templar had departed from Lincoln, he would be able to accept his master's absence with more equanimity. But, for now, he felt a comfort in remembrance of the days when the Templar had been by his side. Closing his eyes, he felt himself relax, and was soon fast asleep.

IN THE PRECEPTORY, AS ROGET HAD FORESEEN, EMILIUS WAS deeply mourned. With Preceptor d'Arderon, Bascot undertook the task of cleansing and readying the draper's corpse for burial. Since the Lincoln preceptory did not have a cemetery within its confines, it was decided that Emilius would be taken to the burial ground of a much larger enclave a few miles south of Lincoln. Until arrangements for the ceremony could be made, the men of the next contingent would stay in the preceptory and, along with the brothers regularly based in the commandery, keep vigil over the draper's bier.

Twenty-nine

◆━◆

On the morning of the third day after his untimely death, Emilius's coffin was secured to the bed of a large dray and the men who would form the escort lined up alongside to accompany the draper's body on its last earthly journey. Temple Bruer, where they were bound, was situated in a lonely stretch of land in Lincoln Heath, a property that had been donated to the Order some fifty years before. It had then been a desolate place, inhabited only by the sheep that provided wool for the preceptory's main source of income, but the brothers' arrival had enlivened it with their presence. To reach it, the cortege needed to travel down the track that led outside the eastern wall of Lincoln town, cross over the River Witham and onto the southbound stretch of Ermine Street. After a few miles, where Ermine Street ran along the edge of Lincoln Cliff, they would reach the western edge of the preceptory's property and could travel down a forked track, one arm of which led south to Byard's Leap, where the enclave's horses were exercised, and the other eastward to the Temple Bruer preceptory.

Bascot and d'Arderon led the funeral procession, riding

at the head of the column in front of the cart on which Emilius's coffin, draped with his own white surcoat, lay cushioned on thick blankets. A man-at-arms held the reins of the two horses hitched to the dray and Brother John, the priest of the enclave, rode beside him. At the end, riding two abreast, were six brothers from the Lincoln preceptory. Serjeant Hamo had been left behind to take temporary command in d'Arderon's absence. Tears had trickled down the dour serjeant's face as he had watched the cortege exit through the preceptory gate. He, along with the lay brothers and servants and the men of the contingent, had stood in a solemn line as the procession passed by.

As the cortege neared the suburb of Butwerk, they could see that a great number of Lincoln townsfolk had gathered along the track. Stretching down along the city walls past Pottergate and along to the banks of the River Witham, they stood respectfully silent as the procession came near, many of the women weeping and the men with bowed heads. One small group was composed entirely of prostitutes. Terese stood at the front of the women, holding Elfie's little daughter, Ducette, in her arms. The child's eyes were round with wonder as she gazed at the sober-faced Templars, all clad in full armour covered by surcoats with the blood red cross of the Order emblazoned on the chest.

Tears blinded Bascot's eye as he saw the sorrow on the faces of the people they passed. Throughout the murder investigation that had led to Emilius's death, the draper had always been fearful that the reputation of the Templar Order would be defiled, tainted by a shroud of dishonour that could never be expunged. Along with the majority of Templar brothers, Emilius had an unshakeable belief in the rightness of their cause, and had never doubted that his duty lay to fight for

Christ in defending Christian lands against the encroachment of the Saracens and to protect the pilgrims who wished to visit the places Our Lord had sanctified with his presence. But one rogue Templar like Jacques Roulan could, in the eyes of the Christian populace, give a false impression of corruption. The grieving presence of the townspeople gathered along the path proved that had not happened. The draper's sacrifice of his life in commission of his duty had, instead, inspired admiration and respect for his memory and, in so doing, for the Order to which he belonged. Emilius had not died in vain.

WHEN THE MEN OF THE ESCORT RETURNED TO LINCOLN TWO days later, a Templar messenger from London was waiting for d'Arderon. On the day that Bascot had returned to the preceptory with Emilius's body, the preceptor had sent a letter to Thomas Berard relating all the sad details of what had passed. He had also appended a note of his intention to allow the departure of the long delayed contingent for Portugal. The messenger waiting in the enclave had brought Master Berard's reply.

D'Arderon, his shoulders still slumped with sorrow, went to his office to open the letter, asking Bascot to accompany him. Once he had read the missive, the preceptor laid it on the table in front of him and stood without speaking for several moments. Finally, he said quietly, "Master Berard conveys his condolences on Emilius's death and tells me that a requiem Mass for the draper was held in London the day after my message reached him."

The preceptor then paced slowly across the room to the window, adding as he did so that a note had been made of the departure of the contingent and a boat would be waiting for their arrival in Portsmouth to carry them across the Narrow Sea to Portugal.

When d'Arderon reached the casement he turned and gave Bascot a direct look. "Master Berard also deals with another matter in his missive. Another knight must be chosen to fill the office of draper and your name has been suggested for the post." He paused for a moment, his eyes searching Bascot's countenance for the younger knight's reaction. "Master Berard can command you to the position," d'Arderon said finally, "but he would rather you took up the duty with a willing heart. What say you?"

Bascot was taken aback. He had fully expected to leave for Portugal shortly after they had returned from Temple Bruer. Now his mind whirled with the implications of the unexpected offer. To be awarded the post of draper was an honour that was not to be lightly decried, but it would mean that he would, for the foreseeable future at least, not be considered for active duty. He was not sure how to respond.

D'Arderon saw the younger knight's confusion and sought a way to ease it. "I know it is a difficult decision to make, Bascot, and one that requires certainty of commitment. Perhaps you would like to spend some time in prayer to aid your reflection."

"I would, Preceptor," Bascot replied thankfully.

"So be it," d'Arderon replied understandingly. "The contingent will leave at first light tomorrow. You have until then to give me your answer."

AFTER THE REST OF THE ENCLAVE HAD RETIRED TO THEIR pallets, Bascot spent the hours between Compline and Matins in the preceptory chapel praying for guidance. After Emilius's interment, Bascot had consoled himself with the thought that he would soon go to Portugal and take up the fight for Christendom in the draper's stead. Emilius had often spoken of his time there and how he wished that he was still fit enough to stand by his brethren in Tomar as they waged an ongoing battle to rid the Iberian peninsula of the Moorish invaders. If Bascot accepted the draper's post and stayed in Lincoln, that goal would not be realised. But was not the work that Emilius had done here in the preceptory just as critical for the defence of Portugal as his time on active duty? Without a constant supply of trained men and arms, the defence of the land around Tomar and Almourol would be impossible. Was Bascot putting his own selfish desires before the needs of his brethren?

Above him the candle on the altar burned brightly, casting shadows from the pillars that encircled the interior of the church. To one side was a life-size image of the Virgin Mary cradling the infant Jesus in her arms, and the faint aroma of incense filled the air. Nearby was the door to the vestry where the body of Elfreda had been found and where Emilius had kept the clothing for which he was responsible. The post of draper was an important one and Bascot knew that his education made him suitable for the responsibilities. But was it truly God's will for him to take up the post, or was he being influenced by the awareness that if he stayed in Lincoln, he would remain in close proximity to Gianni, the boy he loved so dearly? He had to admit that when d'Arderon had told him of the appointment, that had been the first thought that had flashed through his mind. Was he letting his affection for the boy cloud his judgement?

He brought up his hands to clasp them before him as he

once again bowed his head in prayer and, as he did so, his fingers brushed the small leather scrip he wore at his belt. Other than the few silver pennies each brother was allowed to carry in case of emergencies, it also contained a small piece of Lincolnshire stone. He remembered well the night he had picked it up. It had been a few months before, just after the time of Christ's Mass, when he had been standing alone on the top step of the forebuilding of the keep in Lincoln castle and pondering his return to the Order in a few months time. The piece of stone must have become dislodged from the façade of the keep and fallen onto the ground near his feet. His purpose in keeping it had been because he had thought that no matter how far away he travelled from the town he had come to regard as home, and from the young lad he loved like a son, he would always carry a piece of solid remembrance with him. Now he took the stone out of his scrip and held it up to the radiance of the candle. The fragment was about the size of the palm of his hand, flat and smooth on the side where it had fractured from a much larger piece, the surface covered with tiny wavering striations in different shades of light and dark grey. The uneven lines reminded him of how difficult the passage of a man's life could be and that, as so often happens, it could undulate from confident resolution to dithering uncertainty in a matter of moments.

Still holding the stone in his hand, he turned his gaze to the crucifix above the altar and realised he had found the answer to his dilemma. It was not God who made life-altering decisions difficult, but man himself. God's ways were simple and direct. If His intention had been otherwise, the offer of the draper's post would not have been made. Bascot rose from his knees and went into the vestry, then opened the chest where the knights' surcoats were kept. Carefully lifting out the piles of clothing that Emilius had folded so neatly, he laid them to one side and placed the piece of stone on the bottom of the coffer. Then he repacked the garments with the same care that Emilius would have taken and closed the lid.

Leaving the vestry he genuflected in front of the altar and went out into the compound to give d'Arderon his answer. Until, and unless, Our Lord decreed otherwise, he would remain in Lincoln.

Author's Note

SETTING

The setting for *Shroud of Dishonour* is an authentic one. Nicolaa de la Haye was hereditary castellan of Lincoln castle during this period, and her husband, Gerard Camville, was sheriff of Lincoln. The personalities they have been given in the story have been formed from conclusions the author has drawn from events during the reigns of King Richard I and King John.

TEMPLAR HEIRARCHY

In all the reference material I have consulted, three social classifications are given to the men who served within the Templar Order—knight, priest and serjeant. Each class wore garments of a colour that denoted their status—white surcoats for knights, green for priests and black or brown for serjeants. While I have been writing the Bascot de Marins series, I have separated the rank of serjeant into two, that of serjeant and ordinary man-at-arms. Since there are many more scenes taking place in the Templar enclave in *Shroud of Dishonour* than in the previous books in the series, I would like to include here, for those readers who are interested, an explanation of my reason for this distinction.

The word serjeant is derived from the Old French word *sergent*, which comes from the Latin *servient*, the present participle stem of *servire* ("serve"), which implies the simple designation of "servant." The term "serjeant" or "sergeant" was not accorded military status until three centuries after my Templar Knight Mysteries take place. All words, however, have some root in the distant past and it is quite possible that the word was used in its modern connotation long before it was accorded official recognition. I have, therefore, given it a separate grade because, just as a hierarchy of commanders was included within those of knight's rank—master, preceptor, draper, marshal, etc.—brothers of a lower social class held posts such as under-marshall and standard bearer. In any military force, whether medieval or modern, common sense dictates that men of more experience and longer service are selected to take charge of troops who are unseasoned or have less capability. A parallel can be drawn from our present day armies where the ranks of corporal and sergeant are accorded to non-commissioned officers. I have, therefore, used the term to denote this difference. Since two colours of surcoat, brown and black, are always mentioned in the annals as being worn by Templar serjeants, I have taken the liberty of assigning the former to those of higher rank and the latter to the rest.

CANONICAL HOURS

The following is an abbreviated list taken from The Monastic Horarium according to the *Regularis Concordia: The Mo-*

nastic Order in England by Dom David Knowles (Cambridge University Press).

Winter	Summer
6 a.m. approx.—Matins	3:30 or 4 a.m. approx.—Matins

(The service of Matins was not to begin until break of day.)

6:45 a.m.—Prime	6 a.m.—Prime

(Prime was to be conducted in full daylight.)

8 a.m.—Terce	8 a.m.—Terce
12 Noon—Sext	11:30 a.m.—Sext
1:30 p.m.— None	2:30 p.m.—None
4:15 p.m.—Vespers	6:00 p.m.—Vespers
6:15 p.m.—Compline	8 p.m.—Compline

For details of medieval Lincoln and the Order of the Knights Templar, I am much indebted to the following:

Medieval Lincoln by J.W.F. Hill (Cambridge University Press)

Dungeon, Fire and Sword—The Knights Templar in the Crusades by John J. Robinson (M. Evans and Company, Inc.)

In Search of the Knights Templar—A Guide to the Sites in Britain by Simon Brighton (Weidenfeld & Nicolson)